On The Big Hill

On The Big Hill

A Non-Climber's Everest

Mark Anderson

faber and faber

LONDON · BOSTON

First published in 1988
by Faber and Faber Limited
3 Queen Square London WCIN 3AU

Photoset by Parker Typesetting Service Leicester
Printed in Great Britain by
Richard Clay Ltd Bungay Suffolk

*British Library Cataloguing in Publication Data
is available*

ISBN 0–571–15381–X

This book is for all those
who were with me, in body or spirit,
on the British Services Everest Expedition 1988.

Contents

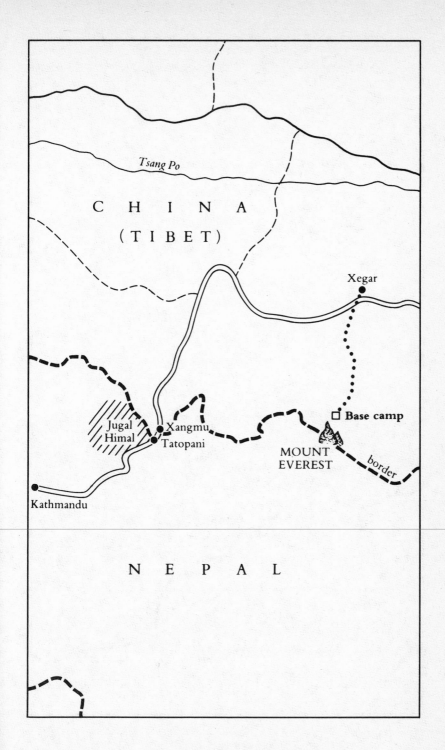

'A wide-shot of the Himalayas'

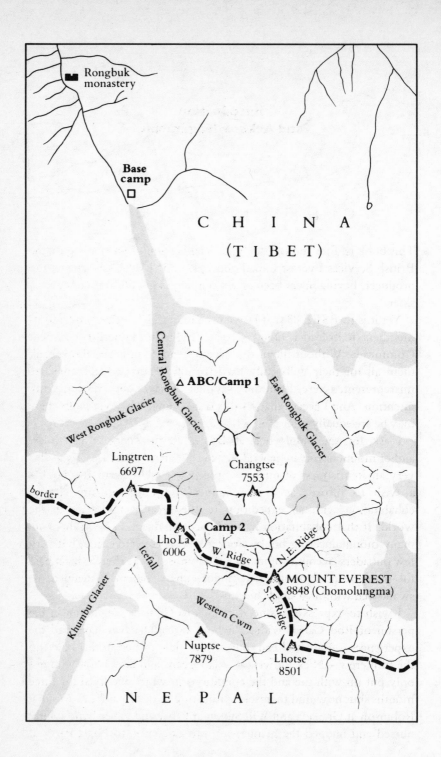

'A close-up of Everest'

Introduction
and Acknowledgements

This book is, first and last, an 'unofficial version'. I went along on the British Services Everest Expedition 1988 – BSEE 88 – as a television producer, having never been on a mountain in my life. I am not even a skier.

Yet it is to BSEE 88 that I owe my greatest debt of gratitude: to its members, to its leader, Dougie Keelan, and to its Higher Management Committee. Without them, this account could not exist, and I thank them all for their willy-nilly participation. If anyone feels they are misrepresented here, I can only say that this was not, of course, my intention. And I accept that, as this is my view, whatever faults there may be are equally mine.

I ask for the indulgence of BSEE 88 members in particular, and of mountaineers in general, for the 'amateur' tone. But it was this very amateurishness of mine that prompted me to write this book – a wish to record, as a non-climber and observer, my curious cohabitation with an expedition to the greatest mountain in the world. If that cohabitation has spawned a hybrid, so be it: there are many mountaineering books worthy of that collective title, but very few outsiders' accounts of major expeditions. I hope there is meat here for many readers, although I cannot expect the entire menu to be swallowed without a single hiccup.

I wish to express my sincere thanks to Granada Television in the person of Rod Caird, without whom I would never have had the experiences – good and bad, but invaluable – related in this book; to the film crew – Nick Plowright, Alan Evans and Ian Hills – who not only put up with me and the conditions in which we lived for three months, but now find themselves featuring in these pages; to Andrew Robinson at Granada and Will Sulkin at Faber and Faber, who jointly nursed and nudged the manuscript into existence; to Nigel Parry at

Faber and Faber, who designed this book and guided my selection of the photographs; to those who kindly allowed me to add their pictures to my own: Nick Plowright (Plates 23, 25, 27, 29, 31, 34, 60, 61, 62), Alan Evans (Plates 2, 9, 12, 39, 51, 52, 53, 54), Roger Antolik (Plates 1, 22, 40, 50), Dave Nicholls (Plate 55), Merv Middleton (Plate 56), Terry Moore (Plate 57), Richard Pelly (Plate 33); and, last but by no means least, to Vicky Price, who has supported me with her presence and advice throughout the writing as she did with her letters when I was at the foot of Mount Everest.

The Beginning and the End

December 1987/June 1988
London

The living-room floor was strewn with paper. Selected extracts from television interviews – pure content – were gradually taking on form: cut-up spinal vertebrae stretched across the carpet, hinting at the whole skeleton still only in our minds.

'This bit of Stuart Hall really belongs in the legacies section – but it follows Scruton so well, and he needs qualification here.'

Orly and I were struggling with a long documentary on the students' revolt of 1968. It was all but done, needing only the interviews to be integrated into a programme of archive material already assembled. And in two days' time we would not be scrabbling around her floor pulling out the plums from hours of interview transcripts, but picking from plates of turkey, chestnut stuffing and all the trimmings of Christmas dinner.

The phone rang.

I cursed silently. Any disruption, breaking a fragile train of thought, could add a half-hour to our labours.

'It's for you, Mark.'

Irritation edged Orly's summons from the kitchen. I picked a careful course across the archipelago of paper, to be greeted by a Manchester accent.

'Great, I've found you – I've been chasing round everywhere for you.' Then, almost as an afterthought:

'It's Rod Caird's secretary at Granada Television – he'd like a word with you'. Pause.

'Mark, it's Rod. We're thinking of doing a documentary series about a group of soldiers climbing Everest. They're leaving in about six weeks. Would you be free?'

Quick calculations – mid-February; I would just about have finished with 1968. Then the realization – Everest!

'Yes, I think I'd be available. But *me* on Everest? I've never done any mountaineering. And, as you know, we TV directors tend to go for the luxuries of life!'

'Well, I'd like you to think about it seriously. Nobody's expecting you to go to the top – it's experience in making documentaries we're after, not climbing mountains. And of course I'm not expecting a yes or a no here on the phone. Give me a ring this evening.'

'Fine, Rod. Obviously, it's a fantastic opportunity. But it is a bit of a surprise. I'll talk to you later.'

Orly was still knee-deep in 1968.

'So – Granada want me to go up Everest with a whole bunch of soldiers. Can you think of any director you know less suitable than me?'

'You've *got* to do it, Mark. It's the chance of a lifetime! And you can get along fine with the Services – you've done it before.'

Orly was right, on both counts. And she was reacting more swiftly than I was. Already I knew that not only would I say yes – I'd be bitterly disappointed if it all fell through. Whatever the hardships, the personal deprivations for a forty-five-year-old habitual smoker and drinker, I just had to do it. Within minutes, my mind was made up. Only the details remained to be disentangled, drawn into a plan for a documentary series with a difference: a soap opera set on the highest mountain in the world – 'On The Big Hill'.

On the shortest day of the year just before Christmas I had no idea what was coming my way. Now, as I write this passage six months later, it is coincidentally the longest day. And it's all over. Life has returned to what I call normal – running water and fresh fruit, beds and electric lights, a car. A dozen paces no longer induce exhaustion. And above all I'm fully occupied, fully fed and warm. Now the pressures are familiar: to bring in finished versions of both book and TV series in what seem absurdly short periods. Ironically, out in Tibet I frequently had time on my hands; but the inclination and capacity to organize and formulate immediate experience into the written word totally escaped me. It may have been the absence of practical aids – a table, a bottle of scotch; or more probably, the absence of perspective and hindsight, the ability to put the experience in a frame, stand back and view it complete, albeit from a short distance.

What remain most obviously are the physical effects – I lost over two stone of surplus flesh at altitude and only slowly, now at near sea level, are they reappearing. But the more permanent legacy is in the mind, a host of jumbled memories:

— near-frozen toes thawing out in my Redline sleeping bag, thanks to down-filled bootees and a metal drinking bottle filled with hot boiled snow. Frostnip still keeps several toes and all my finger tips in a state of semi-numbness;

— the sound of spindrift – blown loose snow crystals – blasting my tent in 100 m.p.h. gusts of wind, uncannily like English rain drops falling on the leaves of a tree;

— the elemental simplicity of vacating the bowels, squatting hunched on an icy slab of stone;

— the physical agony, on the edge of exhaustion, of putting one foot in front of another;

— the taste of tinned steak and kidney pudding – known for indeterminate reasons as 'babies' heads' by the servicemen – as I forced myself to eat, and thereby maintain essential bodily functions;

— watching an indifferent movie for the third time on our Granada perk, a battery-driven Video-8 monitor, whose primary function was to replay footage shot on our lightweight cameras by the climbers high on the hill;

— and the landscapes, so many mental snapshots of distant ranges and close-up peaks, soaring faces of snow and rock, awe-inspiring cwms and cols, rifts and ridges, rising thousands of feet above me into the crystal blue.

Already memories recede into a kaleidoscope that needs a mental shake to form a clearcut picture. But now and then the kaleidoscope invades and colonizes my consciousness, drawing me back from recollection to experience, causing a psychosomatic shiver on warm June nights, or a constriction of the throat as a maverick memory of army 'compo' out-tastes the food on my plate at home. So, I'm going to shake the kaleidoscope into a pattern that tells a story, sort out the images like shots in a sequence of film, and begin at the beginning.

First Feelers

Christmas Eve to 17 February
London/the Lakes/Scotland

I had some serious studying to do if I was to get a sense of what was in store. Stanford's map- and bookshop in London's Long Acre proved to be the path to enlightenment. Spending a fair sum of money – Everest books are expensive – I bought Bonington, Hornbein, Hall, Tilman, two guides to trekking in Nepal, and two maps: a wide-shot of the Himalayas, and a close-up of Everest. The saddlebags of my bike could barely accommodate my new mountaineering library.

I knew from further conversations with Rod Caird that the chosen route for this expedition was an approach from the North – Tibet – along the Rongbuk Glacier to the Lhola, and up the West Ridge to the summit. Put like that, it sounded simple enough. But I also knew it was one of the more difficult routes, and had never been climbed successfully by a British team. Tom Hornbein, an American, had done it in 1963 with Willi Unsoeld – so his was the book I first chose to read properly. But not before leafing through the others, to get the 'feel'. Lincoln Hall's *White Limbo*, an account of the 1984 Australian ascent of the North Face, has the most stunning photographs. I use the word advisedly. As I looked at shot after shot, the enormity of the mountain itself, of this expedition's undertaking, and of our task in attempting to make a record of it was increasingly borne in on me. The clichés are as inescapable as the snow, the cold, the wind: the insignificance of man faced with the awesome grandeur of nature – yet equally, human determination conquering inhuman environment. How would we all shape up when, singly, the time came to take on the mountain? My initial fears – discomfort, no sanitary facilities, even no cigarettes – seemed to fade away as I tried to imagine *myself*, not unknown others, in these pictures. Conflicting feelings, confusing fears and a mounting sense of excitement fought in my imagination. And all too soon, I knew, imagination would be overtaken by experience.

I picked up Tom Hornbein's narrative of the battle up the Couloir that now bears his name, where our expedition was to follow. Cheating forgivably, I turned to the later chapters in which Hornbein and Unsoeld achieve their goal – at the cost of total physical and mental exhaustion, and frostbite. *Chomolungma*, as the Tibetans call Everest – Goddess Mother of Earth – is a cruel deity. Even if I had no possibility or intention of going to the summit, I stood in genuine awe of those who had, and those who now hoped to follow in their footsteps.

Hall's *White Limbo* raised another consideration: leadership. The Australian climb was essentially leaderless, decisions being taken in a microcosm of personalized democracy. Ours would be the antithesis, I imagined, though I had not met Dougie Keelan, the leader. But a Joint Services Expedition – Army, Navy, Air Force and Royal Marines – must be inescapably imbued with hierarchy, authority and rank. As outsiders, we would not be subject to military discipline; but as *de facto* expedition members, we must be as obedient to the leader's word as any serviceman. Our lives, in the final analysis, were in Dougie Keelan's hands. I saw this certainty as surely as I anticipated conflicts of interest between him and me, and made a mental note, there and then in London, to remind myself of that fact on the mountain to come.

Meanwhile, I had been getting a lot of stick from my family and friends. Over Christmas, spent with my eighteen-year-old son Sam, my daughter Polly, two years younger, and my ex-wife Jean, I had announced the possibility of my 'going up Everest'. Sam's response was spontaneous: a howl of incredulous and derisive laughter, followed by a clutch of sarcastic comments about stocking up on alcohol over Christmas to compensate for future deprivations. I knew that underneath he was torn between anxiety on his own behalf and excitement on mine. Polly and Jean were more muted, but hit the same tone.

'But do you think you'll survive it, Dad? Not your life, I mean, but your life *style*? It couldn't be further from your usual alcohol and nicotine diet! Look at you now!'

True, I had a glass of wine and my normal untipped cigarette in my hands. As other filter-free, serious smokers occasionally quipped: 'We're a dying breed, Mark!' I had no real answer – I knew I should stop smoking, whether I was going to Everest or not; I knew it would

be sensible to drink a little less. My problem was, I didn't want to stop –
unless Everest were to do it for me, another bonus from this extra-
ordinary assignment. But I had decided to take some cigarettes, and
some scotch, 'just in case'. It wasn't as though I could nip across the
road to the corner shop or the off-licence for a top-up!

My mother was more transparent in her concern for my safety.
Mothers often are. Her few serious questions, and her instinctive
understanding that this was something I genuinely wanted to do, was
going to do, reminded me once again (as if I needed it) that now my
father was dead, my mother alone played that greatest of parental roles:
concerned but unequivocal support. She sensed more completely than
anyone my excitement, tinged with a *frisson* of fear. And I for my part
knew the two horrors she struggled successfully to keep unspoken: that
in my four-month absence, I might die by accident, or she by due
process of age. My mother is seventy-six.

And there was Vicky, my girlfriend – a silly and inadequate word for
a woman I've known for eight years – who is a film editor at Granada,
where I first met her. She lives near Manchester, I live in London, and
we conduct a long-distance relationship that seems to thrive on intermittent contact – as well as keeping British Telecom solvent! Vicky's
initial response, on that unsatisfactory but inevitable telephone, was
fear, followed in short order by enthusiasm when I told her it was a
Granada project. I flattered myself that this was due to the extended
period we would spend together when I returned from the mountain: I
always stay at her house when I am editing at Granada. But I was
wrong. In fact she was nervous that this project might be 'independent',
and lack the support-system of a large television company such as
Granada. Perhaps, I like to think, we were both right.

As for friends, their assorted guffaws added to the rising tide of
derision. I was getting close to saturation-point on the 'What, *you*!'
version. One close friend, another television director, was I think alone
in her immediate encouragement – even outright envy.

'Well, if anything stops you doing it, I'll be there like a shot.' I
wondered idly how she would manage as the only woman amongst
forty men, then quickly banished the thought. She would manage. I
confess I hoped she would never have occasion to find out by reason of
my inability to go. And then, a split second later came that echo-
thought which was becoming automatic: 'But will I still think the same
once I'm there?'

With only weeks to go before we left, Everest by no means monopolized my thoughts: the 1968 programme was in its final throes of editing, and Orly and I were putting in very full days to meet the deadline. But I ploughed ahead with the reading, and began to build a mental picture resting on fact and research, rather than on the vivid imaginings of the first few days. Not that I found the facts any more reassuring than the fiction; but the gradual clothing of my fantasies in the reality of others' experience was permitting me a growing familiarity with my subject – and that I *did* find reassuring. The unknown always carries with it greater fears than the known; and, perhaps unlike some, I find illusions uncomfortable companions in professional, as in personal, life. If I was not altogether ready, I was better prepared for my first encounter with the expedition members.

Wednesday 30 December: De Heems pub, Macclesfield Street, London

I had arranged to meet Roger – Captain R. M. Antolik – at one o'clock; or, as he put it, 13.00 hours. He was not difficult to spot – a clean-cut head above the lunchtime regulars. His open, fresh face with its neat moustache – a whisker too long properly to be called military – looked about and above the crush at the bar. A serious anorak over a navy guernsey sweater (I noticed later a discreet emblem denoting a previous Himalayan expedition) topped long, long legs clad in Rohan-type 'bags'. Those legs, I was to learn later, had qualified Roger for the British Olympics high jump team until, tragically, he broke his back before the competition took place. It seems to have mended itself completely, thanks to the skilfully inserted steel pins, and, I suspect, the matching strength of Roger's own iron determination.

We greeted each other, mutually tentative. It was my first face-to-face discussion with a member of the thirty-six strong team. And Roger had been assigned the unenviable task of liaison with the film crew and Granada TV; up to now, he had been 'first reserve' on the highly competitive expedition roll call. We both recognized that our starting points were quite different: his, to deal with the many problems and requests we would throw up, and find a formula that would reflect the Combined Services' climb in the best light; mine, to make what we hoped would turn out to be six half-hour programmes in the 'fly on the wall' tradition.

We took refuge in practicalities: dates, routes, and timetables, the added weight of the film equipment, the extra high-altitude mountain clothing for the four-man crew. The make-up of the Granada team had established itself quite simply. The first member was Alan Evans, a videotape cameraman and a well-known rock climber in his own right. He had initially been approached by the expedition to take a sabbatical from Granada and make a short film for them, combining his two skills. Then Granada had come in on the act, sniffing a story too good to lose. The private, half-hour expedition film had become a full-blown, prime-time TV documentary series – with the dubious acquiescence of the expedition's Higher Management Committee. Next, since this was to be a series primarily on film rather than tape, came Nick Plowright; he had shot many and varied programmes for Granada, and was still only thirty-one. He was also, as it happened, the son of Granada's Chairman, David Plowright. On sound would be Ian Hills, again an excellent compromise between age, experience and attitude. And finally, myself – almost the oldest man on the expedition, but the same age, Roger told me, as the leader, Dougie Keelan – a Lieutenant-Colonel from the legendarily tough Royal Marines. I hoped the coincidence of our age was a reassuring omen – that it would start us off from our differing departure points on an equal footing. I gave Roger a copy of my CV, which listed a varied bag of documentaries, embracing subjects as different as hole-in-the-heart operations, Miami murder trials, and the death throes of the British Empire.

Over a pint and a pie – the first of many such meals – Roger and I went over the ground. There was an element of the preliminary skirmish in an affair, in the sense that we both knew this was only the first of many, many discussions yet to come, and it was important to both of us that we understood each other – even, but far more ambitiously, got on well.

Much of our hour-long chat had to do with the immediate future – the run-down to departure on 19 February. A weekend in January had been set aside for the whole expedition to come together in Cumbria, some of the members meeting each other for the first time, and everyone bringing their wives or girlfriends for the occasion. It was to be the first, and most important, of a series of briefings. Unavoidably, I was committed that weekend to my 1968 programme, and could not get to the Lakes. This was a blow, particularly for me personally, as it would be the all-important first confrontation between climbers and cameras – them and us. But the other three, Nick, Alan and Ian, would be there meeting, greeting – and filming. And Rod Caird, as executive producer, hoped to attend to see fair play.

Roger accepted the inevitable. 'Well, it's a pity, Mark. But there's another meeting at the Royal Geographical Society on 6 January – a week today. Colonel Keelan, the leader, will be coming, and I know he's very anxious to meet you.'

I could well believe he was – although I wondered exactly what anxieties he had.

'That's going to be OK, Roger. I'm sure I can spare half a day. And I'm not uninterested in meeting the expedition leader myself! We're going to have a few differences to sort out over the next few months, so the sooner we start, the better.'

'Between us, Mark, can we see if we can get your team together for that meeting? I must ask them, and you, to fill in some forms for clothing sizes, visas and so on – 11.30 hours, then, at the RGS.'

The first bridge had been built. We parted, each to our respective worlds, which all too soon were to become one.

Wednesday 6 January: Royal Geographical Society, London

Knowing Dougie Keelan to be a Marines Colonel, I expected a 'tough nut'; but I had not expected such a diminutive tough nut. Compact and wiry, with a definite twang of 'officer class', Dougie Keelan struck me immediately as a no-nonsense merchant. A handshake belying his stature greeted my formal 'Glad to meet you, Colonel Keelan.'

'Dougie,' he replied. A promising sign. 'Let's get down to business,' he continued, offering me, and the crew who had managed to get down to London from Manchester, seats round a table. We had barely put bum to chair when Dougie went straight for the journalistic jugular.

'I know this is to be a "warts and all" programme. But it's equally a Combined Services expedition, of which I am the leader. How do you anticipate resolving the inherent contradictions, and dealing with the question of intrusion?'

I swallowed and delivered my standard piece.

'We'll want, and expect, to film *everything*, and argue afterwards – if necessary. We will, inevitably, be a nuisance to put it mildly, and quite possibly a downright menace. We'll ask awkward questions, we'll be present – I hope – at crucial times, we'll eavesdrop on critical decision-making. I don't expect you, or your team, to enjoy every moment of this enterprise. But only if we have a common acceptance of what is involved will the series begin to approach what we both would wish it to be – different though that may be.'

I hope it all sounded less pompous spoken than it reads on the page. Either way, the chips were down. But Dougie played the Ace of Spades.

'We cannot rule out the possibility of casualties, even fatalities. Where will you draw the line?'

'I see no line. We must attempt to cover tragedy just as we would happiness or humour. The crunch will come later, in the editing. It would be wrong of me to give my word here and now, since Granada have editorial control in the last analysis, but I would stake my reputation on your having no real disagreements with us at that stage. Even in the event of a death, which of course we all hope won't occur, I would be surprised and disappointed if you, and also the bereaved family, do not support the way in which the tragedy is presented.'

'I accept that. As long as we feel we can communicate, both on the hill and afterwards, we should be able to iron out any problems.'

The understanding, in both letter and spirit, was typical of Dougie.

Later, but before leaving for Everest, I felt I had been less than totally honest, less than totally accurate. In the first place, the journal-ist in me knew that a casualty would be 'good copy' – 'bad news is good news', as the cynical slogan goes. But there is always the question of degree, and of the story's outcome. The contradictions will bear, I hope, a little elaboration.

Imagine that this were a feature film rather than a documentary – fiction rather than fact. An ideal scenario might well run thus: two men, on a problematic leg of the climb, are late checking in on their two-way radio. Concern mounts. As night falls and there is still no word either from them or from the camp above at which they were due to arrive, concern becomes genuine and well grounded fear. At both camps, everyone eventually turns in; there is no value in risking further danger sending out search parties in darkness. Few members of the expedition sleep soundly: each knows it might well have been him out there in temperatures of down to minus 40 degrees centigrade with only a sleeping bag – albeit the best bag in the world. Then, soon after sun-up, the radio from the high camp crackles into life: the two have struggled in. There have been problems, but they are safe; they may have frostbite, but they are alive.

This has happened in fact, as well as in my imagined fiction. But I am dealing here with documentary, and its very essence is that, in starting a story at the beginning, you do not and cannot know the end until it arrives. Mankind, it seems, savours the spice of a mystery menu. Why do we read thrillers, go to horror movies, attend motor racing? To know the outcome, for sure; but also, to share vicariously in the risk? To be, in short, a voyeur?

So the expectation, in theory, of 'something going wrong' is only what any journalist or documentary maker will welcome; but, in practice – and especially on a project as essentially co-operative as this – one's sense of involvement with the common aim, and, more importantly, with the participants themselves, means that the shock of major mishap affects everyone equally (excepting, of course, family). But what is missed when it occurs, is gone for ever; what is 'in the can' is there to be evaluated, used or rejected as sober reflection demands. What one has recorded primarily as a journalist, one edits and presents as a fellow human being. I write with the experience of having applied this principle, and never found it wanting.

It is in this respect that I felt I had been inaccurate; I should have expressed to Dougie what the benefit of time has allowed me to attempt to articulate here: in sum, we from Granada must become so intrinsically part of the expedition as a whole that we would feel a loss of life as keenly as any serviceman.

If I failed myself on that day, what I *had* managed to say Dougie seemed to accept. And now the 'heavy' session was at an end. We were all invited over to the Royal Geographical Society's model of Mount Everest, a six-foot-square relief version of the mountain in miniature.

The first victorious ascent by Sir Edmund Hillary and Sherpa Tenzing in 1953 was marked permanently. Now, thirty-five years and many conquests later, the Combined Services climb was etched in red tape on the papier mâché. As with my first browse through the photographs, the enormity of the endeavour seemed suddenly over-powering – for all of us on the film crew, I found out later. Dougie's confidence was scant comfort, as we studied our intended route. Alan was determined to get as high as possible – on top of the West Shoulder at around 24,000 feet – with a Video-8 camera, if he couldn't carry the thirty-pound film camera. Not for the last time, we were told about the problems of altitude and acclimatization. In the increasingly oxygen-deprived atmosphere of the upper reaches, a few ounces seem like as many pounds; every few yards as many miles. We would have oxygen with us, but only for the final stages.

Foolishly, I had dreamed of helicopters to fly us in, if not to hover triumphantly over the successful summiteers! My hopes were grounded as surely as the helicopter would be: no chopper can operate at such altitudes, and if we were to survive at all, even at Base Camp, gradual acclimatization was the only way. Accordingly, the whole party – including, of course, us – was to start with a ten-day trek soon after arrival in Kathmandu, Nepal. Indeed, we were going to Nepal, rather than direct to Tibet, partly so that we could, literally step by step, get used to the conditions. Kathmandu is at 4,000 feet, and we were going to walk to 16,000 before even crossing the Tibetan border. For one whose principal exercise is a six-mile cycle ride to work, the prospect sounded horrendous. I asked myself – and only myself – whether I could make it, could keep pace with thirty-seven servicemen obviously all far fitter than I.

I could not restrain pangs of regret that our route did not take in Lhasa and the Dalai Lama's citadel of the Potala, let alone Beijing. (I knew an advance party, led by deputy leader Col. Henry Day, would be going in via Hong Kong, Beijing and Lhasa, concluding negotiations for the expedition's *laisser-passer* with the Chinese Mountaineering Association, the CMA.) But *my* visit to these exotic places would have to wait; and Kathmandu was not such a bad consolation prize! I had the feeling that looking on the bright side would be a very useful lesson to rehearse here at home, and take with me 'on the hill'.

Roger Antolik appeared, armed with the promised forms. We greeted him with comments about quadruplicates and army red tape, which he took in good part.

'But you'll be the losers', he added, 'when you find all this gear doesn't fit properly. I can't change it out there you know!'

So, dutifully enough, we all set about recording waist and chest diameters, inside leg measurements and boot sizes, scrawling digits in vertical columns until we felt more like some piece of computer software than a regular film crew.

'What's this then, Roger? Willy-warmers, XS to XXL? Even the army has a sense of humour then?'

A wry smile answered my query about the last line on the form.

'Just fill it in as you see fit, Mark. But I'll tell you now, we've run out of the XXLs!'

I guessed that Roger had probably been the perpetrator of the bogus entry. Or was it Pat Parsons, who was i/c equipment?* (I was already getting quite fluent with the jargon.) Disregarding whatever indignities it might entail, I put a circle round the XS willy-warmer and handed over my form. Passports, Nepalese visa forms, and four photos of each of us soon joined Roger's swelling file marked 'Granada'. Greatly to my relief, Roger had undertaken to buy, cajole or extort all the equipment from the many well-wishing firms which manufactured it. Famous names in mountaineering gear had offered generous discounts or freebies, and I discovered that many other concerns less conspicuously involved had made large contributions to the £250,000 cost of the expedition.

Now it was time to repair to a watering hole well-known to another member of both the team and the organizing committee, one Capt. Giles Gittings of the Coldstream Guards. He proved to be an archetypal Guards officer, complete with recently acquired Seychelles tan, a Porsche, and a bevy of female friends. At the pub, he confided in me that he had a problem about our filming at the weekend in the Lakes; his companion in the Seychelles was to be replaced by a well-known model, and she was under an exclusive TV contract to a certain agency. I remained unsure whether the contract with the model, or the conflict with *la Seychelloise* was uppermost in his mind.

Another new face belonged to Major John Fitzgerald, the Project Officer. He had spent two years getting the expedition on its administrative rails – raising money, coordinating policy, liaising with the 'big-wigs' of the Higher Management Committee. Like Giles, John Fitzgerald was every inch the officer: clipped, confident, and scarcely credible to the jaundiced eye of the TV journalist. But, unlike Giles, he had a practised line in understatement. This must be an art acquired as you rise up the ranks. Dougie had it off to a T, and John's *sotto voce* disclaimers were well on the way.

'Of course, there are one or two expedition members whose units

*in charge of equipment

we don't mention. In public they appear in civvies, but on duty they're often bursting into the Iranian Embassy or somewhere.'

I took the hint. I had met men from the same special service on a previous film in Belize, and I knew their unspoken ambition: to get the job done, come what may. I made a mental note to watch out for these gentlemen, likely summiteers if anyone was.

The invariable pint and pie were finished. I approached Dougie to bid my farewells, hand extended. He shook it firmly, but warmly. Leaving the pub for his Range Rover and a long drive to his home in Scotland, his parting shot found its mark.

'We're going to knock the bastard off – we're right on line. It's going to be a good one!'

I returned his handshake and his optimism.

'It will be, Dougie, in so far as I can influence it.'

I meant it.

Friday 16 January to Saturday 17 January: Windermere

The weekend in the Lakes went off well, as I know from the film shot over those two days. Almost all the expedition members were present, and with them their wives or girlfriends. There were to be no women at all on the expedition and the Lakes weekend provided the opportunity not only for the mountaineers to meet each other if they had not already done so, but also their families, who would be left behind in Britain but could at least keep in contact with each other over the months to come. Much metaphorical ice was broken, particularly the climbers' natural suspicions about having a film crew with them, before we faced the all too literal ice of Everest. Nick, Alan and Ian must have done a grand job in this respect, judging by the relaxed and jokey repartee of the conversations recorded. Pat Parsons, a Royal Marines captain and natural clown who was to figure prominently in the weeks to come, brought the house down with his explanation of the high-altitude clothing purchased for the expedition – especially when demonstrating, up to a point, the purpose of the double-ended zip that ran from the neck to the small of the back of the one piece down suit. This essential feature of the design, known universally, I was to discover, as the 'crap hatch', elicited laughter from the climbers' wives and knowing smiles of approval from the men who would be making use of it.

But there was also business of a more serious nature. On the first evening the Chairman of the Higher Management Committee, Air Marshal Sir John Sutton, addressed the assembled company by way of introduction to the weekend's proceedings. Here, and on many occasions throughout this book, I shall quote selectively from our transcripts of the event, as recorded on film. They add a quality of veracity, of 'thereness', with which no recounting of mine can compete, and the words used by the men themselves – sometimes at moments of high tension – reveal not only what happened, but how it felt for *them*, the expedition members.

Not that there was any great tension about that Friday at the Beech Hotel, Windermere; it was a relaxed and comradely affair, as I have said, and Sir John opened, in time-honoured fashion, on a light-hearted note.

SIR JOHN SUTTON Knowing I had to say a few words at this important gathering this evening, and wondering how I might start, I thought perhaps it might be helpful if I found out whether today was a significant anniversary of anything. But when I discovered that the two major events recorded were the failure of Shackleton to reach the South Pole in 1909 and the day before Prohibition started in America in 1920, I could see it was not at all appropriate . . .

No project of this size can proceed without financial backing, and from the start therefore we've had the problem of finding about two hundred thousand pounds to foot all the bills. Well, the soldiers', sailors', marines' and airmen's funds of various kinds have all made major contributions to the costs, as have the Services' mountaineering organizations, and not least you yourselves, the members. But these contributions, although very important, are of course not nearly enough to mount an expedition of this kind and so we have had to seek commercial sponsorship, and I am therefore most grateful to have the opportunity this evening to publicly thank all of our sponsors and I am delighted that some of them have managed to join us at our table tonight . . .

Clearly no venture of this kind should be without a record of the events, or a tremendous opportunity would be lost. Fortunately for us Granada Television were alive to the opportunity and as you can see they are here with us this evening, and I use the phrase 'with us' deliberately because even though they are going to produce a film for their own purposes they will achieve that result as an integral part of the team. We welcome you aboard . . .

Dougie Keelan and I had already agreed this principle, and I was glad to have it recognized by the Chairman of the Higher Management Committee. There was no doubt that they were taking a risk: this was to be a 'warts and all' production and they knew it, but I had stressed that we too were making an act of faith, in that if the climbers chose not to co-operate with us, we would be backing a sure loser and at considerable cost, both financial and physical. So the principle of team work, of shared rather than separate ambitions, was not only desirable – it was essential. And by and large it was to work out that way, and well.

The *pièce de résistance* of the weekend was a long briefing by Dougie Keelan of all those present – some of it aimed at the wives, some at the mountaineers. He spelt out the background of the expedition, its timetable for the future, the arrangements for the once-a-month mail deliveries, and the way in which he had planned the expedition from a practical point of view. Dougie was to end his briefing on a note of life and death significance to the expedition, but he began, for those who might not know them, with a few harmless facts.

DOUGIE Well, first a little bit, if I may, about Everest and its broad background. In spite of snippets in the press a year or so ago about K2, the second highest mountain in the world, getting bigger and Everest perhaps getting smaller – they have now actually validated it all and I can assure you that not only has Everest got a bit bigger but K2 has in fact got a little smaller, so there is absolutely no doubt that we are going to climb the highest mountain in the world.

Britain as a nation has always had a great interest in Mount Everest, and some of the very earliest expeditions and reconnaissances starting in 1921 were British. It was climbed of course for the first time in 1953 by a British expedition, for the second time in '75 by the British, by Chris Bonington's team on the South West Face, and again in '76 by a British Army team lead by Colonel Tony Streather. Henry Day and I were on that expedition. Are we the only two, Henry?

HENRY And Dick.

DOUGIE And Dick Hardie, of course. Dick, Henry and I are the only three who were on that expedition, and are also on this one. Now there have been something like, I think it's nineteen British expeditions to Mount Everest, and it's only those three that have been successful. And not one of them has been successful from the north or the Chinese approach; all three were done from the Nepalese side. Now it would be wrong of me to say that we're planning to do what has not been done before. It has been done before, not often, and indeed with great difficulty, and it has always been very weather dependent. But it will be, assuming we're successful, the first time that anybody British will have got to the top from the north, in other words from the Chinese side, and that is the great plug that we make to the press. It's a long route, and a hard route, as all of you who are mountaineers will know from the landmarks – the French Spur, the West Shoulder, the Diagonal Ditch, the Hornbein Couloir and the Yellow Band . . .

Now we are of course a large expedition and there is no way that I, or Henry the deputy leader, can possibly manage to control the expedition if we are dealing not only with thirty-six different climbers, but with a TV crew, an artist, and all the other conflicting requirements, unless we split it down into groups. And following the good old infantry principle of building on bricks of four, we are going to work on those broad teams . . .

Here, Dougie indicated the team lists pinned up on a noticeboard. It was apparent on more than one face in his audience that this particular strategy of Dougie's did not find favour. Old friends from earlier expeditions had expected to live and work together. But Dougie had anticipated the dissatisfaction.

DOUGIE Now if you cast your eye down the composition of those teams, and a lot of thought has gone into it, you will notice that we have done our best to split the Services up, and the ranks up, and the previous expedition cliques if you like. Cliques is probably the wrong word, but the cliques that might develop because of a bond of previous experience. We've done our best to try and break that down, so that instead of having lots of separate little expeditions we've got one big one. Now I suspect that one or two of you will be sucking your teeth, not aloud I hope, and thinking, 'now why the devil have they done that? why can't I be with my oppo?' Well, if you think through the logic of that, I am sure you will agree that I am right – at least at first. Now things will change, people will get sick, somebody perhaps will find they can't possibly share a tent with whoever it is they are meant to be sharing for whatever personal reasons there may be, and there is room for negotiation and room for change. But in a broad sense, right at the beginning, I ask you please to accept this breakdown . . .

Servicemen are disciplined, and obey orders whether they like them or not. The knowing glances and raised eyebrows that had preceded Dougie's explanation now gave way to impassive expressions. It was impossible to discern whether Dougie had won over his men to his point of view, or whether they recognized a *fait accompli* when they saw one. In the event, it was never to be an issue. The teams did work together on the mountain, and willingly; but as Dougie had predicted, sickness and circumstance soon dictated changes, and by the end not one team had remained intact. There was, however, another reason why the teams might alter. Dougie now turned to this subject, and across the room, the tension tightened.

DOUGIE Now I want to dwell on something which I am sure it won't be necessary to dwell on ever again during the life of this expedition – and that is the business of casualties. We have all been in the Himalayas before, we have all lost friends in the high hills at one time or another – and we all go to the high mountains for whatever our personal and individual motivation may be. I do believe it's important just to make a brief statement once only at the beginning of an expedition like this, so that we all have said what has to be said and it's out of the way, but none the less underlining it so that we have a basic common understanding. I think I can speak for all of us when I say that if we're careful – and we are a careful, well selected crew with lots of experience – we should not have accidents in a subjective sense. It's the objective ones which of course we can't cater for, and it's the objective ones which we must do our level best to limit, by careful route selection, by following the rules, and by not cutting corners. None the less – Murphy's Law – a group this size statistically does stand to take a casualty or two. You've thought of this, I certainly have, and we are going to just get shot of this subject once and for all, now. I believe I speak for all of us when I say that in the event of there being casualties, or a casualty, there can be no question of abandoning the expedition. We're here to get to the top, and only in the event of a major disaster would we think of turning back, letting down our sponsors and so on. I am, I can assure you, an extremely cautious and safe person by nature, and I think most people in this room are as well. It should not happen; but if it does, let us proceed with regret that it's happened but mindful none the less we're there to climb the mountain. If there is a disaster on the other hand, then it's another story, and we will talk collectively amongst ourselves in that event. Now is there anything that anyone wants to say? I said that I was only going to raise this once throughout the whole expedition and that is so, but I would like to give the floor to anybody else that has a view on this . . .

There was a long pause.

DOUGIE Grand, OK. Let's pretend now that that conversation hasn't happened. But it has, and it's at the bottom of our minds, and I believe that it's right that we've actually had it . . .

There was a hush as Dougie concluded his speech. Everyone present knew the reality, the statistical likelihood of three and a half deaths among the assembled mountaineers. In the history of Everest ascents, one in ten climbers never return. The wives and girlfriends, who could only wait anxiously back home for the one piece of news they least wanted to hear, bit their lips even more than their menfolk. It was a sombre moment, in stark contrast to the hilarity of most of the weekend. But mountaineering, as one of the men was to tell me much later, is about extremes. By then I knew what he meant; for now, I would have to make do with a dress rehearsal in Scotland.

Monday 1 February to Wednesday 3 February: Glencoe

The automatic Departures board clacked impersonally: 'platform 13, 20.55, terminating at Fort William. No restaurant or buffet facilities available on this train.' Thirteen hours on a sleeper, and not even a British Rail sandwich to watch curl at the edges!

Humping my new – too new – rucksack, I found my reserved couchette. The train seemed fairly empty, so the chances of keeping the compartment to myself looked good. Swinging the rucksack off my back and onto the lower bunk, I cracked my head on the upper. Perhaps a tent had some merits?

I was *en route* to join Roger Antolik and his colleague, Simon Lowe, in a Glencoe guest house for a taste of training. Nick, Alan and Ian were making their own way from Manchester, together with the film gear, 'winterized' and packed in adapted rucksacks for so-called simple transport – on our backs.

There proved to be a certain irony in Roger's invitation, 'Come up and give the gear and yourselves a dry run'. As the train drew into Fort William, diagonal sleet slashed at the windows. Soon I had joined the others at the bed and breakfast in Ballachulish. I can imagine it's a beautiful spot, but this Tuesday morning the snow-topped hills disappeared into thick clouds the colour of lead. As we looked out, our hearts weren't much lighter. The prospect of climbing those hills could not have been less inviting.

Roger had been to my house a few days before to deliver my 'wardrobe', a garish conglomeration of garments with names quaintly outlandish: Shell jacket, Javelin sallopets, Scarpa boots, Gortex gaiters, Grivel crampons. We had a quick rehearsal of which items went inside which, and how *I* got inside *them*. Solving a Chinese puzzle might well have been simpler.

And now, it was for real. For the first time, I struggled into clothing that would be my cover and companion for months on end.

The first leg of this Highland dry run I backed wholeheartedly: into two cars and a couple of miles along the road through the glen, to the bottom of an endless scree- and snow-covered hillside, ascending at about one-in-one to the heavens. Miraculously, maniacal mountain-climbers were already dotted up the gully and ridge, orange specks in a sea of white. A party in well-worn climbing gear laughed uproariously at our spick and span outfits.

Roger and Simon set off, Alan keeping up confidently with the leaders, and Nick not too far behind. Then came a long gap between the advance party and myself and Ian, both gasping in the rear. It was a pattern, did I but know it, that was to be repeated – not only over the next two days, but the hundred that were to come on the Rongbuk Glacier leading up to Mount Everest.

Thoughts about the driving sleet and bitter wind blew away in seconds as our bodies became breathing machines first and last, and very inefficient ones at that. My only consolation was the surprising discovery that a few minutes' pause recharged the batteries completely. Having climbed around 1,000 feet, Roger, Simon and Alan stopped and waited for the stragglers. We looked down at the cars, Dinky toys in a model landscape. Even in the sleet, by now more solid

1. The thirty-six climbing members of BSEE 88 with Project Officer John Fitzgerald and Artist Lincoln Rowe in the garden of the Summit Hotel, Kathmandu. *Top*: (L to R): Dave (Howie), Dave (Orange), Al (Miller), Lincoln, Simon (Gray), Simon (Lowe), John (Fitzgerald), Tug, Bill, Jim, Martin, Laurie, Giles, Johnny, Al (McLeod), John (Vlasto), Steve (Bell), Dave (Maxwell), Andy (Hughes), Richard. *Middle*: Pat, Nev, Dave (Nicholls), Henry (Deputy Leader), Dougie (Leader), Keith, Kit, Nigel, Merv. *Bottom*: Ted, Duncan, Dave (Torrington), Steve (Last), Luke, Charlie, Terry, Andy (Edington), Dick. *Missing*: Roger, who took the photo. (For a full list of names, ranks, Services and regiments, see Appendix B.)

2. 'The Summit Hotel had laid on a special Nepali welcome' – Nick Plowright does his bit towards building up the £500 beer bill.

3. From the Summit Hotel: Kathmandu and the Himalayas.

4. Everest and the West Ridge from the Pilatus Porter at 20,000 feet plus. '…it looked both like a model, and yet unimaginably immense.'

5. Nick surveys our equipment bound for Base Camp. About as much went with us on the trek.

6. 'Nepal is nothing if not green – in the valleys.'

7. Pat Parsons and his rucksack on the acclimatizing trek.

8. Dougie Keelan, the expedition leader, takes a breather on the trek to reflect on the future.

9. Luke Hughes, in the Jugal Himal, with an egg in a shell. Soon eggs would be in powder form.

10. A rest-stop on the trek. Ian jots down what he has recorded, while the two Andys – Hughes and Edington – top up the bodily fluids.

11. Nick and Al filming on the trek: 'all too often the very next valley offered an even better backdrop.'

12. One of our two 'filming porters' beats us up a hillside.

13. The end of another exhausting day – the Himalayas from a campsite on the trek.

14. Xegar – the old village and the ruined 'Dzong', or fort, above it.

15. Tibet – 'children ... held out hands black with dirt ... Empty tins were the most popular.'

snow, I had to grant a begrudging admiration for the scenery – bleak and unrelenting to the human body, but vastly impressive to the soul. And this was only Scotland – a microcosm, if that, of the Himalayas. An eagle soared high above us, grandly impervious to the buffeting wind and driving snow.

We set off again, and now came my next surprise – second wind. It was still very hard, I still panted like a grampus, but I felt unmistakably less consumed by the one activity of catching breath. We scaled a small rockface – not difficult climbing, but quite enough for *this* doubtful débutant. The wet and icy surface seemed to offer little purchase to the awkward, unbending climbing boots. Cold aside, I would have been far happier in supple gym shoes, and with bare hands instead of waterproof mittens over inner gloves.

At 2,500 feet, or so Roger maintained, we called a halt. The cloud covered the hilltops ahead of us, and I for one was quite happy to turn round. It had been harder by far than any walking for pleasure in the Peak District with Vicky, or following the cliff path in Cornwall. But it could have been worse. That was a solid crumb of comfort. With this, at least, I could cope. It may not have been much, but a pathetic exhilaration accompanied me back down. Was I beginning to get an inkling of what it was that drove men, and some women, to the top of Everest? It was not, surely, just that 'it was there', as Mallory had claimed in the 1920s; but that it could be beaten, that inanimate mountain, by a mere mortal. I made another entry in my mental notebook – to film a few 'vox pops' on the subject with the expedition members. Perhaps one might express in a nutshell what was still to me elusive – the rationale of mountaineering.

The next fortnight was spent in a furious farrago of farewells, jabs for strange diseases, final post-production work on the 1968 project, and small but significant arrangements like making a will, and delivering my pet lovebird to my mother for safe-keeping. I did feel it necessary, and perhaps I was being over-dramatic, to write two letters to my children telling them how much they meant to me, and that I would be thinking of them often. Not being given to praying, I trusted that my good fortune to date would continue, and that these would be *au revoirs* and not *adieus*. There was little time for reflection, but now and then an attack of nerves punctuated the humdrum crescendo of preparation – long moments of silence in the storm. They should have been a warning of what was to come.

Up, Up and Away

And then, inevitably, the day arrived. I left London, rucksack and kit bag packed and re-packed with a personal medical supply sufficient to stock an average high street chemist, and even a Christmas cake against the direst of eventualities. Driven by Vicky, I arrived at Brize Norton in Oxfordshire, the RAF airfield from which we were to fly to Kathmandu the next day. The last farewell is often the worst, and this was no exception: Vicky bore the brunt of my anxiety and emotion, and yet, whatever her own feelings, managed to be a comfort at the same time. It was not a moment to prolong, and she was soon on her way back home, nursing, as she was to write in a letter I would not receive for a month, her own fears and feelings for my safety and our three-month enforced separation. At the bar, I found the film crew and around half the expedition members, almost all new faces and unfamiliar names. Roger Antolik, aided by Nick, Alan and Ian who had already met most of them in the Lake District, introduced me.

'This is Andy Hughes, one of the doctors.' (A good one to remember, I thought.)

'And Martin Bazire, in charge of catering.' (What a thankless task, I guessed correctly, not knowing then that he was also the nephew of one of my mother's greatest friends.)

'And Steve Bell, an ex-Marine now turned Himalayan trek entrepreneur . . .'

Quietly, Alan Evans, versed in climbing culture, explained that Steve was a well-known figure with an enviable record under his ice axe, and on the face of it a likely summiteer. In the event, the most predictable and the most ridiculous of reasons were to cheat him of that distinction – bad weather, followed by a severely sunburnt bum at the critical moment.

Innocent in these early days, I pushed Steve on who else was on his list of Everest-eaters. He was reticent, quite rightly I now realize, when so many imponderable factors play their part. I mentioned names I had heard, but as yet had no faces to put to them.

'Merv Middleton, Dave Maxwell, Dave Nicholls?' Steve agreed they were possibilities, and we were both right.

'Henry Day, the deputy leader?' I had at least met Henry in the helter-skelter of the last few days, and his single-mindedness had made an impression.

'Yes – well, let's say he desperately wants to get to the top. But if I know Henry, he may not get much moral support from the other lads.' I sensed a story here. What had Henry Day done?

'Well, wait and tell me more when we're filming, Steve. Perhaps there's more to this than meets the eye?'

'No chance,' he smiled. 'When that camera's going I'll clam up like the proverbial Trappist.'

'OK, your prerogative. But I'm sure we'll find someone who's prepared to give us the gen.'

'Or do you mean dish the dirt?' Another enigmatic smile from Steve. I didn't mean that, and I was right that someone would be prepared to say more than Steve. But I made a mental note to be more diplomatic. These were, after all, servicemen, schooled to silence in front of the media.

The talk switched to the state of the road between Kathmandu and the Tibetan base camp area. There were rumours of a twenty-kilometre stretch of landslide just over the Tibetan border, totally impassible, even in trucks. From my guidebook, I knew this to be a long, steep ascent of some 6,000 feet up a succession of hairpins, noted in the book for its stunning views. I thought first of the expedition's seventeen tons of equipment and stores, including all our camera gear and film stock. Porters abounded, it was said. They would need to.

We, the film crew, wondered amongst ourselves what to call the expedition members as a collective noun: 'expedition members' was obviously too cumbersome, and other possibilities tended to sound patronizing. The problem was solved inadvertently by Dougie Keelan, who asked me with genuine concern how things were going with the lads. That was it. From then on it would be 'the leader and the lads'.

My mind boggling over such momentous practical problems, I

eventually made my way to bed. Darkness brought different and deeper thoughts – family and friends, comfort and home – now all to be cut away in exchange for an adventure with the unknown.

Friday 19 February: Brize Norton to Kathmandu

The flight was scheduled to leave at two o'clock, or 1400 as I was learning to call it. While the VC 10 was being loaded with all the equipment – it would take up half the seating area of the plane – we were desperately trying to locate batteries for our Video-8 cameras. Roger Antolik had picked up two V90s, the latest and most sophisticated model from Sony, the day before; but on opening the cases we found they had only one spare battery. This is adequate for use in a normal world of electrical power points – you just plug in the charging unit supplied with the camera. But we would be relying on solar panels to recharge batteries, and we were unsure how effective they would be, and how the low temperatures would affect the batteries themselves. We set about telephoning all the hi-fi and photography shops in the Brize Norton area – not a very protracted business. It became quickly apparent that the V90 was so new that no one stocked it, let alone spare batteries for it. In desperation we contacted Sony in Staines. Yes, they had four, and that was all. Getting Granada to organize a motorbike pick-up and delivery, we sat back, fingers crossed that the batteries would arrive before the plane left. They did – when we had gone through customs and were just on the point of leaving the terminal to walk across to the aircraft.

The RAF, in its capacity as an airline, is unique in two respects: it boasts an accident-free record, and it sits you facing backwards on its planes. The two are in fact connected: if there were to be a crash, the seat back would take the strain of impact. But it is a strange sensation when the surge of power for take-off throws you forward out of your seat, rather than back into it.

There was the usual announcement about life jackets and ensuring your seatback is in an upright position, and we were off. Facing a huge pile of boxes and crates netted down like captured big game was a change from the conventional view of row upon row of seats, but acceptable enough. Less welcome was the RAF practice of forbidding alcohol on their flights – but it would be good training for the mountain, I consoled myself. And of course there was no in-flight movie.

So we set about making our own movie and got in everybody's way wandering up and down the aisle with our Arriflex and Nagra. I kicked off, predictably enough, with Dougie Keelan. Why *this* mountain? I asked him.

DOUGIE Everest is of course the highest mountain in the world and because it is just that, inevitably it is going to lure people towards it – most particularly the sort of people to whom a challenge of this sort is something they can't resist. I think if you were to go round and talk to all the men on this expedition they see the 'Big E' as the ultimate challenge to strive for . . .

I did as the leader suggested. Dave Maxwell had been fingered as a likely lad for the summit, so we stuck the gun mike under his nose, put the camera in front of his face, and clapped the clapperboard. They would all have to get used to this, so it might as well be sooner rather than later! I put the standard question, and got the standard answer.

DAVE (MAXWELL) It's the highest mountain in the world and therefore it has its own attraction, you know, and it must be the ultimate goal for any climber to want to go to tackle it, I suppose.

MARK Any special training recently?

DAVE Just the normal fitness training, gymnasium training. And we've been up in Scotland a couple of times. The weather wasn't too good, as you probably found yourselves, and that's about it.

MARK If I was to twist your arm, what chances would you put on your getting up there?

DAVE Me personally, I've got as good a chance as anybody else, you know. And hopefully if I am going strong enough at the time, I'll get the opportunity.

MARK No cold feet then?

DAVE Oh no! I'll be going for it! . . .

Cold feet, I had reckoned smugly, was an apt enough question in the circumstances. I had tried it on Dougie as well.

DOUGIE I think cold feet is really the wrong way to describe it. I think I would be less than honest if I said I am not slightly apprehensive about it, but that's hardly surprising, is it? We have got fifty-one, fifty-two in fact, in the party including Lincoln Rowe our artist and yourselves and the ten Sherpas, and yes, I am apprehensive. But I am confident as well, and I feel that that's realistic, and I hope an encouraging way to approach our problem. They're all a smashing gang, as you see . . .

Having an artist on the expedition struck me as an interesting sideline, providing us with a visual running theme with a difference. Little did I know – and nor could Lincoln – that visa problems were to beset the unfortunate artist and dictate a very different plan of action from the one he envisaged.

LINCOLN ROWE Well, I have been invited along as the expedition artist, and this is a job I've done twice before. I have got to be here for the entire expedition, but I'm only going to be on the north side until about the end of April. The plan then is for me to go back round and onto the south side of Everest to paint and record the south side, and I hope we also get to do the Tenzing family, to do some portraiture. And so at the end of the day, my brief really is to cover the whole Everest theme, you know. But I also intend hopefully getting up as high as possible. I'll certainly be working my passage by carrying loads as I have done before, and on the way I'll do my own sketching and work for the pictures.

MARK In these days of cameras and video and so on, isn't there something charmingly antiquated about you going along like someone from the *Illustrated London News*?

LINCOLN Well, yes, it's an old tradition obviously, and it's a nice revival of it. I think people nowadays are becoming a little saturated with the photographic image. We are bombarded with it right, left and centre, and as you say there is something rather charming about having an artist along . . .

At this early stage I was on the lookout for 'characters', climbers who had a natural bent for coming across larger-than-life on television. Across from Lincoln was Ted Atkins, an outspoken Geordie in the RAF and destined to be the expedition joker. I could not know this then, but I might have taken Ted's unlikely apparel as a pointer: while everyone else wore an open neck shirt, Ted sported a fulsome bow-tie and, on his head, a magnificent straw boater.

MARK What's the special gear for? Is it just for fun?

TED Well, the hat is just daft, but my mate's wife Wendy Taylor made me this bow-tie. It's made from an ordinary tie and it's the only one in existence, I believe.

MARK As a bow-tie?

TED As a bow-tie, yes.

MARK Can you try to put into words what's so special about the 'Big E', as Dougie calls Mount Everest?

TED The 'Big E'? It's going to be a big challenge because it's so fearsome, it's just mega, immense, a challenge. It's not just the technical difficulties, it's getting up there as far as you can without using oxygen. It's just an immense challenge. You've got the wind, you've got the mountain, you've got the conditions, you've got avalanches and the actual climbing itself, and on top of that it's the highest mountain in the world at the end of the day . . .

As a parting shot – it was already getting dark, making further filming out of the question – I decided to pick up Steve Bell's challenge of the previous evening and see whether he would indeed clam up when faced with the camera. To my relief he played along with our game.

STEVE Just going to Tibet is quite something, but you know Everest is the highest lump of rock in the world and that's a good enough reason for me.

MARK Who is going to be there on the top?

STEVE Oh, I certainly hope it will be me, amongst others, but I'm sure that most of the thirty-six members also hope it will be them. We'll just have to wait and see.

MARK Have you got any kind of cold feet? Are you leaving wives or kids behind?

STEVE Certainly no wives, probably no kids! So I've got no ties back home.

MARK So you're all set.

STEVE Very much so! . . .

As the sun set in front of us (this flying backwards continued to feel disorienting) we all tried to grab some sleep. I dozed fitfully, my head tucked into the one-foot-square airline pillow. I have to confess that, prompted by the example of others, I took this little pillow with me when I left the plane, and very glad of it I was. As I moved from camp to camp up and down the Rongbuk Glacier, the pillow went with me, providing the one soft surface my aching body enjoyed. I have it now, filthy and still unwashed, as a silent but sobering reminder of those nights on the ice.

Bahrain when we got there – our only stop – was anything but icy, although it was the middle of the night. But the terminal was an air-conditioned oasis of marble in the surrounding flat desert, and it had a duty-free shop. Bemoaning the fact that it was not Dubai, the cheapest duty-free shop in the world and only a gallon or two of jet fuel away, I set out to stock up on cigarettes and scotch, and encountered my first setback in the catalogue of deprivation to come. They had no unfiltered cigarettes! Gritting my teeth, I made my selection from the spatted varieties. A quick bit of mental arithmetic informed me that a thousand would see me through the first month at least, by which time some alternative system of supply might be devised. As for the alcohol, I made do with two litres, trusting to top them up with my fair share of the expedition's Famous Grouse, thoughtfully made available by its manufacturers at a bargain price. Loaded with plastic bags, and earning not a few caustic comments, I returned to the VC 10.

Kathmandu is five hours ahead of the UK, so the night was short – mercifully so, as I failed to get any proper sleep. The air terminal at Kathmandu is no match for Bahrain – more a series of concrete sheds than an international airport concourse. But it does much the same job as any other, while a new and far grander building is being constructed alongside it, with foreign aid. We all filed through, lugging our rucksacks and nervously checking on the continued existence of our twenty-nine boxes of film equipment. All present and correct – so far, so good! Having loaded the heavy gear on to the backs of trucks, we loaded ourselves on to a spectacularly decorated bus, all blues and golds and scarlets. So this was it: Kathmandu, once a haven for hippies and still sporting a Freak Street in their honour, now more a Mecca for trekkers who come from all over the Western world to test their legs and lungs in the high Himalayas.

The bus driver skirted round a cow passively chewing its cud in the middle of the dual carriageway from airport to city centre, and eagerly threw himself, his bus, and us into the frantic competition that characterizes Kathmandu traffic. Someone with a neat sense of humour installed the few traffic lights in Kathmandu. They operate on the unique and endearing system of all going red in every direction for pedestrians to cross in relative safety; then they go green, all of them at once. Cars, ancient and battered Toyota taxis, rickshaws pedalled furiously by young Nepalis, trolleybuses built and donated by China, and bicycles sold by India, all make a sudden rush for the centre of the intersection where they then spend the next few minutes before the lights go red again doing their best to disengage one from the other. Remarkably, I never saw an accident in all my time in Kathmandu.

20–26 February: A week in Kathmandu

The Summit Hotel had laid on a special Nepali welcome. One by one – leader, lads and camera crew alike – necks were garlanded with flowers, faces anointed with a vermilion powder, and stomachs assailed with distilled rice firewater and a hard-boiled egg. Feeling a little foolish at being greeted in this fashion, I failed to inquire into the symbolism and significance of it all. But the lads entered into the spirit of the greeting, perhaps enlivened by the first of many local beers. Before the evening was through, the somewhat astonished Dutch hotel manager, Willem, found his cellars drunk dry to the tune of five hundred pounds worth of Star and Iceberg. I took this serious-minded application to the task in hand as an auspicious omen for the expedition – I, too, had had a few beers.

The Summit Hotel was only a staging post, but a delightful one. Looking over the city of Kathmandu to the distant snows of the Himalayas, the hotel also focuses inwards on a beautiful garden around which the rooms form a courtyard. We would have a week or so here before business started in earnest – an interlude as tourists, interspersed with briefings, equipment checks and working parties to load 'compo' food rations into lorries. The weather, for a group one day away from an English February, was glorious – sunny 70s and a pleasant breeze. It was difficult to imagine that some seventy miles away horizontally, plus a couple vertically, the temperature would never rise above freezing and the wind would make it feel a lot less. But for the time being we all basked in the balmy climate. While the lads played tourist, we filmed a travelogue: the Monkey Temple with its garish colours and countless prayer wheels; the old capital of Bhaktapur, beautifully built in the eighteenth century and rich in elaborate hand-carved wood on houses and temples alike; and the bazaar area of Tamal – tiny alleyways singing with bright colours: polythene buckets and bags next to the deep hues of traditional spices, technicoloured dreamcoats in local fashion beside second-hand climbing clothes, and the purples and ambers of Sherpani shawls complementing the beaten brass and copper vessels used everywhere for carrying water. And not only the eyes were assailed. With every step, sounds and smells overtook us – some familiar such as the ubiquitous tinkling of bicycle bells and the pungent aroma of curry, and some unidentifiable and possibly best left so.

Filming in the bazaar with three of the lads, we stopped with them to look in the window of one of the many shops which deal in expedition cast-offs, sold second-hand to trekkers and would-be mountaineers. It is acknowledged practice for the Sherpas who accompany serious expeditions to hoard as much as possible of the clothing and equipment with which they are always issued, and, subsequently, to sell it to these establishments. They thus jack up their expedition pay, which is, by Western standards at any rate, very modest. One of our number, Johnny Garratt of the Grenadier Guards, had been on an expedition – led by our deputy leader, Henry Day – to Shisha Bangma, a lesser Himalayan peak than Everest, the previous autumn. His trekking boots, used for the walk-in, had been assigned to a porter to be carried down along with other gear while the mountain proper was climbed in the heavy, rigid plastic boots used for serious assaults. When the time came to revert to flexible leather – no boots: lost, all knowledge of them denied, never seen them, said the Sherpas. Sanguine, Johnny wrote them off – a casualty that could be coped with. So he was perplexed by a certain familiarity about one pair of boots in this window. Determined to settle the question, he went in and examined them more closely. We filmed. To me, one pair of trekking boots looks very like another, especially when well worn. Not to Johnny Garratt. He looked inside and suddenly exclaimed triumphantly: 'I knew it! You see . . . my army number. I put it on with an indelible marker, and here it is.' Turning to the shopkeeper, he inquired the price.

'Three thousand rupees.' About seventy-five pounds. He declined the opportunity to buy them a second time.

I must say that, in defence of all Sherpas and most porters, I never heard of any such disappearance throughout the whole of our expedition – which is, I think, quite remarkable when the going daily rate for a porter in Nepal is around one pound sterling, and a pair of boots can be sold for more than twenty (the shopkeepers make the most profit). It is one of the many massive contrasts, even contradictions, that seem inevitable when the First World encounters the Third; and money is the medium that brings the clash most tellingly to the surface. What deeper effects, culturally and sociologically, are experienced by a traditional subsistence farming society such as the Sherpas', is incalculable. When Sherpa Tenzing accompanied Hillary to the summit of Everest in 1953, he unwittingly led his compatriots into a new world of wages and Western values. For better or worse, Sherpas, like the rest of us, now want the latest Toyota and Zanussi, even if the likelihood of their getting it is significantly less than yours or mine.

Back from the press of humanity in Kathmandu, I took a shower and donned the expedition-issue pale grey trousers and discreetly embroidered navy blue sweater for the social climax of our stay – drinks at the British Ambassador's Residence. The film crew would have to mix business with pleasure – such an occasion called for cameras. The Residence proved worthy of the title: an imposing cross between Regency and Colonial styles, set grandly in its extensive grounds. The British believed in doing things properly in those days. But Nepal had the Gurkhas, and the Gurkha Regiment had many times proved its worth to the British. Nepal has never been other than fiercely independent, unlike its massively larger neighbour, India, and yet the Gurkha Regiment still has British officers today. It would be appealing to see the Ambassador's Residence as a symbol of British estimation for their host nation, but perhaps a little naïve. Either way, it makes an excellent venue for a drinks party and the lads set out to do it justice.

While we ran around trying to manoeuvre people into the small patches of subtle lighting offered by the wall sconces, the lads hovered, like moths about a candle, round one Kathy, a British woman working in Kathmandu as a secretary. Seldom can anyone have received such undivided attention. Eventually it dawned on me that if we wanted to film the expedition members having a good time at the British Embassy, the trick was to move Kathy to wherever there was light enough to film. It worked. But it didn't stop the drinking. It was rumoured that, once again, the beer stopped only when stocks were no more. Or was it that the Ambassador, surely a prudent diplomat, gave the nod to his major-domo at the critical moment?

The journey back to the Summit was rowdy: people were passed around the bus like parcels in the children's game – some were dropped, others had layers removed, all to the accompaniment of a vigorous but ill-tuned male voice choir. It was, of course, too dark to film, and not a little risky. We had anticipated hazards on the mountain, but not losing a camera before we even got there.

For me, personally, the social highlight of the week in Kathmandu was unlikely and unplanned. I had agreed a rendezvous with Giles Gittings, the Coldstream Guardsman, and Luke Hughes, a furniture designer and part-time soldier in the TA (Territorial Army) when he was not climbing some Himalayan peak. The year before, Luke had almost reached the summit of Shisha Bangma on the expedition led by Henry Day. We met in Kathmandu's most famous watering hole, the Rum Doodle. This bar, immortalized in Bill Bowman's book *The Ascent of the Rum Doodle*, is a lodestar to mountaineers passing through the Nepalese capital. Competing for wall space, messages and drawings by every famous name in Himalayan ascents provide a record of their passing through – Messner, Bonington, Hillary and Sherpa Tenzing, Scott, Hornbein – the catalogue is endless. Some scribbles poignantly remind the casual drinker that Everest, and its acolytes along the highest range in the world, all too frequently exact the ultimate sacrifice. But perhaps the lighthearted tone of Joe Tasker's and Peter Boardman's contributions is their most fitting memorial. All mountaineers know the risk they take; why they take it is another matter – a question I am still unable to answer to my satisfaction. But I am no mountaineer.

When I arrived Giles and Luke were not alone. Fast movers, I thought to myself, admiring their two female companions. But I was wrong. Once again coincidence had intervened, and the Nepali in earnest conversation with Luke was the friend of a friend, as well as being a princess in the Nepalese Royal Family. Jyoti and her friend Emma, an English traveller, proved charming and delightful companions through what was to be a long evening. Topics of conversation ranged from the position of the monarchy in Nepal – the population had voted to maintain the King's paramount power, rejecting on his behalf a more constitutional role – to the beauties of the English countryside. Jyoti had a house in Winchester and a daughter at school in England, and Emma came from Wiltshire. There was something paradoxical about sitting in a Kathmandu pub reflecting on the rolling downs of Wessex – they seemed immeasurably remote. And perhaps prompted by some of the framed farewells around me, I indulged an over-dramatic inclination to wonder whether I'd ever see those hills again. I suspect the reason was in fact more prosaic: the conversation was being washed along with waves of local beer. Eventually, somebody suggested eating. Certainly a little solid sustenance was a welcome prospect, and we all piled out into the narrow streets of Tamal where, incongruously, Joti produced a chauffeur-driven Mercedes.

Jyoti took us to a Nepalese restaurant called Adaina's Place, where the food was excellent and akin to Indian. In mid-meal two friends of Jyoti's appeared unexpectedly, an architect called Raja and his businessman friend, Bitol. Raja had undoubtedly spent the earlier part of the evening competing with even our considerable consumption of beer, and insisted on providing yet more to quench the fire of the curry. It would be churlish to argue, I reasoned, and apparently Giles and Luke agreed. Awash with alcohol, we wandered out into the street after midnight, at which point the more sensible members of the party repaired to their beds. But Emma insisted the night was young and the casino was beckoning.

We went for it, of course – by rickshaw! Emma commandeered two likely locals and instigated a race by promising the winner untold wealth – about five dollars. Giles and Luke mounted the first rickshaw, Emma and I the second, perching ourselves precariously on the double seat, high above the back of the straining cyclist. Kathmandu rickshaws have no gears, so we dismounted when we encountered uphill slopes, and, running behind the rickshaw, pushed it to the top. The hush of slipping through the deserted streets, across Durbar Square, past shuttered shops and temples bedecked with fluttering prayer-flags, was all too frequently interrupted by yet another incline and the effort of an uphill push. Giles and Luke, to our glee, were having problems with their rickshaw – the chain kept coming off, and they were forced to push their carriage on all but downhill runs.

Thanks to the failing chain of our competitors, Emma and I won the race, and the rickshaw lad was duly paid off. He had entered into the spirit of the event with gusto, and appeared to be delighted with his reward. We had probably disrupted the rickshaw drivers' economy by setting a dangerous precedent – another incidence of West meets East and buys its way onward.

While Emma advised Giles where to place his bets on the roulette table, with unreasonably successful results, Luke and I settled into a conversation about the project ahead. I was anxious to know how the lads felt about being the subject of a TV series. I had addressed them all earlier that day in the hotel garden and pleaded earnestly for their co-operation, without which the documentary would be doomed. They had all listened; but what did they think? Luke could not, of course, speak for everyone, but he assured me, as had Dougie Keelan, that the general feeling was that, given we were there and the thing was going to happen willy-nilly, they might as well go along with it. It was as much as I could expect and I knew much would depend on our own attitude and actions. Once we gained the lads' confidence, which must take its time, we would be on surer ground. Almost every one of them had been on Himalayan expeditions before. They knew what they were doing on mountains, and I flattered myself that we knew what we were doing on film. The trick would be to marry the two, and nothing was more certain than the fact that we needed them far, far more than they needed us.

What Luke, perhaps wisely, did *not* tell me that evening in the Kathmandu casino was potentially far more damaging, and only came out later because I asked him specifically to jot down some thoughts on the subject.

LUKE Nick was foolish enough to leave a postcard lying around on the VC 10 on the way to Kathmandu:

Dear Mum and Dad,

Finally we're on our way, my first taste of military service has so far been OK . . . we always seem to end up hoping things will go wrong . . . For the first two weeks people will be walking, eating and sleeping albeit in picturesque countryside, but I hope there's some disasters. We hope to make two episodes out of it.

So it was true. All the suspicions held by expedition members and aired in preceding months were justified. This realization highlighted two things. First, with the camera around no one would want to be seen to be at the wrong end of any disaster, either as victim or as the man responsible. Who would? Second, however hard the camera crew might declare their intent to become integrated with the team, there was always going to be suspicion and reservation.

The effect of the first undoubtedly distorted behaviour on the mountain. Military personnel are traditionally wary of the press. Experience in the Falklands or in Ulster justified this caution and has taught them again and again that the mere presence of a camera can inflame, incite, or inhibit the normal course of events. Many of the boys had had direct and unfortunate experiences.

To some extent this wariness was part of another syndrome: servicemen's anxiety about history. Official histories of Service activities have a tendency to glamorize *pour encourager les autres*. The VC citation of H. Jones's performance at Goose Green, for example, bears little resemblance to what eye witnesses can relate. In fact, little of Service life is 'active' any longer. Mess chat revolves around a mixture of gossip, myth, and legend. Absolute truth should never be allowed to get in the way of a good story, so the adage goes. The Everest trip, with all the hype associated with a Joint Service Venture, with such a high profile, such a large team, and such a high degree of public interest was just the kind of event from which official histories, not to mention the gossip, myths and legends, were likely to emanate. What might come out of the cutting room might just tell a less massaged story . . .

How close, then, should we pitch our metaphorical tent? We needed to be in constant contact, but not to invade privacies jealously preserved. We needed to get to know them, each and every one, on film, without prying so deep that people exercised their prerogative in any documentary of this nature, and brought down the shutters by declining to answer.

A case in point had already arisen: Dougie Keelan had suggested to me that on the acclimatizing trek on which we were to embark in a couple of days, he and I should share a tent. It was a kind thought, generously intended, with a view to our being able to chat through potential problems from our respective points of view. Luke felt I should accept the offer, but I was apprehensive on several counts. Firstly, it was still very early days and I needed to build a working relationship with my own crew – I knew none of them personally or professionally before embarking on this trip, and time spent sharing a tent and chatting through our intentions with Nick, Alan and Ian would be an investment that could only pay dividends. Secondly, I sensed it might be wiser to preserve a little distance between myself and Dougie: to be seen by the lads to be almost literally in the leader's pocket would perhaps give the impression that in my estimation he mattered more than they did.

But I knew that if I were honest with myself, what figured most prominently in my considerations were purely personal concerns. Since my arrival in Kathmandu I had been sleeping badly, and frequently turned to a book and a cigarette at ungodly hours – all very well in a hotel bedroom shared with an indulgent Nick, who also smoked, but unacceptably anti-social, I felt, in the confines of a small tent. And on several occasions I had suffered more than just insomnia. I am not given to attacks of nerves, but the natural apprehensions I had felt in England had developed in Kathmandu into quite irrational panics, especially when night fell. I had experienced nothing like it since the occasional nightmares of childhood, and I did not like it. As soon as I switched out the light by the bed and turned over to sleep, I was seized by a sense of terror that had nothing to do with any identifiable problem, but quite completely took over my consciousness. I tried in vain to reason with myself, to count to ten and breathe deeply, to tell myself to get a grip, to reassure my errant imagination that all was under control. But manifestly it wasn't, or at least I wasn't, and it was the knowledge that I could find no means of coping with this sense of panic that fuelled it further. I had tried getting up and wandering around the hotel garden, but the nagging fear that if these symptoms persisted I could hardly expect to trot about the Rongbuk Glacier in temperatures of minus 20 degrees centigrade or less, only added to my predicament. Putting on the light at least postponed the problem, but I knew I should be getting some sleep if I was to do my job properly.

In the end, after two or three such nights, I turned to one of the doctors, Andy Hughes, and asked for a sleeping pill. I had never taken drugs for sleep in forty-five years and resented my need for them now, but it proved to be the solution. A small handful of what were known as 'yellow bombers' (Temazepam) brought me the peace of mind and the sleep that had escaped me. Strangely, once I knew the pills would work, I frequently managed without them; just having them available seemed to settle my uncontrollable subconscious. It was to be an experience that kept recurring in the months on the mountain, but as time passed I found myself more able to deal with it and, *in extremis*, I could turn to my little yellow capsules.

In the early days in Kathmandu, I suspect the cause was my anticipation of the unknown and, in some ways, the unimaginable. I told myself what experience on many previous occasions had taught me – that events seldom match up to expectations, good or bad. Yet it failed dismally to convince. But if I felt *I* was having a bad time, and I can honestly claim that self-pity was not a factor, our sound-recordist, Ian Hills, was faring worse.

The first morning in Kathmandu, I was recounting my nocturnal neuroses to Nick, when Alan Evans came in from next door asking us both to come to see Ian. The poor guy was lying in bed, shaking so violently the bed itself was moving. Our attempts at providing some soothing words failed as miserably as had Alan's a little earlier. I suspected that Ian was experiencing a more extreme version of my own syndrome and sympathized deeply.

The one difference between our symptoms, aside from the obvious fact that his were persisting into daylight hours, was that he claimed to identify a cause: his concern about his sound-recording equipment, its adequacy for the task in hand and, in particular, the effect of the extreme cold on the batteries that provided the power for the three types of tape recorder he had with him. This, at least, offered us a chance to provide tangible assistance. First, Nick assured Ian that we had sufficient lithium batteries, which were supposedly unaffected by temperature, to cover his needs, although they would need minor adaptation to do so. And second, we could surely purchase more batteries in Kathmandu if necessary.

I was not at all surprised when these assurances failed to have the desired effect. No rationale would meet the need. But obviously we had to do what we could, and buying more batteries was the easiest course. Over the next few days we cleared Kathmandu of AA cells, adding yet more pounds to the overall weight of our equipment, but doing little, unfortunately, to allay Ian's anxiety. He did stop shaking, and often reverted to his normal self; but the attacks, like mine, kept recurring, and it was not long before Dougie Keelan asked me whether everything was all right with Ian. I tried to reassure him, while being impressed that, with so many concerns of his own as leader of the expedition, he should be so observant.

I sensed that what was at the back of Dougie's mind was what bothered me too – that once we were over the border in Tibet, at Base Camp and higher, it would be extremely difficult to get Ian out, let alone a replacement in. It had taken many weeks for China to grant the necessary visas, and there was the problem of acclimatization, even if we got a new visa. I resolved to talk to Ian about the possibility of his returning before it was too late, if the symptoms continued. They did, and a few days later, just before we left Kathmandu, I put it to him that he could get back home to his wife Lynn, herself half way through her first pregnancy, which can hardly have helped Ian in his predicament. I tried to assure him that no disgrace or lack of professionalism would be involved – in fact, if anything, the opposite. It would be better, and less trouble in every way, if he accepted that this was fate rather than failure. He considered for a short time and then said, no, he could and would continue; he was the sound man on the assignment, and he would do his job to the best of his ability. It was typical of his dedication, and there were to be many occasions when it was this dedication that carried him through what, I feel sure, must have been one of his worst, most protracted periods of unhappiness. Both psychologically and physi-cally, Ian had by far the hardest time of the four of us. My enduring mental picture of Ian is with his head bent down deep in his hands, symbolically shutting out both sight and sound of the hostile world around him. Yet he never failed to cope professionally – a feat of both mind and body over matter that it is difficult for any of us to imagine.

But Ian was not always the one to suffer. One ordeal he sailed through, while it left not only the rest of us 'Granadas' but several servicemen rather green about the gills, was a flight to Everest in a fourteen-seater Twin Otter. Excited anticipation preceded the trip, and still cameras of every style and size competed with our one movie camera, operated on this occasion by Alan. The plane was not pressur-ized; it was going to 20,000 feet; and it was full. A beleaguered air hostess, having failed with the standard issue of boiled sweets as we took off, administered the one bottle of oxygen to those most in need – particularly John Fitzgerald, who had a very nasty time, constantly on the verge of unconsciousness. I felt pretty rough and, unsure of the symptoms of oxygen starvation, put it down to airsickness. Certainly, the one whiff of oxygen I had did nothing to help. Whether it was my

queasiness, the rarified atmosphere, or the exceedingly unsettling
sound and smell of paper bags being filled by those worse afflicted
than me – while their other ends, soldiers being soldiers, raucously
attempted to equalize the air pressure in their intestines and in the
aeroplane – Everest, when we saw it, failed dismally to impress. My
one thought was 'When will we turn back and get down to the
ground?' The unfortunate Alan, trying to film the view through the
window – which is known by all cameramen to induce airsickness at
the best of times – eventually succumbed to the inevitable, and concentrated on aiming at the opening in the paper bag rather than at any
mountain outside. To my surprise, the very active contents of my
stomach stayed where they were.

It sounds insensitive, even churlish, to fly past the highest mountain
in the world – 'home' for the next few months – and be almost
exclusively concerned with my guts. And it would be wrong to imply
that Mount Everest made no impression. I wrote in my diary when I
returned:

*My first view of the monster for real. Everest looked totally forbidding,
breathtakingly imposing, and, from the air, placid. No doubt less so at closer
contact. One surprise: Everest did not stand out as I had imagined, only
slightly higher than its neighbours, Nuptse, Lhotse and Changtse behind.
Daddy bear, perhaps, but very big mummy bear and baby bears in the family.*

However, it would be an understatement to say that the flight had
not been a success; and more to the point, we had got no footage
worth using. I had anticipated getting a potential title sequence for the
series in the can, plus some excellent aerials on top. So we made
inquiries at Kathmandu airport about other options, as the Twin Otter
was ill-suited structurally to aerial photography, even if we had not
felt so sick. A Pilatus Porter was available, I was told: far smaller, with
much bigger windows, able to go higher, and with oxygen on permanent supply. This sounded more like it. We reserved it for the
following morning. But in the event, having got up at six to catch the
supposedly clear morning light, the mountain pulled its punches and
shrouded itself in cloud. The same the next morning. We had one
chance left, as we and the lads were due to leave Kathmandu for the
acclimatizing trek on that day – Friday, 26 February. And this time,
the fates were with us. The diary again:

Perfect weather: low cloud over Kathmandu but Himalayas as clear as a bell. Flew in far closer to Everest, across the Lhola and looking along the West Ridge and our route. Whole flight fantastically exciting. Now see its unique qualities as an individual peak, not only the biggest but the greatest. And the challenge – theirs to climb it, ours to record that attempt, and make a worthwhile series. Seeing the subject in close-up, I feel a step nearer. Can't pretend to be confident, but can better define the task to myself, in abstract terms if not shots. Dougie Keelan over the moon and seemed even moved as we flew away – very quiet and thoughtful.

We had been recording sound as well as filming the view through the window, and Dougie's outpourings as we approached the mountain are an eloquent testimony to his excitement.

DOUGIE We have just flown over Lukla, that tiny little airstrip tucked into the side of the hill. It has many memories, this, flying up this valley, from my last Everest expedition in '76. Then, they had the wrecks of other aeroplanes that hadn't made it lying all around. Very disheartening. But I'm glad to see they've done a clear-up job since then. This is exciting – it's a very clear day really, and there's a tiny plume of snow to the side going off the top of Everest. But it's certainly clear to me that this has been a mild winter, because those rocks on the Shoulder are very bare. The South West Face is almost completely clear of snow. I've never seen it set back quite like that. That very dominant ridge that runs across the front of the Everest summit approach is the Lhotse–Nuptse ridge which runs along at twenty-five thousand feet – that's still ten thousand feet above our height at the moment, although it doesn't look it . . .

The Nepal–Tibet border runs behind Lhotse and Nuptse from the summit of Everest along its West Ridge and across the old trading pass, the Lhola, at the foot of Everest's West Shoulder. We were, of course, approaching Everest from the south, and no Nepalese-registered plane is permitted into Chinese airspace. My problem was that we were seeing the whole panorama as though in a mirror. On the ground, we would be looking at the mountain from the north, and the majority of the huge 8,000-metre peaks in front of us now would be hidden by the even greater bulk of Everest itself. Furiously trying to orientate myself, I had to make do with a tantalizing glimpse of the Rongbuk Glacier, where I would be living for three months, as we banked back into a permissible flight path over the Lhola. Dougie, far more familiar of course than I with the topography, had none of my conceptual contortions and seemed to be in seventh heaven.

DOUGIE What a place this is! And what a whizzing day it is, isn't it? Smashing! . . . Now we're at eighteen thousand seven hundred feet, according to my pocket altimeter here, and still climbing. Nineteen thousand eight hundred now, and I think he's going to take us up the Khumbu glacier, over towards the Lhola, and then head back above the southern approach to Everest Base Camp – we can just see it ahead to the right. This *is* exciting.

There's our ridge, very clearly ahead now, and the Lhola down below, very bare . . . One of our dilemmas is whether to get on to the West Ridge directly up from the Lhola, or to go up the French Spur there which leads up from further round to the north. This very prominent West Ridge which we can see, and along which we will be traversing, looks quite short and easy. In fact, it's well over a mile long, probably nearer a mile and a half. One has little idea of scale . . .

I knew what Dougie meant. But for me, the vista made conflicting demands: as we skirted round the peaks, it looked both like a model, and yet unimaginably immense. It was impossible to think of a man, all six feet of him, measured against the 29,000 plus feet of this mountain. Even from the Lhola or the Khumbu glacier below us – the lowest point in the whole panorama – it was a good 9,000 feet to the summit. Almost two miles, I told myself, not that I would be taking *that* bit on. But Dougie was getting altogether proprietorial.

DOUGIE You can see down there to our right the Khumbu ice fall – it looks horrible and it's clear why people don't like going through it. I reckon I've been through about eight times. You say your prayers at the bottom, in the middle and again at the top . . .

Dougie laughed wryly.

DOUGIE Well, if ever there was a millionaire's view, it's this – both sides of Everest so dramatically revealed. There we are, coming up to twenty-four thousand feet now. Looks very still, very clear, settled I'd say. It's still the end of the winter, so temperatures would be at least minus thirty-five centigrade, I reckon . . .

I hope I'm not speaking out of turn here, but it does seem to me that the avalanche risk at the moment is not particularly great because of the lack of snow; but time will tell, and we're certainly going to be as careful as we can be . . .

Andy Hughes, my saviour with the yellow bombers, had taken the one spare seat next to the pilot, and was clicking away with his camera throughout. Again for the first time, I had an inkling of what mountains mean to mountaineers, and Everest above all. The excitement is infectious, the sense of challenge almost tangible. I returned from that flight with Andy and Dougie with a new perception of what was in store: a sense of reverence and privilege, as though one had met, albeit briefly, a great and justly famous human being.

Our pilot, an Indian by the name of Aran, exhibited no such deference. As we took off from Kathmandu, asking anxiously about the oxygen, he told us he had once taken Rheinhold Messner on such a flight, and he too had had a cameraman with him. As they got high, around 20,000 feet, the cameraman – who could not both film and keep his mask on – suddenly slumped forward. To help revive him, Aran passed the man his own mask, at which Messner, known for nothing if not his instinct for survival, grabbed the mask back off the unfortunate cameraman and forced it on Aran, saying, 'I'm still here and still alive, and I need you to be the same. You're the one flying me!'

The Jugal Himal Trek

Friday 26 February to Saturday 5 March
The Jugal Himal

Back at the Summit Hotel from the flight, we had little time to sort
our gear and personal baggage. It is no simple matter to be packed and
prepared for a three-month trip, let alone to Mount Everest, and still
keep a camera, recorder and their awkward accessories ready to film at
any moment. To make matters worse, we or the film crew intended
to split our forces half way through the trek, as there were to be two
trekking groups of around twenty mountaineers each. The first party
had already left Kathmandu, and was on its foot-slogging way up the
Jugal Himal. The film crew was to leave now with the second party
and eventually catch up with the others at the highest camp on the
trek. The plan was that everyone would spend a few days at altitude,
acclimatizing; but Nick, Ian, Dougie Keelan and I would miss out on
this, and set off down almost immediately to cross over into Tibet
with the first group, leaving Alan Evans and Roger Antolik to cover
the remainder of the trek and follow us through to Base Camp in due
course. The net result of all this complex 'boxing and coxing' was that
we would need not one, but two 'sync' camera channels at the ready.

Much of the film equipment, the heavy film-stock and high-altitude
clothing had already been loaded onto lorries with the seventeen tons
of expedition gear. But there seemed to be a frightening amount still
left and we 'Granadas' looked at it and each other in some dismay at
the prospect of portering it over the next ten days. We each had a
good-sized rucksack with a sleeping bag, roll-up mattress and warmer
clothing for when we hit the snow line – difficult to imagine in the
delightful summery weather of Kathmandu. We also had smaller
rucksacks for daily needs – water-bottle, thin anorak, our own still
cameras and so forth. Then there were the filming rucksacks, one each
for camera and sound with specially prepared padded interiors to take
the rough and tumble of trekking; a horrendously heavy box

containing the fifty rolls of film we anticipated using on the trek alone; sound tapes, spare batteries, filters, telephoto lenses and microphones; a film-changing bag; and the two metal magazines in which the film fitted on to the camera. Then there was the tripod and, lastly, the clapperboard. And we were doing our level best to travel light, knowing that some unfortunate Nepali villagers would be following us with this lot on their backs.

We had planned and discussed for hours what we could omit and what was essential, the major problem being that none of us knew quite what to expect. Yes, we would be on foot; yes, we were climbing some 10,000 feet overall; yes, we would have to cover everything from huge panoramas to intimate close-ups. But what would it be like? How would we *feel*, television softies that we were, more used after a hard day's filming to expense account restaurants and luxury hotels than putting up a tent on snow, washing in a stream and squatting behind some rock?

I had made a conscious effort to enjoy my shower that morning, knowing it would be the last I would have for three months or more. But a shower is only a shower, and it failed to impress me as it rinsed away what might be the only shampoo my thinning hair would see until the end of May. Almost more important to me is the well-established routine of taking my morning constitutional on the loo, a deliberately slow and ruminative procedure, during which, while yesterday's detritus falls away, I contemplate what today might hold in store. The prospect of whistling winds and insecure, icy footholds boded ill for peace of mind during the essential evacuation. And the probability of company at this peculiarly private ceremony gave me the horrors. What if my bowels, used to taking their time in comfort, foreclosed on me? Or, perhaps worse, what if dire necessity imposed impromptu squats at times and places that, even allowing for the circumstances, were indisputably ill-suited?

Then there was the matter of food and drink. I am fortunate enough, financially speaking, to be able to indulge my enjoyment of both. I positively relish cooking, even when alone, and like one of my favourite recipe writers, Keith Floyd, I tend to titillate the taste buds with a strongish scotch or a glass or two of wine. Those of you who share a genuine delight in good food and drink, preferably in company of your own choosing, may well sympathize. Others will just have to believe me when I say that I viewed with indescribable dismay the culinary desert that lay before me. No fresh, crisp vegetables; no succulent meats and tender fishes; no piquant sauces; no fruit in its familiar form, complete with pith and peel; and not a single glass of wine.

I knew that wine was out: it would freeze and crack its bottle long before it even reached Base Camp. So would beer. And both were bulky and unacceptably heavy. There was, however, a small crumb of comfort to an ageing addict like myself: the dozen cases of Famous Grouse. A hundred and forty-four bottles eked out over almost as many days and a quarter as many thirsty throats could not do more than offer occasional solace at moments of extreme need, but it was much better, I reckoned, than nothing.

I doubt a day has passed in the last twenty years in which there was not the opportunity or inclination for a glass of something alcoholic – usually several. So it proved to be a genuine surprise to me that, on Everest, the lack of a drink was never to be a problem, or even greatly missed. I enjoyed the occasions when the scotch was handed round at Base Camp, and I took my share along with the others. But at Camp Two, at the head of the Rongbuk glacier, where at one stage I was to spend the best part of a month continuously, there was nothing stronger than powdered orange juice. And I cannot remember a single sigh for something with which to spike it. My liver and kidneys must have found the sudden stop to their normal heavy duty a slight shock, but they did not complain any more than I did.

My other addiction I *could* cater for; I had already bought 1,000 cigarettes at the duty-free shop in Bahrain, and had ascertained that the monthly mail run from Base Camp to the border of Tibet could furnish further supplies as required. I entertained a tiny, and in the event vain, hope that perhaps smoking, in the exalted air of Everest, would give *me* up, as I had always failed at normal atmospheric pressures to give *it* ip. But, in case it didn't, I had to be prepared. And I can now assert that smoking cigarettes was one of the few physical comforts I could continue from my life-as-normally-lived into that time-out-of-time up on the Everest glacier.

I was not alone in killing myself with nicotine. A few – very few – of the climbers found it as necessary and as pleasurable as I, notably Dave Orange, master baker turned PT instructor turned mountaineer, who besides being a delightful man to talk to, was a hero to each and every one of us on the expedition because he first baked

himself – and then taught the Sherpa cooks to bake – fresh bread.
Daily bread, when it is the only fresh food of any kind, and even
accompanied by tinned jam or processed cheese, is pure pleasure. The
aroma when the loaves arrive to be cut, the squidgy resistance to the
knife, and finally the mouth-watering, honest-to-goodness taste and
texture, runs the gamut of sensations. Everest had its unexpected
bonuses, and the inevitable deprivations did mean that ordinary
simple pleasures stepped into another league. Fresh bread was only
one of those experiences. Recovering one's breath after a lung-
cracking climb was another. Feeling one's body warm through in a
sleeping bag, another. Seeing a bird or an animal, indeed any living
creature other than ourselves, another. And seeing something green
and growing, had it ever happened, would surely have been one more.

But setting off from Kathmandu, I could not anticipate all this.
Nepal is nothing if not green – in the valleys. And we were driving
along the valley of the Bhote Kosi, its banks luxuriously verdant even
in February, its water occasionally a striking bright turquoise akin to
Cornwall's china clay pools. The soil of the Kathmandu valley area is
a strong deep red – Devon sprang to mind – which doubtless accounts
for the ubiquity of red brick buildings. High standards of construction
are not restricted to cities such as Bhaktapur; little villages along the
valleys boast brick buildings with finely carved wooden windows and
roof support beams; and everywhere, in every conceivable patch that
could be levelled to something approaching the horizontal, are tiny
terraces of cultivation, sometimes barely bigger than a bed. Each
square yard that can is growing a crop, destined to be harvested before
the monsoon comes in June and all too frequently washes away not
only the top soil but the supporting walls of each terrace. Over the
next few days we were to see at close quarters the industry that went
into this intensive agriculture. But from our bus, the impression was
more one of patchwork patterns framed by the retaining walls, here
electric green where the rice had sprouted, there russet red, giving
way to stony grey higher up the valleys.

We 'de-bussed' by a bridge over one of the many feeder streams of
the Bhote Kosi. Now the fun was to start – an easy walk, I was
assured, for this the first day. Only five miles or so, with little
climbing. I tried to tell myself the stifling heat – we had dropped 2,000
feet from Kathmandu – should be relished not resented; there would
be little enough of *that* all too soon.

The first problem presented itself: not enough porters. And as we were the slowest to get going, it was our stuff that stood on the roadside. One of the Sherpas who would be with us throughout the expedition, a charming and strikingly handsome twenty-two year old called Bhadri, had been deputed by Dougie to find more porters and follow us up the track. Dougie and the lads had already started and were disappearing fast. Most worrying was that the rushes from the flight, our precious aerial footage, were amongst the gear left stranded. Nick and I could not face leaving it and split the load between our rucksacks, an unwelcome extra weight. Bhadri, who spoke the best English of the six Sherpas, assured us all would be well – more porters were coming, he would make sure everything was collected. Having no evidence to go on, good or bad, but little alternative, we left him to deal with the problem. He did, and ended up at the first campsite some two hours behind us, accompanied by well-loaded local porters.

The walk to the camp was hot and sweaty, but to me surprisingly easy. I had expected worse, being used only to cycling and shortish country walks that always end in friendly pubs. And the scenery, daily more dramatic, was spectacularly special! I began to understand why people flew all the way from England and America to come trekking in Nepal. Villages carefully paved in stone some centuries ago hung on the steep sides of the little valley – one, to my amazement, sporting a bank. And this some miles off the nearest road!

With considerable trepidation and a lot of clammy hand-holding, we crossed a swinging rope-bridge barely wide enough to take a porter and his load. They trot across merrily enough, but to the uninitiated the possibility of freefall seems all too real. Frustratingly, our camera was one of the loads that *had* found a back to hang on and was way ahead of us. We made a mental note to make sure this didn't happen again, but could do nothing about filming there and then. I was sure we would come across another such bridge, affording an obvious sequence as our lads negotiated the precarious crossing. But we never did. Sod's Law!

We reached the camp, already set up by the Sherpas, about five o'clock – a little over two hours for the five-mile trek. Not bad, I thought, relishing the offer of a mug of tea and a patch of grass to sit on. The little river that formed a half-circle around the clutch of tents looked irresistibly inviting - until you stepped into it. Fed by melting snows higher up the valley, it cannot have been much above freezing.

Skimpily, we splashed our sweaty armpits and quickly cooled our swollen feet. I felt the need to clean my teeth, and did so. Only as I finished did Roger Antolik, braver than I and stripped naked in mid-stream while I perched on the bank, shout across:

'All the villages up the stream use this as a natural sewer, Mark. You'll probably be dead by morning.'

I didn't even get the runs!

We ate – and, on the trek, ate well – at what seemed the ridiculously early hour of six o'clock, whereupon all the lads promptly disappeared into their 'pits' to get as much sleep as possible before the six a.m. reveille. We could not accommodate so quickly, and the film crew was to be heard, night after night, chatting through today's dilemmas and tomorrow's tribulations. Once *they* were out of the way, we would turn to more personal topics – Nick to his sporting activities, which embraced anything from rugby to pheasant shooting; Alan to his rock-climbing, beer-drinking exploits in the Peak District; Ian to his days as sound-effects man in a repertory theatre, or his penchant for antiques auctions; and I, hopping sparrow-fashion from subject to subject, to my plans to convert a cowshed in the South of France to a holiday house, or my childrens' ambitions to go to Art School, or the impossibility, as I saw it, of supporting any of the existing political parties . . . Before the trip was out, we would have exhausted every issue, and learnt a lot more about each other. But these were early days, and we frequently found ourselves discussing nothing more momentous than the conditions in which we existed.

That first night of the trek, we four 'Granadas' were to share an octagonal tent, which seemed neither too cramped nor too spacious, even with our extra 'filming' rucksacks. We all unrolled our bedding: a half-inch inflatable mattress called a Thermarest and, as a concession to our tender bodies, a further half-inch of solid foam – a Ridgerest. They seemed to make no difference at all to the uneven stony ground when I lay down to test them out. I told myself firmly that I would get used to this, and I was right. There is a knack of not lying directly on your hip-bone, but tucking it slightly behind you so that thigh and rib-cage share the load. Or, if you're lucky, you can sleep on your back. I can't.

Soon, I counted myself lucky if I slept at all. I noted in my diary:

To sleep at ten, but wide-awake at twelve. Up for cigarette, pee and wander round. Eventually back to sleep four-thirty, but had to get up at six to leave. Both hips feel like well-beaten veal escalopes.

It was little different on subsequent nights and, as we climbed higher and higher, considerably less inviting to get out of the sleeping bag, let alone out of the tent. Within three days we were at 12,000 feet, and our maximum/minimum thermometer read minus 10 degrees centigrade inside the tent when we reluctantly struggled out of our bags at six o'clock.

This was my first experience of being unable to get away from the cold. I have filmed in Moscow, in temperatures of minus 30 centigrade, but there was always the haven of a centrally heated hotel to return to. Camped on a frozen lake bowl – we had quickly climbed above the snow line – there was no escaping the bitter wind and biting cold, short of staying permanently mummified in my Redline bag.

I had taken the decision to bring the heavier-weight Redline on the trek, while the other three had opted for their Lightlines, and regretted it. They all slept with three or four layers of clothing – string vest, thermal vest, shirt and sweater – inside their bags, and still felt chilly. The cold seeps up through the foam mattress at any pressure point, and if you move or roll over, a new freezing patch awaits you. Worst of all was answering a call of nature. We had all been issued with pee bottles – one-litre wide-topped polythene jars – but mine was still at this stage full of duty-free scotch. My diary:

Nipped out for a pee at four a.m. Christ, was it cold! Had snowed an inch or so, but now under full moon and crystal clear starry sky the campsite on the lake looked magical. Moon hanging over the Himalayas, and so many stars as to be unreal. Half of me wished I was anywhere warmer; the other half stood transfixed at the scene – but not for long!

During the day it was different. Although the air temperature is normally around zero, the radiant strength of the sun is such that in it one felt hot, and the sun shone brightly for nine days out of ten on average. This pattern, established on the trek, continued on the Rongbuk glacier. If at all possible you stayed in your bag until the sun hit the tent, when the temperature soared dramatically; and when the sun set you dived for cover, trusting to stay in it.

I have no idea whether the more experienced mountaineers found the extreme cold as much of a shock, however expected, as we did.

Certainly the porters, born and bred in the mountain villages, seemed unaffected. Some wore plastic flip-flops; others even went barefoot in the thick snow. The soles of their feet must be as tough as the proverbial old boots. We filmed one porter warming up his foot in the flames of a fire for minutes on end. One unfortunate man did admittedly suffer from minor frostbite before the trek was over, but he seemed more surprised than any of us at this painful turn of events.

The lot of the Nepalese porter, to Western eyes, is not a happy one. For little financial reward, both men and women shoulder massive loads of up to one hundred pounds, frequently so stacked-up that from behind the only visible part of the body beneath the load is two feet and a short section of leg. Bent below this burden, which hangs on a leather or woven belt across the forehead, they negotiate steep slopes often barely recognizable as paths, so boulder-strewn and indistinct are they. But the porters are as sure-footed as the mountain goats that careered across the scree as we approached; I never saw one slip, while we were constantly correcting our balance with an outstretched hand or supporting ski-pole.

My 'personal' porter, who carried my larger rucksack, was a young lad called Karmi. He was probably only twelve, but claimed to be seventeen. Grateful though I was to have him, rather than me, carrying the sack, every morning pangs of guilt assailed me as his diminutive frame disappeared behind the green Berghaus which was almost as tall and certainly broader than he was. To make matters worse, as Karmi was the youngest porter of the lot, his seniors would load him with extras they chose not to carry, so that frequently he resembled a travelling tinker, bedecked with pots and pans, ropes and tent poles, and any other inconvenient object that no one else wanted. Yet he never seemed to complain, and wore a happy smile throughout, except for one day when he contracted a stomach disorder and quite obviously felt very wretched. Andy Hughes came to the rescue with a pill or two, but Karmi still did his day's carry; there was no one to take his place.

We had two 'filming porters' expressly to carry camera and sound gear in their respective rucksacks, and stay close to us throughout the day. We didn't want a repeat of the first day's fiasco. They quickly entered into the spirit of the enterprise, and within a day were able between them to set up the tripod, mount the camera on it, and stand there smiling, offering us the clapperboard. Nepalis never seem to be other than cheerful, and are consequently delightful companions. I wish I could say the same of the Tibetans – but that was yet to come.

As the days passed we developed a routine for the filming. Up early and off before the lads, to be ahead of them when we found a suitably scenic spot for them to file by. This necessitated seeking assistance with the tents, and the Sherpas soon learnt that we were peculiarly cack-handed at getting our tent down, folded and packed. In what was to become an expedition catchphrase – albeit one prompted by guilt and verging on the offensive – I tried to encourage the Sherpas by exclaiming: 'We may be slow, but at least we're rich!' – hoping that Granada-staked tips-to-come would build up a fund of good will. I now know this was quite unnecessary: the Sherpas were endlessly willing from the trek to the final pull-out from Everest. But they did get their tip.

One of the problems with our filming was never knowing what lay around the next bend or over the next ridge. On many occasions we would set up our camera with a stunning landscape as our background, and record this panorama as the lads struggled up and past, only to discover, once they had all disappeared out of shot and into the distance, that the far end of the village or the very next valley offered an even better backdrop. If there was a pause, a stop for lunch, it was always for us a short one, as once again we laboured up ahead. But the rewards were worth it. Day by day the landscape changed and unfolded, revealing new and unexpected vistas as we climbed ever higher. Initially, terraces, fields and villages abounded, this one Hindu, that Buddhist. We passed small groups chanting at a shrine, we walked dutifully to the left of the Buddhist Mani stones with their delicate carving (Buddhists always do it clockwise – at least so far as their religion is concerned), we skirted round the fields of bamboo, rice and maize, and fought our way through jungles of rhododendron, their blooms just beginning to burst open. In a month's time, I reflected sadly, this 1,000-foot horizontal belt of hillside would be a blaze of blood red and shocking pink. Wild primroses were trodden unavoidably under foot, and now and then tiny orchids winked from their root-holds in the forks of trees.

Inexorably, day by day, we climbed up and up. Here and there, the path was clear and rose gradually. More frequently, it was only by keeping in sight whoever was in front that we knew where we were aiming – except, of course, that it was upwards. Stone steps, cut often eighteen inches high in the raw rock of the hills, were a challenge no four-wheel drive vehicle could even contemplate. But they were easier going for our pairs of legs than the one-in-one hillside devoid of man-made modifications. Gasping what seemed to me to be perilously close to a death rattle, I would reach the top of a ridge and collapse for a cigarette – only to contemplate the downhill slither immediately in front of me and the even higher ridge that followed it. It was not uncommon to scale the equivalent of Ben Nevis between dawn and dusk, a feat I found truly remarkable when I had the energy to think at all. I had never known exhaustion like it, and my diary is littered with expressions of utter disbelief.

Just about done in by the final climb. Never been so exhausted and breathless, yet within five minutes of resting quite recovered. Very strange.

And later:

Filming immediately on top of today's climb a superhuman effort – true victory of will over instinct. Will never forget leap day 1988 – and it can only get worse.

On the next day:

Must try to record my sense of being totally all-in. Moved like some automaton driven by necessity. Could barely lift one foot up the rough-hewn steps frequently over a foot in height. Panting like an asthmatic in a marathon – my Waterloo. Ought to find some spot of humour to relate, but that's pretty difficult to do right now. Yet far from unhappy, good sense of achievement.

It now reads slightly like whingeing, punctuated by self-congratulation. But I can clearly remember my genuine surprise that I managed to arrive at all at this or that campsite, let alone know where I was. So I asked the leader.

DOUGIE Last night we were behind the main peak which I am pointing out with my pipe. To the left – you've got a subsidiary peak, go left again and you've got another peak, and we were between the two, somewhere in there. We have come round the back of many of these bumps – bumps is probably a misnomer because as we have discovered from the sweat on our brow, some of them are quite big. But we've been over many of them and round others, and I think by any standards today has been a good demanding trekking day. We've

16. Prayer flags on the Pang La, the 16,800-foot pass that guards the northern approach to Everest. Probably at any altitude, and certainly at this, a breathtaking view.

17. 'We filmed in wide shot, we filmed in close-up, but we knew that any picture we could put on celluloid would be a poor substitute for the real thing.'

18. From the sublime to the ridiculous. And when we passed by on the return journey, my scratched stone had disappeared!

19. The Rongbuk lamasery, now rebuilt and reoccupied after a decade of desolation during the Chinese Cultural Revolution.

20. Inside the lamasery, a nervous Nick hands over to a Tibetan.

21. 'Nick needed foreground to complement Everest fifteen miles up the valley, and I was deputed to herd some yaks into shot.'

22. Base Camp soon after our arrival on 9 March.

23. 'At Base Camp, I had my own chair ... a stroke of pre-planning genius.' Ian appears to have found one of the few others!

24. Everest may loom large, but to the addict, cigarettes can dominate even more!

25. '... and finally, stark naked, I sat in the bowl of now disgustingly scummy water.'

26. Filming the 'puja' organized by Chowang, the Sherpa Sirdar. 'I quashed a passing thought that offering a bottle of the Expedition's Famous Grouse was extending generosity too far.'

27. 'When the sun goes down, you dive for cover' – keeping the diary up to date in our 12' x 12' tent.

29. Ian on the 'path' to Advance Base Camp.

28. 'In a uniformly grey-white landscape,
flashes of colour caught the eye.'

come up from six three to eight three, then we dropped down to about seven eight and now we've come up to ten thousand six hundred – ten thousand seven hundred according to my altimeter, to be exact. Which isn't a bad sort of height – and over a distance of about twelve miles.

MARK Glad I didn't know that at the time! . . .

Another surprise, and just as reassuring, was that the ordeal of squatting in the open air turned out to be no ordeal at all. Steep hillsides could be a problem. I had to choose between facing downhill, enjoying spectacular views: this went some way towards compensating for the lack of a porcelain pew but had the disadvantage of allowing errant undergrowth to spike me in the most tender of places; or facing into the slope – boring, but offering the security of a handhold. There were, too, the hazards of the countryside. I remember one occasion when my peace was interrupted by a herd of cattle, curious to see what this strange crouching figure was up to, and hotly pursued by their female cow-herd, who tactfully took another path while I scrambled to my feet.

As a topic of conversation, the needs of the bowels were second only to sex. I asked one of the climbers, an experienced mountaineer and a Major in the Gurkhas, why these two bodily functions were of such obsessive interest.

KIT SPENCER Well, you can only think about one, and you've got to do the other. I suppose on any trip like this, you get a whole group of men together and it's fairly inevitable that those two fairly basic functions should feature in conversation. It gets worse too; I mean we're only two or three days out. Just wait for a couple of months.

MARK How are you coping generally? Do you turn your mind off? Do you think about things when you're trudging up?

KIT Well, I try not to. It's probably a lack of imagination or something. I'm just thinking about how much further I've got to go before the next cigarette stop.

MARK You and I are more or less the only smokers, I think, or maybe there are one or two others.

KIT You wait, we'll burn everyone else off. Don't worry about that! . . .

On the morning after we hit the snow line for the first time (and also for the first time set about the routine of melting snow for each and every drop of water – a practice which was soon to become monotonous in the extreme), one of the more ebullient of the lads, Pat Parsons, sliced open his leg on the spike of an ice axe protruding from fellow climber Charlie Hattersley's rucksack. Pat's language was soon bluer than the view, especially when he saw us coming with the camera.

PAT Can I tell you lot to fuck off?

CHARLIE What did you do, just tripped on the axe, did you?

PAT I fucking walked straight into it, it was next to your . . .

CHARLIE Just by the tent, wasn't it? Just jammed down in the edge of the tent?

PAT It was jammed up next to your rucksack. I just brushed passed the rucksack and it went right in, right fucking in.

CHARLIE Yeah, well, I told you, you should have watched out.

PAT Should have bloody filed it down a bit.

ANDY HUGHES Get him a biting bar, Charlie.

CHARLIE He's had two already.

PAT Fuck off, Hattersley.

CHARLIE At least you've got a good doctor this time.

PAT I'll let you know about that.

NICK Someone stand by with a new camera battery, please.

PAT Emergency Ward Ten, this is.

NICK Battery, camera battery . . . OK, all right, thanks . . .

As Pat was skilfully stitched up by Andy Hughes (by the end of the trip there was a neat but barely perceptible scar on Pat's shin), Dougie Keelan hovered round making acerbic remarks about scab-lifters – his soubriquet for all doctors. It was clear that this was no major disaster. Painful indeed for Pat, and lively material for our camera, as they were quick to remark, but if no one fared worse than this, the expedition would be very lucky.

And in fact the next accident came only two days later, on the steep descent to the little border village of Tatopani. The victim was Giles Gittings, the Porsche-driving Coldstream Guardsman. With unconscious irony, he had talked to us only the day before about the dangers of trekking accidents.

MARK Has the trek had its desired effect, do you feel a lot fitter? Does anyone have a real struggle?

GILES A couple of people who will remain nameless had to hand their packs to porters, but on the whole I think that most people needed this sort of burn-out to get rid of their home fat, and just get back out into the hills and get walking.

MARK Who was that then, why can't you name them?

GILES Well, OK, one was Ted Atkins – the guy with the boater – but he was carrying a ridiculously heavy load, and it's important, you don't want to damage yourself at this stage of the game, especially if you want to get on to the hill. That's the trouble with coming downhill carrying a heavy pack, you don't want to fall over and twist an ankle, turn a knee, when you've got a chance to climb Everest in a couple of weeks' time. The very last thing you want is to injure yourself at this early stage . . .

Giles was tempting fate too far. First thing in the morning, he slipped on the loose, shale-covered, one-in-one slope, and was immediately reduced to an agonizing crawl on all fours if he was to make any progress at all. As luck would have it, he was at the rear of our well spread-out procession. But Merv Middleton was with him, and Merv was a trained paramedic. He scribbled a note on the inside of a Kodak stills film box – 'Giles sprained or broken ankle. Needs rescue party' – and sent it with a Sherpa to Dougie Keelan ahead in the valley below. Merv then ripped a removable thick aluminium frame support from his rucksack, bent it into a U and taped it under Giles's boot and up round his ankle, which was already visibly swelling. Giles was on the very limit of consciousness, and every attempted or accidental movement of his damaged joint pushed him momentarily over the edge. There was nothing to do but wait for the note to reach Dougie, and the rescue party to arrive. It would be an excruciating several hours.

The Sherpa messenger knew a short cut down to the road, even more precipitous than the near vertical 'path' we had been following, and arrived well before Dougie Keelan. We stopped filming a local village boy delighting in the miracle of a personal stereo lent to him by one of the lads, and set ourselves up to eavesdrop on Dougie receiving the bad news.

Dougie acted quickly and resolutely, appointing to the rescue party the two strongest Sherpas, Gombu and Gopal, both built – as one of the climbers was to put it later – 'like a brick shit-house'. He sent them back up the knackering hillside with a woven bamboo basket. Six hours later, having covered most of the return journey in darkness, Gombu and Gopal staggered into our riverside camp. The fifteen-stone Giles was perched, bum in basket and legs through cut-out holes, on Gombu's back. Taking it in turns to carry their load, the two Sherpas had negotiated the perilous descent without dropping him once. They were on the verge of collapse, and Giles himself was pale with pain. It was a truly heroic effort, and a testament to the physical strength and mental determination of all three concerned. As soon as he could summon speech, Giles thanked Gombu and Gopal fulsomely, realizing all too vividly that without their assistance he would have spent a night out bivouacking – in his state a very dangerous alternative.

The expedition carried no X-ray equipment, so Al Miller – one of two other doctors beside Andy Hughes – did all he could do in the circumstances and securely taped up the ankle. Giles was given the option of returning to Kathmandu and more thorough medical examination, or continuing with us over the frontier into Tibet and on to the mountain. He chose the latter course, despite what turned out, only months later in the UK, to be a fracture rather than a sprain. His injury did preclude Giles's participation in climbing, but he acted as an essential and efficient manager of Base Camp, even at one stage walking the arduous six or seven miles to Advance Base to do the same job there.

Meanwhile the proximity of a village, and therefore of bars and beers, was too much for the rest of the lads. It had been ten abstemious days since Kathmandu, and it might well be the last opportunity for months; tomorrow we crossed into Communist China, and no one knew for sure what alcohol would be available there.

But before dousing the dust inside, there was a chance for a much needed wash of our outsides. Tatopani, which means 'hot water' in Nepali, is a natural spa, and five jets of scalding water run continuously into a communal stone trough. I must stress that Tatopani is no Cheltenham or Harrogate; it is scruffy and poor, with an open sewer running down the side of its one street – a dirt track lined by ramshackle hovels. There are a few more solid structures in the ubiquitous brick of Nepal, and it is behind one of these that the 'spa waters' flow. In briefs or boxer shorts, we all joined the local Sherpani women, swathed for decency's sake in saris. Unaccountably Simon Gray, due after the expedition to marry his fiancée Louise in Hong Kong, induced one of them to scrub his back for him, and sat there under the steaming spout for far longer than was strictly necessary.

Set deep in the thickly wooded valley of the river, Tatopani is a hot and airless village, and the lads needed no encouragement to quench their thirst. Monopolizing the few available bars – dark cupboards off the main street, selling a bewildering variety of brightly packaged goods as well as beer – the lads set about drinking Tatopani out of beer, as they had done the Summit Hotel and the British Embassy. I cannot record with certainty that they succeeded, but the carousing and the careering soldiery that somehow found its way back to the campsite had manifestly done its best. Much swaying and singing prolonged the business of getting into tent and sleeping bag. But when Johnny Garratt went just too far with a spot of horseplay at the expense of Dave Maxwell, he was sharply reminded of that officer's particular training. Despite his virtual inability to remain upright, Max (as he was known, to distinguish him from assorted other Daves) spun Johnny like a top, and in a split second had a foot on his throat. It was all in the same spirit of fun as Johnny's attack on him, but Max was very obviously not a man to meddle with over anything serious. I hoped he would never have cause to lose his patience with me.

It would be quite wrong to give the impression that none of us in the TV crew had indulged at all, and I think I can speak for all of us when I say I was more than happy, for once, to be tucked into my bag, and horizontal. We had had a good time in Nepal, and this last evening there had been a fitting swansong. But the rehearsals were now at an end, and tomorrow the curtain went up for real. Tomorrow we crossed into Tibet, and set out in earnest for our goal – Mount Everest.

To Everest Base Camp

5–19 March
Tibet

I imagine entry into China is never a simple matter. In our case, it was made far more complex by the amount of expedition equipment in general, and of Granada's filming gear in particular. Our two radio microphones excited special interest. If they were transmitters, where and over what distance would they transmit? And why? I was convinced they thought we were posing as a film crew making an Everest series, while really we had far more sinister intentions; and I could not at that stage know that in the Tibetan capital, Lhasa, demonstrations against Chinese rule and in favour of the exiled Dalai Lama were to break out in the next few days. Eventually the customs officers were satisfied, and with much form-filling we entered China. The border town of Xangmu, spread up a steep hillside, gives an impression of organization and purpose that totally escapes the Nepalese equivalent of Tatopani – no children rolling metal hoops in wire hooks down dusty streets, no meandering pigs, goats, dogs and chickens scratching a meagre meal from the roadside rubbish. Here in Xangmu, concrete and glass predominated over wood and clay, even if tarmac had not yet established its supremacy over mud roads. Earlier in the year, there had been a serious landslip carrying away several houses and totally obliterating sections of the road through the town and on up the valley. This necessitated a 1,000-foot climb for all of us, accompanied by an army of porters bent below the seventeen tons of equipment. As at the customs, the aid of our specially appointed liaison officer Mr Mah and his interpreter Mr Deng was essential. The most populous nation in the world is surely also the most bureaucratic, and seemed to solve its potential unemployment problem by absorbing any surplus labour in officialdom. Mr Deng explained that his superior, who spoke no English at all, was 'an officer'; but in what I never established. Between them they represented the Chinese

Mountaineering Association – the CMA. The CMA governs every attempt on Everest with a rod of relentless exploitation, solving problems of their own making and charging massively in sterling or US dollars for so doing. The 'registration fee' for our expedition was £1,000, and by the end of the trip their total bill would exceed £30,000. Mr Mah, a charming moon-faced man with a permanent toothy smile, dealt with every inquiry in the same way. 'This is necessary. That is impossible.' It was fruitless ever to ask why; the concept of questioning the authorities did not exist. This problem had surfaced immediately: part of the contract with the CMA was the provision of transport to Base Camp, and four lorries had been ordered – the requisite number, by their own estimate. However, only three had appeared. No explanation. 'There are three.' Other lorries abounded, and were available for hire. 'Not possible. They are not CMA lorries.' Their solution: to make two journeys. So a massive stack of boxes and barrels was left under the eye of four unfortunate expedition members, while the majority loaded the three available trucks and finally climbed into the bus set aside for bodies.

To facilitate filming, we had ordered a Land Cruiser which would, we hoped, allow us to get ahead of the main convoy, film them approaching through suitable scenery, and then overtake them to repeat the performance further along the trail. We had not bargained on Messrs Mah and Deng, with the jeep driver, taking up the front row of seats, leaving the rear seat for the three of us (Alan was still with the second trekking group yet to cross into Tibet) and all our camera gear. But we all got in somehow, and set off up the 7,000-foot ascent to Nylam, the next town of any size or importance, and our destination for that night.

It was undoubtedly one of the more dramatic drives I have experienced. Hairpin followed hairpin, pot holes competed for depth and breadth, and frequent halts to remove from our path boulders fallen from the hillside above punctuated our progress. The Chinese driver – the CMA favours their own people rather than the local Tibetans – had perfected a driving technique guaranteed to make the journey as memorable as possible for his passengers. This involved taking the sharp bends flat out, and then slowing down to a crawl over the short straights in between. Mr Mah sat impassively in the front; he had seen it all before. His continued existence offered some consolation, along with the fact that I was in the back, and therefore slightly safer in the event of a head-on collision, which seemed certain if any other traffic used the road. I need not have worried – it didn't. Being in the back would not of course have been much help when we went over the edge, but at least I would not have long to contemplate that disadvantage; the drop down the hillside gained depth and potential for destruction with every kilometre we climbed, and I reckoned that I would surely be pulped to death long before the Land Cruiser came to rest at the bottom of the valley.

It was, then, with some relief that I saw the small town of Nylam approaching over the horizon. We had now emerged on to the 12,000-foot-high plateau that extends across Tibet, and surrounds Lhasa – the highest capital city in the world, and still almost 1,000 kilometres away. Under the auspices of the CMA, we were booked into a hotel which Dougie Keelan had informed me would cost us eighty US dollars per person for evening meal, bed and breakfast. This sounded expensive, being way above the rate of the Summit Hotel in Kathmandu, but perhaps it would be worth it, holding some pleasant surprise in store.

It *was* a surprise: a concrete barracks with no heating at all in sub-zero temperatures, and the only available water in puddles on the floor. The Nylam hotel was not luxurious. Its manager, Tashi, informed us that we were his first guests for three months. 'I wonder why,' I idly remarked. But Tashi proved to be a resourceful hotelier, exploiting the one area in which he could make any profit under the conditions imposed upon him by the authorities. He had installed a bar in a lock-up cupboard; local beer, wine and brandy were available. We tried all three. The wine might just pass in the quantities offered from a communion chalice; the brandy, tried and rejected with a salty Royal Marines' expression by Dougie Keelan, found favour with some of the lads, whose stomachs, like my own, were Polystrippa-proof. But the beer proved to be the best bet, and had just enough alcohol content to prevent it freezing in the bottle in front of you.

Tashi cleverly delayed the serving of the meal until we had consumed the contents of his cupboard, and miraculously succeeded in presenting a good Chinese dinner. Warmed by the alcohol and the hot food, I crawled into my bag and gave silent thanks for the bed beneath me.

China has one time zone for the whole country, and in the winter Beijing time is two and a quarter hours ahead of Kathmandu time. So it was pitch dark and freezing hard inside the bedrooms when we got up shortly before eight a.m. Back in the Land Cruiser we set off across the bleakest landscape I have ever witnessed. Rolling hills the colour of chocolate sponge topped with white icing receded into the distance where the Himalayas, all-over Christmas cake, rose majestically into the gentian sky. Stones are what I most remember of the Tibetan plateau: mile after mile of stony terrain with little or no cultivation, stone roads rhythmically ribbed to send vibrations up the spine, stone walls around the village compounds when we occasionally passed some sign of habitation. A cold and unrelenting environment, Tibet has trained its inhabitants in survival. Children, staring silently at our convoy, held out hands black with dirt for any offering we might put in them.

When we stopped for lunch, the empty tins from the compo rations were unaccountably the most popular gift – the contents were spurned suspiciously. But these kids were no innocents. When we brought out our cameras, both cine and still, they smartly hid their faces until some reward was received. Only then would they pose for a shot, their brief smiles revealing gaps in the teeth of even the teenagers. I wondered at the severity of their lives, only barely imaginable to the cosseted Westerner, and the cast of mind that centuries of hardship had engen-dered. There was both acceptance and resilience in their eyes, the sense that little could surprise them, as conditions could hardly get harsher. I admired these Tibetan villagers, but could not like them. Like the stones all around them, they were hard and gave little – so completely in contrast with their Nepalese neighbours on the other side of the Himalayas. But Nepal is green and fertile right up to the foothills, and the ready laughter of a Sherpa or a Tamang is a likely legacy of a kinder climate.

In the afternoon we reached Xegar. A modern concrete town spreads out across the plain, while the old village nestles under a steep bluff dominated by a 'dzong', or fort, snaking up the hillside from the dwellings and the monastery, or more properly lamasery, it was built to protect. The brick and stone walls are now semi-ruined. A famed but distant view of Everest is sufficient to prompt most visitors to Xegar to climb up to the 'dzong', and was so for us. Carrying camera and tripod, we slipped and slithered up the steep shale. Looking down, I found, was not advisable, and I have to confess that the prospect of getting back without mishap to myself or the camera prompted me to call a halt once Everest was visible, but before we reached the top. The altitude of Xegar, approximately 14,000 feet, may also have been a factor, as we gasped in vain for lungs full of oxygen. A few of the lads were hardier and more determined, and waved at us disparagingly from the summit. We filmed them, and waved back.

After Nylam, we were prepared for the Xegar hotel to be equally spartan, and we were not disappointed. The only difference was the bedroom floors, here made simply of earth rather than concrete. As I lay on my bed – the last time I would do so for the next hundred nights – I listened to the BBC World Service reporting ten deaths in the Lhasa riots. It was difficult to take the implications as seriously as they warranted; our expedition felt so cut-off from the real world. Tibetan nationalism, although erupting on to the streets only 500 miles away, seemed to exist in another timescale from our own. Of course, I know it was we who were in the time-warp but, in our circumstances, experience had a quality defined more by physical realities to hand than any perceptions of the mind.

The 'road' into the Everest Base Camp area can best be described as horrendous. Frequently we were catapulted into the roof by the pitching jeep, as it negotiated a course across the boulders. Driving up and down the escalators at Holborn would be more comfortable. We bounced and slithered up and up to the Pang La ('La' means 'Pass') at 16,800 feet, cursing volubly and aching in every bone. But it was worth it – a 100-mile-wide panorama of the Himalayas is something special. No photograph can quite catch the immensity of this mountain range, or express the elemental force that threw it up in such geologically recent times, a mere fifty million years ago. The adjectives have all been tried and found wanting. However prepared I was, I still was not ready for this quite literally breathtaking view. There was no mistaking Everest now, plumed with blown spindrift and rising head and shoulders above its 8,000-metre-high neighbours. We filmed in wide-shot, we filmed in close-up, we took still photographs, and yet we knew that any picture we could put on celluloid would be a poor substitute for the real thing. Perhaps to reduce the quality of the experience to a more mundane level, Nick and I turned from the sublime to the ridiculous and scratched names and dates on two slaty rocks – 'NICK 8.3.88' 'MARK 8.3.88'. We recorded these graffiti, suitably situated with Everest as their back-drop, through a wide-angle lens. When, on 22 May, we passed by in the opposite direction, I was mortified to find only Nick's memorial still *in situ*. Mine had disappeared.

After a long wait on the top of the pass, we spotted the convoy of trucks, mere dots on the snake of road. It took another hour for them to bump and grind up close enough for us to film their coming. The lads were now all in a lorry, as no bus could survive the punishment meted out by this road surface. I shall always remember the moment when the truckload of would-be Everest conquerors rounded the final hairpin of the ascent, giving its occupants their first glimpse of the view we had been absorbing for the previous two hours. As they had neared the top, everyone had stood up, clinging to the metal frame of the lorry. Then Everest came into sight, and a spontaneous cheer erupted from the lads and rang down the Rongbuk valley towards the mountain, still many miles distant. It was a salutation worthy of the scenery.

Three hours of spine-shattering drive still lay ahead before we arrived at the road-head to choose the exact location of our Base Camp. Our jeep, followed, one by one, by the lorries, forded the half-frozen Rongbuk River and crept along the track through the glacial moraine. I was surprised that the snow was so sparse – only patches remained where outcrops of rock kept it in shadow. Our path was largely across greyish slate and grit, interspersed with larger boulders of granite – a bleak and colourless environment, watched over by the occasional lammergeier soaring high in the bright blue sky. I remembered the eagle in Scotland.

Perhaps more remarkable than the lack of snow were the signs of habitation in days long past. Ruins of little villages or settlements lay to the left and right, and I discovered that 3,000 people once lived in this inhospitable valley. In the monsoon period the Rongbuk River runs fast and deep, but for more than half the year it is frozen over, its water only accessible by breaking through the ice. That the inhabitants eked out a living in these harsh conditions is a testimony to mankind's determination to survive, even if today all but a few yak-herders have given up the unequal struggle. All, that is, except the lamas – the Buddhist priests – who have reoccupied the Rongbuk lamasery after a decade of enforced desertion during the Chinese Cultural Revolution.

At the lamasery we duly stopped to photograph and film. Nick needed foreground to complement the *stupa* standing out against the North Face of Everest some fifteen miles further up the valley, and I was deputed to herd some yaks into shot. While Nick composed his frame and Ian recorded the tinkling of the yak bells, I cajoled and prodded the reluctant beasts into position. Back into our transport and on we went. At long last, the more or less flat plain of the valley floor was barred by mounds of moraine-covered ice. The trucks could go no further – this was it, our 'home' for the next twelve weeks. Dougie and the Sherpas recce'd the area for the best available site, and settled on a stretch of what might later in the year be grass, beside a frozen lake. Between lake and mountain, one of the mounds of moraine obscured the view of Everest, but the Sherpas claimed that, come warmer weather, there would be fresh water here; and the hill offered some protection against the bitter wind which blew down the valley.

We set about unloading our twenty-nine cooler boxes and silver cases carrying our equipment and stock of film and tape. The lads sorted out their tents, and quickly occupied the better spots. When our turn came, the only available location was the furthest from the sheltering hill and the communal cook-tent just beneath it. But by way of compensation, we had the view that proximity to shelter precluded, and, set back at the end of the site, the whole camp lay before us with Mount Everest towering behind. That night, I wrote in my diary:

Surprisingly, both glad to be here and be in such good frame of mind. Had anticipated more trepidation. Exciting day, but what a drive. Unlike James Bond's martinis, I'm shaken physically but stirred emotionally. Want to share this experience with Vicky, and come to think of it, wouldn't say no to a fuck to celebrate our arrival. Fat chance of either.

This was to be the last entry that mentions sex. In total contrast with Kit Spencer's warning of what would occupy our imaginations, I found that my mind subconsciously edited out all such thoughts, and my body acted in sympathy – no wet dreams, no early-morning erections. I checked this later with a cross section of the lads, some of whom were honest enough to admit to the same absence of normal sexuality in themselves. Luke Hughes, who had visited Tibet before and spent some time in Lhasa, told me there was a well-established syndrome known as 'The Tibetan Revenge'. The Chinese officials, sent to Lhasa to supervise Sino-supremacy over the 'autonomous region' of Tibet, had been plagued with an inability to maintain normal relations with their wives. Altitude was held to be responsible. And we were to live half as high again as Lhasa! There's a footnote to all this – I can record (with relief!) that my return to normality at sea-level has been complete.

A big surprise, given that this was a military expedition, was the far from military free-form of Base Camp. Tents were not laid out in serried ranks, presenting a neat line to the eye, with their doors all on one axis. I had had visions of the old prints of the Battle of Waterloo in miniature, with Dougie filling the Wellington role, inspecting his ordered kingdom. I could not have been more wrong. If the tents tended to face one way, it was to avoid the prevailing wind; and common sense dictated that the lie of the land aligned your tent, avoiding this frozen-in rock or that deep depression. Similarly, rank appeared to count for nothing in personal conversations. Everyone was on first name terms and the word 'sir' was used only in irony. I have no comparisons to go by, and assume that Dougie's brand of leadership felt such conventions unnecessary, or positively intrusive. His orders were always accepted, if not without question then certainly without contradiction. Democracy can only go so far on an Everest expedition, but what characterized this expedition was an atmosphere of open discussion and lack of formality in every sphere.

For our communal use, we had what no previous Everest expedition has ever enjoyed – Hunter Huts – devised and developed by RAF Wing-Commander and expedition member, Keith Hunter. The Hunter Hut is constructed of pre-formed sections of rigid plastic foam, faced with fablon-type white paper, and held together by aluminium extrusions, adhesive tape and bolts. Extremely light to transport, it had excellent insulation properties, and was supposedly simple to erect. 'A morning's work,' asserted Keith, as we all gazed at the pile of white sheets in assorted sizes. The Hunter Hut destined for use at Base Camp was the largest – eighteen feet square and high enough inside to stand upright. For higher camps, there were two baby huts only eight feet square and lower in cross-section. The problem with the larger version was more to do with the base, or lack of it, than the hut itself. For all the sections to lock neatly together and meet, as they were designed to, at a central point, it was essential to build on a level platform. The ground at Base Camp was anything but flat, and it became quickly apparent that the hut must be put together on the lake, conveniently frozen and thus level, and then man-handled bodily into its chosen location, where the ground would be built up to meet the horizontal bottom edge. Once this had been appreciated – and it took several vain attempts at erection on site and a very testy and frustrated Keith before the solution was hit upon – it was not difficult to set the Hunter Hut fair and square, and tie it down with guy-ropes. Sloping sides gave it stability and minimized wind resistance, and windows could be cut with a pen-knife and covered with rigid clear polythene. The Hunter Hut was to prove a godsend, far warmer and more rigid than a mess tent, and consequently more convivial.

As for our accommodation, we fared well. Initially, Ian and I shared an octagonal bell tent, comfortably large enough for four, while Nick had a small tent, a Quasar, to himself. A fierce wind, which was a permanent feature of the early weeks at Base Camp, had hampered the erection of the tents and threatened, day and night, to tear down our handiwork. The fact that it was impossible to knock tent pegs more than an inch or so into the deep-frozen ground did little to appease my fears of finding myself, some dark night, flailing around in endless folds of canvas.

In a few days, when the second trekking party arrived to complete our number, we were allocated a 'twelve-by-twelve' – a twelve-foot-square, eight-foot-high, heavy canvas tent on a solid, alloy frame. This sounds like space enough and more for four men and their scant possessions, but throw in the filming gear to which we needed instant access, (the rest lived outside under a tarpaulin), and Roger Antolik with his photographic and climbing equipment (he undoubtedly had more paraphernalia than any other expedition member), and floor space was promptly at a premium. Tempers tend to be short at altitude, and sharp words were exchanged if one of us felt his territory had been invaded. It never came to an outright row, but we all became absurdly jealous of our patch, perhaps just because it was all we had to call our own. By the same token, privacy was respected as far as possible. Tempting though it was to someone employed to plumb the inner depths of the climber's psyche and get it on film, I would never have dreamt of reading anyone's diary, and nobody, to the best of my knowledge, ever looked at mine. One metaphorically knocked on the door by calling 'anyone there?' before entering another's tent, and if one saw a man obviously deep in a book or his thoughts, even in the close quarters of our communal hut, one avoided an interruption. By such small gestures of respect for each other, we co-existed peacefully and I never witnessed an argument that was seriously meant in the whole time on the mountain.

Although we knew we would soon be moving further up the glacier to higher camps, a routine quickly established itself at Base. The day would start, usually around eight a.m. unless some reason dictated otherwise, with the Sherpa cook-boy Manbahadur's cheerful cry of 'Chahi Sahib', as his face appeared through the tent flap, followed by a steaming kettle of thick, sweet liquid: 'bed tea'. There is something of the English Raj about an expedition, I reflected. There can hardly be many occasions, these uncolonial days, when a definite hierarchy of master–servant relations obtains, and is accepted and expected. The Sherpas take great pride in their skill, whether it be carrying or cooking, and the knowledge that their job is well done and appreciated is their satisfaction. If this sounds like boss-talk, I can only record that I found the relationship distasteful to begin with, but grew to respect the Sherpas and their way of life as I perceived it.

'Breakfast ready!' was the next call, accompanied by the beating of an empty kerosene can. At Base Camp and Advance Base Camp all cooking was done by the Sherpa cooks, two to a camp. Breakfast consisted always of porridge and, until it ran out, powdered scrambled egg and fried bacon roll. The egg was better than I expected, but the bacon roll shared little with the crispy rasher of the traditional British breakfast. I remembered fried Spam from childhood, and none too fondly. There were optional extras to this daily fare, supplied by their makers: crunchy, muesli-based cereal, spoiled by the addition of milk made from powder; Appeel, a powdered orange juice, and Marmite or Bovril for when the fresh bread routine was established. In addition I had brought packets of espresso coffee and a coffee machine, and varied my liquid diet by indulging myself every few days. I proved very popular with my coffee, and soon gave up offering to make it myself to avoid spending hours in the cook tent. People laughed at my five kilos of coffee, but they were happy enough to drink the stuff when it came their way!

Lunch was usually potato-based while the fresh spuds lasted, and sometimes included a fresh fried egg until they too disappeared. Then, it was down to tinned processed cheese – 'cheese possessed' – and further inventions based on the bacon roll. Karmi, the chief cook, was a master of making something new out of the same old ingredients and serving it in visually appetizing ways. While he had vegetables to experiment on – peppers, tomatoes, beans – he was a miracle, but even Karmi's imagination stalled when all that was left were tins of wholesome but unappealing 'scram'.*

The main meal was supper, always starting with soup and followed with meat and mash or noodles. Puddings varied: tinned fruit salad was a rare luxury, jelly and custard more frequent, and a form of fruit stodge, the staple. The memory is too recent to allow much enthusiasm to invade my account, and the excellent meals I enjoy between bouts on this book bring back the fantasies we all indulged on the mountain. The early imaginings of rich and elaborate dishes gradually gave way to more down-to-earth yearnings – a good joint of meat, a salad, an egg that came in a shell.

The thankless and unrewarding task of being in charge of catering had fallen to one Martin Bazire. His had been the job, back in the UK, of deciding what the compo rations should consist of; how much should be ordered for forty men for three months (the Sherpas catered for themselves); and what extras would make the meals more palatable and inviting. He had settled on huge quantities of bottled sauces, red and brown, and many varieties of chutney, pickles and the like in jars. Then there was the chocolate – one-gross boxes of Mars and Marathon, Rolos and Twix, and for the more figure-conscious, Trackers and Jordan's Crunchy Bars. Tins of tuna, pilchards and sardines filled the fish quota, and as a special luxury there were occasional tins of coleslaw and other prepared salads.

Although I often wished for a more varied menu, I had only one genuine criticism of Martin's preparations, given what was possible in the circumstances, and this concerned the biscuits. It appeared that only one variety of biscuit had been ordered: Garibaldis. I have nothing against what were always dubbed 'squashed flies', but we had Garibaldis by the ton, and nothing else. Towards the end of the expedition, when pudding stocks ran low, the Garibaldis kept coming in endless supply. Day after day, the heaped-up dish of Garibaldi packets was greeted with mounting derision. And in the final clearout, countless Garibaldis were consigned to the bottom of a crevasse, so that their wrappings should not be distributed down the Rongbuk valley by the alpine choughs or passing yakkers. I doubt I shall ever

*scram (Navy) = scoff (all three Services) = food.

want a Garibaldi biscuit again.

Martin, a tall and lanky individual, was known always as Baz, after television's Basil Fawlty. But whether this was because of his physical resemblance to that harassed hotelier or due to Martin's catering responsibilities was never clear.

Amongst Baz's best buys, to judge by their rate of consumption, were tubes of Nestlé's condensed milk. This went not only in Nescafé and tea, but on Alpen and porridge, puddings of all but the steak and kidney variety, and, when the baking routine started, on fresh bread. But the freezing temperatures made a quick squeeze on a recalcitrant tube a potential hazard. On one memorable occasion Simon Lowe, a Signals captain who went on to distinguish himself first in his communications speciality and subsequently on the upper reaches of the mountain, was having difficulty getting the required squirt by the mere application of finger pressure. He put his whole hand to the task, and gave the tube the crushing equivalent of a wrestler's handshake. It worked. Condensed milk shot out in abundance – but not from the nozzle. The crimped bottom end gave way first, and a gush of goo an inch thick covered Roger Antolik from hair to hands.

Everest Base Camp is not the place to be coated in condensed milk. What was most crucially lacking at this juncture was a bathroom. A tersely silent Roger did his best to wipe off the surplus with tissues that disintegrated, and soon he looked as though he had been tarred and feathered. An abjectly apologetic Simon went for a wet cloth from the cook tent, and the rest of us collapsed in convulsions, interspersed with ribald comments about Simon's male prowess as the creamy rivulets trickled down Roger's upper half.

Roger himself was a master of self-control. In the fractious atmosphere induced by altitude, I could have understood men coming to blows over less, but Roger contented himself with a few choice expletives and a lot of dabbing with a damp cloth. It was days before the weather was kind enough to allow him a hair-wash, and his matted locks began to resemble a nascent Rastafarian's.

Roger was to play the hero in a different context only a few nights later. He had risen at two a.m. in response to a sudden call of nature of the kind that necessitated a smart 200-yard trot down to the 'crapper', an elaborately constructed affair of rocks around a rising pile of excrement. It was a bitterly cold night, brightly starlit and even more windy than usual. I muttered my sympathies as Roger crawled out of the twelve-by-twelve and into the elements, and tried to settle back to sleep, despite the buffeting canvas whip-cracking about me. A particularly vicious gust hit the tent, causing it to clap like a thunderbolt. Through the raging wind, I heard more such sounds further away, but thought nothing of it. Then came even more distant shouts, and cries of alarm. 'Some poor sod's losing their tent,' I thought, and in the same second selfishly decided to leave them to it – after all, by the time I had extracted myself from my bag and put on suitable protective clothing, it would be far too late to offer any asssistance. Perhaps half an hour later, Roger reappeared.

'You bastard, Mark! Where were you?'

'Here, of course! Where should I be at this time of night and in this weather?'

'Didn't you hear me shouting and calling?'

'Well, yes, I did hear someone.'

'It was me, you idiot, shouting for help!' Roger was close to apoplexy. 'There I was in mid-crap, when suddenly I was enveloped in a huge mass of thrashing canvas.'

Roger went on to tell his story. The stores tent had broken loose, and purely by chance had blown on to the 'crapper' down the valley, where he valiantly managed to hold on to it with one hand, while pulling up his pants with the other. It must have been a superhuman feat, especially as the rock on which we squatted had a pronounced downward slope towards the pit, and a nasty habit of icing up. I looked at his boots.

'No mishaps, I hope, Roger?' I inquired.

'Fuck off!' he responded very understandably, climbing back into his sleeping bag. I decided I had better say no more.

Such excitements were the exception rather than the rule, but night time in general continued to present problems. My diary is peppered with 'rotten sleep', 'read 2 to 4 a.m. until too cold to hold book', and 'awake 3 a.m. till bed tea arrived'. But gradually my conscious mind got on top of my subconscious, and I managed to lie peacefully awake, and even think constructively. Normally, my thoughts were to do with the immediate questions presented by the filming. Should we go up or down to another camp? Should we interview this or that climber? Should we tackle Dougie on this or that issue? But I also wondered further afield. One night the idea of redesigning my house in London occurred to me, and I subsequently spent many a sleepless hour running through the options of taking down this wall or re-painting that room. It was good therapy, but I have yet to decide whether to put it into practice. On Everest, thoughts cost nothing.

Construction works were not limited to my imagination, however. The 'crapper' deserves more than a passing nod to its existence. Initially, we had improvised, picking our spot behind a remote rock; but tiptoeing among the turds was getting to be a hazard, and Dougie decreed the immediate necessity of a purpose-built privy to be used obligatorily by one and all. Designed by Dave Nicholls and executed in massive lumps of stone by mountaineers-turned-masons, Ted Atkins and Al McLeod, the new loo was attractively situated on a mound of moraine, a decent distance from the camp proper and down wind, for obvious reasons.

It was decided to have an official opening ceremony presided over by both the leader and deputy leader. Obviously this was an occasion we could not omit from the film, and accordingly we set up our camera and gave Dave Nicholls, MC and architect, the go-ahead.

DAVE Would you like to pass me the loo paper, please? Thanks. Right, Leader Sahib, this is the loo – the finest view in the world, with your Base Camp and Everest behind it. I would now like you please to undo your zips, gentlemen, from the back. Yes, both please. Right, lean back now and take the strain.

HENRY DAY Hang about, I've got to do things properly.

DOUGIE KEELAN I think I can help you there.

DAVE Then take some loo paper in the other hand. Right, now again take the strain, please.

TED How many pieces for you?

HENRY I don't want to tell everybody my secrets, you know. I think I'll have the lot.

DOUGIE Hang on. If I'm going to do what you want, I've got to go like this. Now just make sure that my pockets are secure.

DAVE Right, are you ready? . . .

The grunts and groans of simulated evacuations echoed down the valley, but they were interrupted by Pat Parsons.

PAT I'm just about to do something for real, I can feel it coming on.

DOUGIE (urgently) Let me get out first then, Pat . . .

Dougie raised himself from the bamboo bracer, his cigar still firmly clenched in Churchillian fashion between his teeth. We left Pat to the privacy to which I felt he was entitled. But I was in a minority on this, as I discovered in a recorded chat with Ted Atkins and Steve Bell, the initially camera-shy former Royal Marine.

STEVE There was quite a funny incident this morning, concerning Henry. When I went along to the heads – for those of you who aren't Marines that's the toilets – I found they'd been vastly improved, which I didn't know about. So I went looking for them, and I couldn't see them anywhere. Then suddenly I heard this voice from behind a rock saying 'Wait your turn' and I thought 'Oh yeah', so I located the loos and just sat there quite happily waiting my turn. Then along came Ted, and he just came storming past me. I said, 'Hang on, Ted, wait your turn. I'm next', and he said, 'Well, that's all right, you know, I'll just keep going', and he went on right past me. Henry in the meantime came out, and I ran after Ted and when I got there I said, 'What are you doing? It's my turn next?' But when I got there there was a loo big enough for about three people. But I don't know, perhaps it's shyness, perhaps you have to be on a few expeditions to . . .

TED . . . Before you can all sit comfortably together.

STEVE Yup, all boys together you know, to be able to drop your pants and all go for it on the old trench.

TED Well, Henry unfortunately I think has a bit of the Colonel about him, and he really can't have the troops crapping next to the old Colonel, what! Whereas Steve and I happily sit it out together, pants down, away we go, lovely morning isn't it? isn't this a wonderful idea? etc. etc. . . .

Ted laughed.

STEVE I'm not necessarily all that pally, but it's quite pleasant to exchange a few ideas in the morning. But yes, Henry was a bit stand-offish, wasn't he?

MARK I can't say I blame him.

TED Well, I think it's just something you've got to get used to. It's bloody awkward at first, it really is. I mean, on the walk-in and things, you tend to sort of adopt the conservative British attitude that you must run up the glen for sixteen miles to find the right size boulder to hide behind, where no one could possibly see you before you can, you know, do your toilet.

STEVE What I'm most concerned about is the big thick bamboo bar that you brace yourself against. If you had three people bracing all at once against that bamboo bar, I think there's a pretty good chance of dropping yourself in the proverbial . . .

To the best of my knowledge, no one did.

Within a week of our arrival at Base Camp, Manbahadur, Karmi's assistant cook-boy, was taken suddenly and seriously ill. Andy Hughes was alerted in the middle of the night, and in the morning we found a desperate looking Marni, as we called him for short, hooked up to a drip, and on oxygen. He lay motionless and pale, and looked to me closer to death than life. Andy was non-committal – Marni had pneumonia and/or pulmonary oedema, a potentially fatal form of AMS or Acute Mountain Sickness. The standard treatment for this condition is to get the patient to a lower altitude as quickly as possible, but this was out of the question – we all knew how long and arduous was the drive, and the descent was too gradual. Oxygen and anti-biotics were the only hope. My diary:

Sherpas' attitude interesting. Chowang, the Sirdar,* and Karmi, rubbed Marni's feet to warm them, while another hung a line of prayer-flags from the tent he lay in to the cook-tent. Moving to observe their care and concern, but contradictorily the other Sherpas seemed totally unconcerned and fatalistic, to do perhaps with their Buddhist belief in reincarnation – if Marni's time has come, then so be it. I found his predicament distressing, could not resist temptation to encourage him verbally – 'come on, you can pull through, don't throw in the sponge' – although I knew it meant nothing. If Andy's drugs and the expedition oxygen don't bring him round, he's had it. What a thought!

The treatment worked. In a few days Marni was sitting up and even smiling again. He was a wan shadow of his normal, cheerful self, but he was on the mend. The expedition put our own tribulations in perspective. It was less easy to be self-pitying with the occasional splitting headache, a more normal symptom of AMS than pulmonary oedema, or sheer physical exhaustion. But one could not escape the conclusion that if the treatment available failed, there was little hope of getting down and off the mountain in time – a sobering thought.

We were, though, lucky on the whole. Alan had the worst time

*Sirdar = boss or leader.

with headaches; Nick contracted a nasty chest infection; and Ian coughed relentlessly for three months, and felt frequently well below par. I fared best of the four of us, and half jokingly put it down to smoking. But Dave Orange, the other inveterate smoker and I, agreed that there was perhaps some sense in the claim – if our lungs had had to cope every day with the degree of pollution we imposed on them, then they were used to abuse and oxygen starvation. We didn't know as we discussed this possibility that Dave's own experience on the West Ridge and higher was first to contradict, then dramatically to support our theory. He ended up unable to operate with the oxygen equipment, and carried loads to Camp Five and just above without it, a feat only the lifelong-acclimatized Sherpas could match.

If the inside of my body was inaccessible to a good clean-out, the outer parts were scarcely more so. Personal hygiene is a matter of taste, but I was surprised how readily I convinced myself that I need not strip off and wash, or even clean my teeth each day. The effect of abstinence from washing is not cumulative pro rata – in other words, the first day or two is the worst, and then you learn to live with greasy hair and tacky teeth. But sooner or later action must be taken, and one fine sunny day I strengthened my resolve and asked the cooks for hot water. Pouring a kettle into a wide tin bowl, I ventured outside. A hair shampoo came first, and quickly reduced the water to a grey and scummy solution. But I could not back out now, and first the top half came off for a flannelling of the armpits and neck, and finally, stark naked, I sat in the now disgusting bowl and washed private parts and feet. Almost better than the marked improvement I felt in my body – it has to be experienced to be appreciated – was the exquisite pleasure of clean clothes against the skin. Only then did I realize how stale and sticky the others – worn night and day for a fortnight – had become. I can only say that one can get used to almost anything, and often it is not only the lack of incentive to strip in a freezing wind, but the lack of sufficient water to wash in that enforces long periods in an unwashed state. My diary records another of these periodic ablutions.

A day of perfect weather – bright, clear, cloudless sky, warm sun, and no wind! Amazing. Everyone took to washing – themselves and their clothes. I was appalled to find quite bad athlete's foot – hardly surprising as I can't have washed my feet for ten days – but felt totally regenerated by washing first myself, and then my clothes – underpants, roll-necked top, socks and thermal

*longjohns. Now feeling very virtuous and a damned sight better. The trouble
is, the washing freezes rock solid on the line between two tripods. The
temperature must be below freezing, despite sitting here in shorts and, earlier,
a bare chest. The clothes are directly in the sun, but still they freeze. What to
do? Last night very cold, minus 15 degrees centigrade inside tent; but now, in
the sun, it's too warm in the tent.*

To the yak herders camped nearby, the whole business was
hilarious. They gathered at a barely respectable distance and stared, as
only Tibetans can stare, in disbelief. Themselves black from years of
nomadic tent-living at close quarters with their animals, they quite
obviously did not share my albeit rudimentary principles of hygiene.
Swathed in thick yak-fur jackets and baggy trousers, whose blackness
matched the skin of hands and face, they were a fearsome sight. All
wore long knives, and in their thickly matted hair, solid yak-horn
rings, the size of napkin rings. The yakkers' only concession to
relieving the head-to-toe blackness of their appearance was to sport
bright earrings of metal and woven thread. To their animals, they
allowed more freedom. Many were adorned with tufts of magenta-
dyed hair and made a welcome splash of colour in the uniform
drabness of the grey and white Base Camp.

The presence of the yaks was not accidental, although herds do
wander up and down the valleys of Tibet in search of the meagre
greenery on which they live. But these yaks were here for us,
'ordered' by Messrs Mah and Deng, to carry the bulk of our provisions and equipment to an unspecified point up the valley: the yak
dump. It was hoped that this would be at least as far as Advance Base
Camp, which although as yet uncertain itself, would in all probability
be where Tilman made a camp some fifty years before. It was about
six miles as the crow flies, but with the continuous undulation of the
terrain, half as much again on foot. However, when the weather and
the depth of snow at last allowed the yaks to start their journey, they
were able to go beyond Advance Base Camp and dump their loads on
a bluff beside the 'penitents' – eerie pinnacles of ice thrown up by the
glacier, like a giant jawbone with blue teeth. Much later on, we were
to record some of the lads attempting to scale these ice spikes with our
lightweight video equipment.

Although our documentary series was to be made primarily on
film, we had a second string. Film gear and the film it consumes is

very heavy – a camera loaded with a ten minute magazine of film weighs almost thirty pounds, and operating for any time was already proving a problem at Base Camp, let alone far higher on the mountain. To use up there, and to lend to the climbers to use on our behalf, we had four Video-8 cameras, far lighter and capable of an hour's uninterrupted recording, even if, in terms of quality of picture and sound, they could not match the film camera and recorder. To view the tapes we made, Roger Antolik had begged and borrowed a TV monitor from Sony, and with it a couple of dozen or so pre-recorded feature films and pop videos. We 'Granadas' thereby ingratiated ourselves with the lads, offering movies at night in the communal hut. On one occasion we were running *The Eliminators* (most of the films were truly terrible) when we noticed two yakkers standing in the door with their habitual stare. But this time, it was understandable. They had surely never seen a television at all, let alone here at Everest Base Camp. They stood transfixed, understanding of course not a single word, but glued to the magic of the screen. The Sherpas too shared the yakkers' interest, particularly if there were any salacious scenes – Sherpas pride themselves on their sexual prowess as much as their mountain skills, and seemed very happy, in the absence of the real thing, to live the experience vicariously. One of our films, *The Clan of the Cave Bear*, had a sequence in which the leader of a tribe of cavemen exercised his *droit de seigneur*, but before doing so indicated his intentions by a gesture involving the linking of both hands with fingers hooked together. This sign language the Sherpas quickly grasped, and were often to repeat the gesture, accompanied by much raucous laughter, in their conversations with us. Needless to say, this movie was the Sherpas' favourite, and got many screenings once we had run through the limited repertoire.

We did not make use of the TV monitor every evening by any means. A bridge clique soon developed, with Nick as one of its stalwarts, while Alan and I led a Scrabble faction. There was a considerable library with a high proportion of war books, of which the most popular was undoubtedly *Red Storm Rising* by Tom Clancy; and we had Travellers' Trivial Pursuit, which dispenses with the board and becomes basically a quiz game. One evening, we 'Granadas' challenged teams from each of the four Services represented to a grand tournament, and got off to a promising start. But our luck deserted us when a run of medical and scientific questions came the way of Al

Miller, the doctor who had treated Giles's ankle. The Navy raced into the lead and held it. Granada disgraced itself by coming in last. I trusted our practical ability in making the series would outshine our intellectual skills – it needed to!

If the evenings were often fully occupied – there was always letter writing to friends and family to fill in slack moments – the days frequently yawned with inactivity, particularly for the film crew. We could not film all and every day for obvious reasons – the stock would run out and, more significantly, there was often nothing happening worth filming. The lads were kept busy load-carrying – a monotonous routine of back-packing thirty or forty pounds of food or equipment from one camp to the next. But once we had done a sequence recording this, we depended on chance events to provide a focus for our camera. Between these occasional moments, we occupied our time with the odd interview and shots of the stupendous landscape in varying lights. But there was still time to spare, and my abiding impression of the trip as a whole is the enforced tedium that lay between the spurts of activity, and the exhaustion that such efforts entailed. My diary notes, a week or so after arriving at Base Camp: 'Filming is always a mental release, although physically so demanding.'

I had had the foresight to bring with me a very light aluminium garden chair of my mother's and, wind permitting, was often to be seen sitting comfortably in the sun, reading or writing. The pleasure of being able to sit upright rather than be sprawled on our thin foam mattresses is deeply memorable. Chairs were at a premium – some half-dozen or so for the entire population of Base Camp – and to have my own was proving a stroke of pre-planning genius.

The only fly in the ointment, or more accurately, mote in the eye, was due to the wind. All too often a glorious sunny day of clear sky and radiant warmth was unpredictably interrupted by a sudden gale of an icily cutting ferocity hard to imagine. Grit whipped into the eyes and driven spindrift stung the face and hands as you made for the nearest shelter. And on Saturday 19 March, the mountain excelled itself, breaking all its own records of instant storm-mongering.

This particular Saturday was a special day – we were to be visited by the lama from the Rongbuk lamasery, who would conduct for our benefit a 'puja', blessing the expedition and its endeavours. We had already visited the lamasery to film, as the lamas had come back only recently to rebuild their ruins. Photographs taken a decade ago show broken-down walls and roofless buildings, a scene of devastation wrought by zealots wielding Mao's Little Red Book, and compounded by passing trekkers and expeditioners who used the erstwhile lamasery as lavatory and dumping ground. But the changing political climate has allowed the lamas back, and we found a half-dozen in residence, together with a working party of visitors making votive lamps from yak grease, to the incessant drone of 'Om Mane Padme Hum'. Paying a small fee – the lamas are nothing if not practical – we had duly filmed the proceedings, and were then told of the intended puja.

The day dawned blustery. Already we had had to look to the fixings of our twelve-by-twelve tent, as my diary records:

Woke to find sleeping bag white with snow blown in by the wind, and dust and grit in every orifice – very cold and very unpleasant. A fine, freezing spray of spindrift falling on my face, like being under a huge eau-de-cologne atomizer. Wind getting stronger and stronger before breakfast. Tent flapping dramatically, and the one-and-a-half-inch frame bending like a twig. One gust ripped the whole back section up from the row of rocks that weighted it down. Ian, asleep, sat up as though he'd been stung, and we all grabbed at the canvas to prevent its being blown off down the valley. Had been musing verbally on the impossible alternatives to Base Camp breakfast – fried egg and bacon, or perhaps French bread and coffee, black cherry jam. 'And croissants,' interjected Nick. 'And a French maid to serve it,' – this from Roger Antolik – until a gust of wind got us smartly out of our bags and into instant rescue manoeuvres.

Chowang, the Sherpa Sirdar and a deeply religious man, had great difficulty directing the installation of a massive string of prayer-flags on the hillock above Base Camp. Three twenty-foot streamers led out from a central pole of bamboo two inches thick. But when it was raised against the wind it flexed like a wand of willow. It should have been a warning. About 11 a.m. the lama arrived and installed himself at a small table erected by the Sherpas before an improvised altar of stones on which a fire burned fiercely. The table was laden with specially prepared offerings of food, and even a bottle of the expedition's Famous Grouse. I quashed a passing thought that perhaps this was extending generosity a little too far, and concentrated on our filming of the event. Chanting throughout, although barely audible through the howling wind, the lama took minute morsels of the votive food and drink, tasted it and offered it symbolically to the altar before him. As he held the offertory aloft, the huge prayer-flag construction broke free and crashed down the hill, looking to me suspiciously like a bad omen. But the ceremony was concluded to everyone's satisfaction, and the lama retired to the cook-tent for more solid sustenance.

The wind, however, had not finished its work. My diary again:

Although the wind had been blowing strongly, there was no warning when it suddenly became a serious threat. The first gust flattened Dougie's tent, and as we jumped to save it, the next hit our twelve-by-twelve, bending the inner frame like a cane in the hands of Dickens's Wackford Squeers. The whole tent was on the verge of lifting from its moorings and blowing piecemeal across the lake, when several of the lads joined us inside, hanging on the frame to hold it down. We left them to it, turning to our camera to film. They tried to drop the section of frame that held the windward side to near vertical, so that the angle the tent presented to the wind would offer less resistance. Several times while filming, one leg of the tripod lifted off the ground, and I was forced to hold it down for Nick to get a steady shot. Facing the wind was impossible, blinded by flying snow and grit and, if taken off guard, flattened to the ground. Moved inside the twelve-by-twelve to film the lads reconstructing it for greater safety. One wall suddenly flapped free, catapulting Nick and camera across the tent. Force of these gusts quite incredible. The only thing we've yet to see is one of the lads hang-gliding down the glacier under his tent! Over a third of the octagonal tents have been flattened and/or ripped open, and the camp is in ruins as though hit by an earthquake. Alan's lost his pee bottle; Ian's totally bemused; Nick's excited by the shots he's got; and I'm delighted to have got a sequence that's not engineered in any way. This is the kind of natural disaster I'd envisaged but hasn't happened until now. No injury to anyone, only the tents, but what a day! Exactly one month since we set off from Brize Norton.

Onwards and Upwards

Sunday 20 March to Monday 28 March
The Rongbuk Valley

The next day, Sunday, was in complete contrast: total tranquillity descended on Base Camp, with hardly a breath of wind to raise a tent flap or flutter a prayer-flag. The sun shone down strongly, burning noses, ears and lips as only Everest sun can in the thin atmosphere. And everyone set about repairing the ravages of yesterday. I see from my diary it was a day for taking stock.

I think things are turning a corner, in two senses: first, and most important to me (because the other is inevitable), I am now reconciled emotionally and psychologically to this whole endeavour. It's taken a month, but given the 'culture shock' to someone of my recent history, that's not surprising. Nor do I think I'm completely out of the woods – I'm certain there will be days, and more certain still, nights, when the horrors come back. The physical side I feel confident I can cope with, whether it be the exhaustion (as today when we walked up to the East Rongbuk River and were all, except Alan, knackered to the point of nausea and fainting), or the discomfort – no beds, no electricity, no decent food, etc., etc. All that is just something to face as it comes, grit one's teeth and deal with. The real problem is the other – the emotional/ psychological – which is beyond the control of my willpower, mind, etc., because it's subconscious, and it's this element that I now feel has come to heel, at least to a manageable extent.

After the walk up to the East Rongbuk – ostensibly to film the yak-trail, but they were too speedy for us and so we could never get far enough ahead, a total failure – the mail arrived via Giles from Xangmu. I had four letters from Vicky, two from Peg [my mother], one from Polly [my daughter] and one from Jean [my ex-wife]. Wonderful. A real, almost tangible pleasure to read about things back in England – a touchstone to reality. But also a sobering reminder of both how remote we are and how tenuous that connection is. Waves of homesickness, pangs of envy and regret. Vicky's off to France soon for Easter. How I'd love to be with her – wine, food and all the rest. This is, and will remain, a demanding project in every sense. Wrote quick replies as Roger, Luke and Henry are off to Lhasa. Then, a cop-out, a yellow bomber to get off to sleep after re-reading the letters until nearly 2 a.m. They brought the real world a little too close for my recently adapted psyche.

But letters were not our only means of communication. We called on our Video-8 cameras to record visual 'letters' home, in which we all appeared. Nick usually did the operating, filming everything from the majestic scenery to the Base Camp 'crapper', and even managing to set the camera up on a rock with himself in front of it, holding forth like any professional reporter. We intended these tapes for purely private consumption – our wives and girlfriends – but in the event, they were seen by a wide variety of interested parties, such as my mother, and even David Plowright, Granada's Chairman, by virtue of his being Nick's father. This would have been fine, except that we had been fairly down-to-earth in our 'pieces to camera', and I had visions of being sacked for 'conduct unbecoming to a producer/director'. Phrases such as 'Sod you, Rod Caird, for dropping me in this heap of shit!' were *not* intended to be heard by Rod himself, let alone his boss – even if they were not seriously meant! But I need not have worried; the tapes were taken in the spirit in which they were recorded, and David Plowright even considered using them as publicity material – 'the Granada crew, living and working on the Rongbuk Glacier'! We soon put a stop to *that* one when we heard about it.

The tape messages were also a two-way affair. I had lent my own Video-8 camera to Vicky, who lent it to Nick's wife, Annie, and she sent back a recording of Plowright family life. Nick was delighted, if a little homesick, at the sight and sound of his two-year-old son, Marcus, talking in proper sentences for the first time. There was a weird quality of dislocation about watching, in our remote circumstances, such familiar faces in familiar surroundings. But it was certainly worth the odd pang of almost enjoyable anguish.

Since Video-8 cameras are relatively new, I doubt if previous expeditions have been able to indulge in this particular form of communication with family and friends back home. And we had another Everest 'first' to our credit: Satcom. The expedition had borrowed from Marconi a satellite telephone system, which, thanks to difficulties with the CMA only now sorted out by the industrious Mr

Mah, was about to be put into operation. It required two large solar panels to charge a pair of car batteries, which then gave a good hour's worth per day of working communication with any number in the world connected to the direct dialling system. For the remaining nine weeks of the expedition, we would enjoy the double pleasure of speaking to our 'loved ones' in Britain – if only for a few minutes at a time – and of knowing that, in an emergency, a message could be relayed to us in a matter of hours. This made for considerable peace of mind, which was equally appreciated, we soon learnt, by those at home: should a tragedy occur, or an accident befall one of the lads, an accurate on-the-spot account of it could be given to those most in need of knowing.

Most of the time, though, the airwaves were taken up with the 'I'm fine, miss you, love you' trivia which, from Everest Base Camp, were anything but trivial. But all this was in the future; I had better return to that Red Letter Day of the first phone call, 21 March.

The Satcom was the brainchild of Simon Lowe, a Signals Captain who had successfully persuaded not only Marconi to supply the hardware, but also British Telecom to make us a present of fifteen thousand pounds worth of calls. The normal charge was ten US dollars a minute, so there were a good few hours of free phoning in the bank. Simon now set about connecting up the dish and turning it to beam directly to the satellite over the Indian Ocean. The frequency of a bleep tone indicated an on-target signal, and with a few more cables plugged in, he was on the air. There was a genuine aura of excitement as he test-called the expedition Project Office in Aldershot.

'Hello. It's Captain Lowe here from Everest Base Camp . . . I'm very well. Everyone else is as well . . . Yeah, it's not bad. I'm getting a bit of an echo back, though. Is John there?'

A pause, while John Fitzgerald came to the phone in the military HQ in Surrey.

'Hello, John. How are you? Marvellous, isn't it? Before the batteries run out, I'll hand you over to Dougie.'

It was an impressive moment. Dougie took over the phone.

'Hello, John. Well, we got clearances from the Chinese about three days ago, but we've been charging up the batteries ever since. Now, John, before we talk about lesser things, let me read over a sitrep to you which you can then issue. Right. This is as at the twenty-first of March. "BSEE now firmly set up on Mount Everest stop. Base

Camp established on eighth March, Camp One on eleventh March, Camp Two at the foot of the West Ridge by the twenty-second of March stop. Weather has generally not been good but finally spring seems on the way stop. All members in reasonable health but one Sherpa was critically ill, now recovered, stop."

'OK, John. Super. Well, I mean, it's exactly as I've said on the sitrep – we're in good shape, winter seems to be just about giving its final lurches, and we're all set fair. Absolutely smashing. We've got Henry and Luke who've gone to Lhasa today, and they'll telephone us on this machine if a problem arises. Now, just a warning order for you. You will know that the oxygen in Lhasa we bought off Brummie Stokes. We've heard just a hint, no more than a hint, that he might be trying to have second thoughts about the sale because he might want it himself for a monsoon climbing slot he's been given. Has he accepted any cheques yet? [A pause] But he's accepted the first cheque? OK, now, if there's any problem we'll be coming back to you on this machine, if necessary to get the Crown solicitors on to him. We'll come back to you when Henry gets back in about three days.'

Oxygen, the single most costly commodity the expedition had brought to the mountain, was already causing problems, and the man in charge was Henry Day. It was a key responsibility. Before he had departed in the CMA jeep for Lhasa, I had asked Henry where the oxygen had come from, and why it was in Lhasa.

HENRY We buy our oxygen from two different sources. The major quantity is already in Lhasa and has been for a year or two, and we bought it from Brummie Stokes, who's led his own expedition here, and indeed was on our trip the other side of Everest back in 1976. We've come up against a bit of a problem in order to get the stuff from Lhasa. Apparently a telex has been received by the Chinese Mountaineering Association saying: 'Release none of my kit. I'm Brummie Stokes.' Well, that's fine, because the oxygen we've bought off him is ours and not his. But that is not immediately apparent to the senior official here from the CMA. So we're having to send a rather larger deputation to Lhasa than we would have wished in order to make absolutely certain that there isn't a hold-up in getting that issue. The other source of oxygen we've got is the new, lighter-weight cylinders, fibreglass, which we bought from a firm in the States, and they're a much handier size to carry further up the mountain. The idea is that they'll be used almost exclusively in the Hornbein Couloir higher up. The ones we're getting from Stokes are rather heavier beasts, and if we can get those along the West Ridge and use them for sleeping rather than for daily work, that would be a great help. But the smaller ones are here, and we had to use some of those, of course, when poor Manbahadur got pneumonia and complications. So we're already five of our smaller cylinders down, plus a couple of my specials which I had made a few years ago. The oxygen situation is not as happy as it might be. Until we've actually got them in our own hands, there'll be this worry that there could be some kind of hold-up . . .

Going with Henry Day on the Lhasa trip was Luke Hughes, partly because he knew the city, and more particularly because he had been on Henry's Shisha Bangma expedition the previous autumn, and had left a further small supply of oxygen in a store in the Tibetan capital. Luke had also been deputed to organize the transport of all the oxygen back to Base Camp.

LUKE There are problems with the transport because there are about seventy cylinders, each one weighing about twenty pounds, which is well over seven hundred kilos altogether, about half a truck load's worth. It's a good two days' drive to Lhasa. There are problems in finding transport; problems in getting stuff loaded; problems getting it over all the passes, particularly back here; and you need a particular type of transport for that purpose. There's also the problem with the recent troubles in Lhasa – foreigners are not welcome, although the Chinese have not blamed foreigners for this latest spate of trouble, unlike when we were there in October when they did. So, we have many problems, getting through the police checkpoints and so on, but I think with a little bravado, we ought to be able to pull it off.

MARK Why is it that oxygen is such a critical part of climbing Everest?

LUKE It's been a problem that's plagued expeditions since they first brought oxygen up in the 1930s. It's when you're sleeping that you deteriorate most, and that is not just in terms of your ability to perform on the mountain, but your ability to convert food to be able to keep the blood going round for circulation, to stop things like frostbite, just to stop yourself deteriorating. And, obviously, at anywhere over sixteen thousand feet you always start to die a little, but oxygen helps slow that down. And particularly, as I say, at night . . .

The oxygen saga, did I but know it, was to become a running theme of the expedition, even a running sore, and Henry was to be the butt of many a complaint.

But, for the moment, I was far more concerned about our own imminent departure for Advance Base Camp (ABC). There had been much discussion as to where to site Camp One, as ABC was also known. Merv Middleton, who knew the Rongbuk approach to Everest from a previous expedition, favoured a location nearer to the mountain proper, but Dougie Keelan had exercised his authority as leader and settled on the Tilman site. Merv is a powerful and determined man, as well as an excellent and experienced mountaineer, and I know Dougie weighed Merv's objections carefully before making his decision. Democratic to a degree, he had thrown the discussion open to the eight team leaders he had appointed as his deputies, and secured a majority support from them. Dave Nicholls, another veteran mountaineer with almost as many Alpine ascents under his harness as there were hairs on his bushy moustache, was strongly behind Dougie, and would himself take the decision on where to site Camp Two, the location from which the mountain climbing for real would be launched. Advance Base Camp, as Dougie's sitrep to the Project Office and the Higher Management Committee had reported, had been established for some days now, and only the absence of two porters, ordered through the CMA to carry film equipment exclusively for us but still nowhere to be seen, was holding us up at Base Camp. The problem, we hoped, would soon be resolved, as Roger Antolik had joined the Lhasa party as our liaison man, and was expecting to return with the two errant porters.

We could wait for them no longer, I decided. The two lower camps were well established; the third, Camp Two, was about to be; and any day now the first group, led by Merv Middleton, would be fixing ropes on the French Spur that rises some 4,000 feet to the top of the West Ridge. My diary for 22 March attempts to describe 'the walk' to Advance Base Camp.

Well, this has been quite a day! Taking down our twelve-by-twelve so it could be yakked up here to ABC (which in the end it wasn't), and setting off at 12.30 for the walk up. The first half to East Rongbuk River went rather better and more quickly than on Sunday – less than two hours and less exhausting, although still a pretty hairy walk over loose boulders, stones, snow and ice. Every footstep has to be placed with care to avoid a sprained ankle. East Rongbuk River still frozen and not greatly different from all the surrounding terrain. And then the climb starts, and goes on and on and on. The yaks slowly overtook me, batch by batch, their herders variously asking for cigarettes, motioning me out of the track, which I wasn't on in any case, and rarely greeting me – as I endeavoured to greet them – in a friendly manner.

We all started together, but by the Rongbuk River Alan and Nick were well ahead and set off again as I reached them, and Ian well behind. Dougie Keelan and I did one stretch together, but it was pretty well impossible to hold a conversation, and this was before the climb started. And what a climb it was! Truly horrendous – a matter of putting one foot in front of another, gasping, stopping every dozen or so paces, and in my case, sitting every fifteen or twenty minutes for a five minute break. When you stop it seems OK – breath comes back, heart stops pounding and legs feel as though they might possibly have the odd muscle rather than uncontrollable jelly. Then as soon as you start, it's back to square one – desperate zombie-like wanderings, as step-by-step you climb higher and higher. I was ashamed of staggering around and welcomed a long stretch behind the yaks, completely alone. Ian and Laurie Skoudas were well behind me. My pauses were islands of peace in ever more majestic scenery, but only islands – it was back into the stormy sea of my body's inability to deal with the demands, except that in the end, after ridge upon ridge failed to reveal Advance Base Camp, finally it came into sight.

I found I had taken five hours – more than twice the expected time for expedition members. I had four or five mugs of tea and coffee to re-hydrate, and settled down to discuss yet again how to deal with the filming, as it now appears that good weather has got Merv and his group a day ahead and we must move on to Camp Two and the French Spur as soon as possible, i.e. tomorrow. No rest day! Only after haggling with Dougie Keelan did he magnanimously allocate us two Sherpas to help carry our film equipment, tents, food, stoves and personal kit, including sleeping bags etc., up to Camp Two. It's still going to be another horrendous day, and that on top of today. I only hope we don't all get AMS and collapse. A rest day is normal after a climb like today's, to this altitude – eighteen thousand two hundred feet from sixteen thousand eight hundred.

Looking back on it now, I know that entry makes too much of the climb. It *was* hard for everyone, and especially for us, less fit than the lads; but they did 'carries' from camp to camp for several days running, and walked back to their point of departure the same day. By the end of the expedition, some members were making the trip between Base Camp and Camp One, or Camps One and Two, in well under two hours. And that with a thirty or forty pound load on their backs. For them, it became a routine which for me, thank God, was never necessary. But this difference between them and us was not lost on the lads, as Luke's recollections were to reveal:

LUKE Although it was Mark's expressed intent that the film crew should be part of the team, right at the start he blanched at sharing a tent with Dougie during the trek for fear it would jeopardise his independence. In any case media men are not naturally imbued with team spirit. The Services select people on the strength of it, and are skilful at fostering it in training. Much camaraderie and team spirit is either based on hardship mutually experienced (a former Operation, or even a previous expedition) or on respect for another's similar adventures. As a climber one will naturally find an affinity with a man who has been to the Himalayas four or five times before. The chances are that he knows what he is doing in that environment. The camera crew clearly did not. The daily pantomime of them putting up their tent; their self-pitying misery as victims of altitude sickness; their complaining about the non-existent weight of their sacks; their whingeing about the cold and the conditions; all these contributed to the climbing team feeling the need to behave like a benign host to a parasite.

Allowances clearly had to be made. But it was sometimes difficult to make allowances. One evening, over Scrabble, details were revealed of their formidable earnings whilst on the trip. It was felt this many times compensated for the discomforts of which they complained. It has to be said that Base Camp was the most palatial I have ever lived in. It was also their careers. Ludicrous pay, good prospects . . . what were they complaining about? . . .

At this point I am forced to interrupt in explanation. Our salaries may or not have been higher than those of the servicemen; I know my pay approximates to Dougie Keelan's, and I am freelance while he is permanently employed and pensionable. The lads' real bone of con-tention was the 'buy-out' sum paid to each of us to cover overtime and the expenses allowances normally paid to any film crew – and over more than three months this totted up. So, while we were well rewarded for our pains, the lads had each paid £500 to come on the expedition. It was easy to see their point. But they had chosen, even competed, to be part of BSEE 88, while we were 'only doing our job', and would have been similarly rewarded on any other assignment – if such existed. But, obviously, this distinction between us was a sore point. Enough of my justifications – back to Luke.

LUKE Alan was the most at home, having a climbing background and a passion for fell-running. Nick transpired to be the comfort clown, complaining like a union convenor about his rights and clearly missing the deep leather sofas of the Holiday Inn. Ian seemed totally dazed most of the time and in the early stages had to be bullied to eat, drink, or even take his boots off.

'I think the altitude is slowing down his thought process,' remarked Nick one evening at supper. 'Really?!' said Mark, himself surprisingly equable in the environment. He was, however, not a man going to get out of his bag one night to help rescue a mess tent blown away amidst a clatter of poles and frenzied cries for help.

Inertia ruled. When they did move to Camp One or Two, they were extremely unwilling to move again. At Camp Two, in the early stages, this caused particularly bad feeling amongst the climbing team who had been lugging the food themselves and were more than a little anxious to watch it being wolfed by those who did no carrying. They were also extremely slow. One morning they set off two hours ahead of the main party, thinking it appropriate to film the yaks crossing the East Rongbuk River. Yaks are slow lumbering beasts and it is normal for walkers to move ahead and not wait. In the history of load-carrying, Granada are unique in being overtaken by the yaks even though they had a head start. They didn't have a chance to film . . .

What I remember now from that first experience of walking up the Rongbuk Glacier, a journey I was to do several more times before we left, is as much odd details as the sense of exhaustion. In a uniformly grey-white landscape, flashes of colour caught the eye and remain in the eye of the mind. Spots of bright red on the grey dust or the white snow, recurring every few yards, turned out to be blood from the yaks' hooves, cut by the razor-sharp slaty stone. Here and there, the full imprint of a cloven hoof with its crimson centre bore witness that even the yaks found the going tough. Lichens, now dark terracotta, now brilliant ochre yellow, shone in the sun and seemed to jump out from the grey granite. A flock of tiny birds flew past. What on earth do they find to eat? And then, closer to Advance Base Camp, came the blue teeth – the hundred-foot-high stalagmites of ice, melted into weird contortions by the sun.

Advance Base Camp itself, also known as Camp One or Tilman's Camp or Lake Camp, I found to be a shallow bowl carved out of the valley wall which rose to rocky peaks a good 2,000 feet above it. In the centre of the bowl, a patch of frozen snow would become, in late April and May, a muddy pond. Around this snowy centre, tents were pitched on the mossy ground: all two-men tents up here, with the exception of one twelve-by-twelve for the cooking and the small sized Hunter Hut. And ahead of me, as I staggered into the camp, was Everest, here half-obscured by first a mound of shale and boulders, and far further up the valley, the mass of Changtse joined across a col to Everest itself, and once known as Everest's North Peak. From the camp, the West Ridge and the final summit pyramid were all that could be seen. Opposite, across the valley, a great rift lay deep below Lingtren, a bowl of royal icing cut vertically in half.

Although Advance Base was only 1,500 feet above Base Camp, it was appreciably colder and the facilities more spartan. No chairs at all in the Hunter Hut – just compo boxes on which to squat, balancing your plastic bowl of food on your lap. The Sherpas still did the cooking, but unlike Karmi and Manbahadur at Base Camp, Tenzing and Tashi had no fresh ingredients at all with which to enliven the tinned fare. One small Base Camp luxury was the morning routine of bed tea, still observed up here. Despite having to get up in the coldest hours to melt the massive cauldron of snow, Tashi appeared every morning with a broad grin, brandishing his kettle.

On that first day at Advance Base Camp, I retired to bed early, physically worn-out; but sleep eluded me. Perhaps it was the uninviting prospect of the following day. Little did I know, as I tossed and turned in the cold and tried to sleep, how much worse it would be than my most vivid imaginings.

The first day of real FAILURE. After yesterday's climb we all got up very unwillingly with a lot to do – re-pack for one or two nights at Camp Two; fix the Walkmans to the camera, etc. – and in very cold conditions, at least minus 25 degrees centigrade at 8 a.m. I had been cold in the night despite long-johns, vest and shirt, down boots, and from 3 or 4 a.m. the Light-line over the Redline. Not surprising – it must have touched our best low so far. Wonderfully clear skies, with the moon balanced like a slice of melon on a plate, points level on each side. A new position! The stars are quite unbelievably bright and numerous up here – clouds of galaxies that don't exist in murky London. I slept on and off, and eventually took a pill at 4ish because big day coming and I reckoned I needed the sleep. Bed-tea, supposedly at 7.30, woke me at 7.50. We had a fractious time packing: I must admit I, and everything I touched, was so cold it brought me near to tears. Pushing a recalcitrant sleeping bag into a stuff-sack at minus 25 centigrade is the height of freezing frustration.

Eventually we were ready at 11.15, and set off with two Sherpas, Angnema and Bhadri, carrying film gear, and we carrying our green rucksacks with overnight essentials. At first the track went downhill, steeply and awkwardly, then started slow climb alongside the moraine and suddenly across onto the glacier, in the centre of which are the weird blue teeth towering over you some sixty or eighty feet or more, and occasionally crunching alarmingly as though about to break in half. With the hot sun glinting across the baby-blue ice turrets, it was more like the scenery of some Christmas pantomime than the approach to Everest. Very soon though, the rising heat of the sun in the sheltered valley put paid to any thoughts of simile, as every breath and every footstep took a hundred and ten per cent of my existence. Nick and Alan, as usual, were ahead: Ian, as usual, well behind. Nick and Alan were waiting at the yak dump, tired but OK, although Alan had a bad headache. It was obvious we had pushed ahead too soon. I was done in, could barely struggle out of the rucksack, and collapsed while Tug made a brew of melted snow, and Nick and Alan eventually set off feeling confident. I said I'd wait for Ian, and follow on. Ian didn't come for another hour and was obviously beyond continuing physically, but bravely was determined to do so. Just as we set off, Dougie came down from Camp Two, having misunderstood our discussion the previous evening and very unwilling for the four of us, or even two of us, to stay at Camp Two. It was a welcome relief – I could now go back to Advance Base with Ian, having been forbidden to continue alone for safety's sake in the heat of the day – it was by now 2 p.m. So, swapping a very light sack for mine, I set off back, snapping away with my camera at the blue teeth, a task I had been unable to contemplate on the way up. I had also developed a furious cold – sneezing, running nose, etc. – and a weeping left eye – very infuriating, and still is, as it keeps freezing up.

At 6 p.m. called Nick on the radio intercom: they'd arrived safely, but knackered. Merv had put out two hundred feet of fixed rope on solid blue ice at the bottom of the French Spur, and Nick and Alan were intending to go with him tomorrow. So at least the whole venture was not in vain, even if Ian couldn't be there to record on radio mikes, and I to check out what was worth *filming. I have confidence in Nick though, which is a great relief. I felt a real failure, but also massively let off the hook. I looked forward to that climb like a condemned man the gallows. It's now 10 p.m. and I'll listen to the World Service News.*

But things were not to turn out too well for Nick and Alan either. My entry for the next day:

Gradually the load carriers drift back into Advance Base, bringing word that Nick and Alan are returning, feeling pretty rough and having done no filming of the first ascent on the Ridge. Very annoying. They must have their reasons. Principally, I suppose, how they feel, but it's a real shame to have put in the effort of getting there and then filmed nothing. Still, I am as powerless as I am motionless here, perched against a box in the lee of my tent enjoying the sun and trying to avoid the chilly intermittent wind.

6 p.m. Nick back, Alan 45 minutes later. Not good news. Nick had managed to film half a roll of GVs* but nothing of Merv's climb up the Spur. Too knackered. Both in bad shape on arrival yesterday, and after very cold night Alan still with bad headache and Nick totally exhausted. But it's obvious Camp Two must be our main camp: Advance Base is too far away even with a 1200mm lens, and Camp Two is where the action will be. So we must get stuff up there, preferably with our porters who will, I trust arrive soon. Failing that, I don't know. It's impossible for us to carry personal gear (two rucksacks each), more tents and a lot more filming equipment including the heavy legs, long lenses, more stock, etc. We must get porterage and a.s.a.p. or the whole Ridge will be done. I think that's inevitable. This is the first conflict between what I want, and what I can get.

We were not the only casualties, by any means. Indeed Nicky's and Alan's exhaustion proved very temporary. Ian's cough continued unabated, and the worst I had to endure was a heavy cold and sore throat. The dry, freezing air rasped a raw throat like a Black and Decker sander.

And amongst the lads, the altitude was taking its toll. The first to suffer obviously was Duncan Strutt, who hitherto, when asked how he was doing, invariably replied, 'Tremendous'. Duncan is built like a bridge, solidly supported on massive thighs tuned to maximum power output by cycle racing. But it was not his legs that were causing him problems.

*GVs = General views or scenic shots.

DUNCAN I've just come down from the yak dump, which is half way to Camp Two. The last three or four evenings I've had very bad coughing problems, which kept me awake at night. At this sort of altitude, when you're working high in the day, it has a great debilitating effect. It came to a head last night because I'm sharing a tent with Bill and just after midnight he said, 'It's no good, Dunc, I'm going to bivvy outside.' But being the perpetrator of the crime, I decided it was probably my fault. So I took my sleeping bag and went out amongst all the kit and just sat up all night coughing. So I've come down today to Advance Base and I'm going to push on further down to Base Camp to see if it'll heal up. It might be related to the flu bug I had about three or four days ago. I thought I'd got over that when we left Base Camp, and when I arrived at Advance Base I was feeling great, but I've just been deteriorating since then.

MARK How do you feel now, then?

DUNCAN Well, tremendous. I feel fantastic when I'm not moving, but as soon as I do I'm dead tired, lethargic, just got no energy, and without sleep I just can't keep going. Last night I tried sleeping pills; one is supposed to give you four hours' sleep. I took five, and slept for an hour and a half. So it's not going to work until I get down and actually get out of this dry, cold atmosphere, down to Base Camp where it's a bit warmer and slightly more sheltered.

MARK How do you feel about it personally and emotionally?

DUNCAN Frustrated, very frustrated. You've got to realize it's a very long expedition: we've still got at least another eight weeks here and we're only just starting on the mountain itself. It's pointless burning yourself up in the first ten days, and then having two months when you can't do anything at all. It's a fact of life, you've just got to accept it, so I've got to go down, it's better to be down there, four, five, maybe six days, and have the rest of the expedition feeling good and going well.

MARK How far up do you reckon you'll be able to get? You were telling me the other day you don't necessarily see yourself as going to the top.

DUNCAN Me, I'm a load carrier. I'm quite happy to carry as much as I can, and as high as I can. I'm the new boy to the team out here: it's my first trip to the Himalayas, so I'm quite happy to carry for everybody else. It's just fantastic being here, and I still feel tremendous! . . .

As it happened, I next saw Duncan up at Camp Two – we made it at the next attempt! – some two weeks later. He was determined to carry to Camp Three, half way up the French Spur and a very steep climb up solid ice and dangerously less solid snow. But here he was to meet his Waterloo. I was slurping down the nth cup of tea of the day in the Hunter Hut, when I heard a terrible gasping rattle. Moments later, an almost unrecognizable Duncan appeared at the door, his whole frame heaving as he struggled to draw breath. Foaming at the mouth and with a trickle of blood running down his chin, he half-staggered, half-fell into the Hunter Hut, his legs bending outwards like a baby's on its first unsure steps.

'My God, Dunc, what's happened?' I asked. But he could not speak and collapsed onto a compo-box seat, emitting what sounded like a death rattle. I was seriously alarmed, and there was no doctor at Camp Two at the time. But soon poor Duncan regained some composure, and told his story. He had set out with a load and started the climb up the fixed ropes. But it became quickly apparent from the enforced pauses he found he needed that he could not make it to his destination. He started to climb back down but soon collapsed completely and realized he was in a critical condition. Very sensibly leaving his load attached to the ropes, he tried to make it back to Camp Two, taking over two hours to do the thirty-minute walk across the glacier from the bergschrund at the base of the mountain. He finally made it in the state I have described. On the way he had twice collapsed and lay prostrate on the snow-clad glacier, and only the knowledge that in his condition he could quickly freeze to death had got him back on his wobbly legs. He had, he said, hit his ceiling. Apparently this is a known phenomenon: some mountaineers can be fine at, say, 20,000 feet and completely powerless 1,000 feet higher. The body dictates the level of this ceiling, and there is no argument – you come down below it, or die.

Duncan recovered completely, and stayed on at Camp Two as unofficial camp manager, working wonders as a part-time cook when we managed to eat together in the Hunter Hut. But he now knows his limit and must choose his mountains accordingly in the future.

The next to succumb to AMS was Pat Parsons, he of the ice-axed leg on the trek. Pat is an experienced climber, and tough as an old boot; his Royal Marines' training has ensured that. Normally ebullient and extrovert, the Pat I found packing his rucksack one day at Advance Base was a wretched shadow of his normal self.

PAT I've got a fucking avalanche happening in my head at the moment. Headaches, vomiting, total sort of incapacitation. I can't even speak properly. I just can't do anything. So, got to get some whisky down at Base Camp . . .

The whisky, if indeed he had any, did not solve Pat's problem. Later, when Pat was in a more communicative frame of mind than he had been on his way down to Base Camp, I asked him what had actually happened.

PAT I got up to Camp Three – great, best day of the expedition. You're climbing, and this is what we're all here for, and there was magnificent superb scenery, and then the next morning when I woke up – I was in the tent with Al Miller the scab-lifter – and I was just looking at the DPM pattern, you know, that's the camouflage pattern on the roof of the tent, and all of a sudden, I mean it's complicated enough as it is, it just merged into itself, my eyes went completely sort of cock-shutty and they stayed cockeyed all day. I don't know what it was. So I got out of the tent, and I had no balance, I was stumbling around like a drunken sort of slob, and I was completely incapacitated. So I just went to bed for the rest of the day, and my eyes have never recovered since. I still don't know what it is, I don't know whether it's the altitude, or whether it's some condition, or what. I've got sort of single vision back, but the left eye isn't focusing and I'm still stumbling around like a drunken old fart, which is really frustrating when you're trying to climb Everest. Walking down yesterday from Camp Two, Merv had to go in front of me, you know, like a bloke waving a red flag in front of one of those early cars, to warn people I was coming.

MARK What did the doctors say?

PAT Doctors, Christ the doctors have been a complete waste of time! Al Miller, who I was sharing a tent with when it happened . . . he turned and looked at me and said sort of follow my finger around . . . which I tried to do, and he said, 'bloody hell, mate, you don't half look rough. I hope you don't snuff it tonight,' and that's about all the encouragement I got from him. So they don't know what to say. I mean, Dick Hardie, he doesn't know what it is, he hopes that it's altitude-related. If it is, then presumably it will get better, but I've been told I've just got to rest. I don't like resting down here because the bloody mountain's up there. It's just so frustrating, but you know when it's something to do with your vision it's worrying, and the fact that I don't know what it is, is doubly worrying. And I'm just going to sit round here and going to get bad tempered and bite people's arses and probably not be a lot fun, so it's a good job you're going up the hill.

MARK Have you had such problems before?

PAT I'm just having a bad trip. Sometimes you have good trips, sometimes you have bad trips. The last trip I did, I hadn't any problems whatsoever and I topped out and it was great, and I think largely as a result of that, I've had high expectations of this trip. And because I've been involved in this trip on the planning committee. I've been working on this for two years now, devising all the equipment and clothes, and while you're doing that you inevitably see yourself taking a certain part on the team. I suppose I had too great a vision of my individual part. And because I've had all these sort of problems, and banged into these ceilings head first, one after the other, it's been doubly disappointing. I'm bloody pissed off. But it's early days yet, we're twenty-four thousand feet up an almost thirty thousand foot mountain, so it's a long way to go, and that last six thousand feet is the most difficult six thousand feet. Other people will drop out, you know, with a bit of luck I'll shake this off and I've just got to lower my own personal sights. What I'd like to do now is to go to eight thousand metres, crack that eight thousand metre barrier.

MARK Fingers crossed?

PAT Yeah, fingers crossed, I've just got to sit here and rest for a bit though . . .

Down at Base Camp, where Pat spent a long period of enforced inactivity, he was to be seen staggering around with double vision, setting his sights on, say, the Hunter Hut door, and as often as not crashing into the door frame as he entered. Andy and Al, the doctors, both tried to treat him, but in the end it was only time spent at the lowest camp that allowed his condition to improve. Greatly to his chagrin, Pat never got on to the mountain proper, although he did appear again at Camp Two when the final push was underway.

AMS has many and varied forms, and one of the most unsightly and uncomfortable, if not the most serious, is peripheral oedema. The hands, feet or face swell up alarmingly, the result of water retention. One consolation is that it can be treated with drugs. Alan Evans suffered a mild version for a few days, his puffy face contrasting curiously with his altitude-slimmed frame. But Jim Morning, a quiet and thoughtful Scot and another Marine, got the full works. We set up the camera to talk to him and, rather unfairly, I started by handing him a mirror – a seldom-seen irrelevance on an Everest expedition.

'Christ, I look that bad?' Jim could barely see out of his swollen eyes. We were sympathetic, but this was a very visible symptom of AMS and would obviously speak for itself on film. I pressed Jim on the unseen symptoms.

JIM In the evenings my eyes are quite sore. I get a lot of water running out of my eyes which tends to freeze of course at night, and causes a lot of discomfort round the outside. But apart from that, there's no real problem. Yesterday I managed to take a load up, but today the wind was so cold that when I was walking it was just freezing the tears as they came out of my eyes and I just couldn't see, so I had to come back and take it easy. Hopefully tomorrow I should be OK.

MARK You had a pretty bad spell down at Base Camp but we didn't speak to you then. What had happened there?

JIM Well, I've had a pretty raw deal right from the word go, really. I mean, I started off when we left Tatopani with a sore throat which developed into flu, and that put me out of action for about seven days, and the flu aggravated an old back injury and I ended up with a sore back for about three days, flat on my back. And eventually I managed to get up here and felt fine, and now this has started. So once this goes, I'm just waiting to see what on earth can happen next . . .

As fate would have it, Jim's run of bad luck was over. He went on to provide sterling support in the summit bids, and suffered no more ill effects from altitude, despite climbing many thousand feet higher than Advance Base Camp.

I have already said that we 'Granadas' were fortunate, and had little more than occasional discomfort and the odd splitting headache. Looking back on it, this was just as well – speaking for myself at least, I needed all my strength to survive the rigours of daily life! Towards the end of March we made a one-day sortie up to Camp Two where Nick and Alan had already been, but Ian and I had failed to reach. This time we made it, past the yak dump and the blue teeth, over some very slippery scree which alarmingly kept sliding down into pools of ice many feet below, and gingerly over the criss-cross of crevasses on the glacier. Camp Two, when we reached it, looked minute in the immensity of its surroundings. Dark dots on an all-white landscape, the tents had an air of absurdity about them. I could not escape a feeling of unwantedness, that man had no business on this mountain. But I knew that, on the contrary, we had a job to do, and that was to film Merv Middleton handing over to Dave Nicholls. Each group could only spend a matter of days up on the mountain, labouring to put in the camps, each higher than the last. Logistically, as well as topographically, Everest is a pyramid – broad at the base and pointed at the top. The lower camps, on the glacier, are large and well stocked, albeit slimming off at Camp Two, situated at the foot of the mountain proper. Above this, the camps shrink in size, as do the provisions: at any one stage there is only the minimum necessary for the particular task in hand, such is the magnitude of physical effort required to stock them. Now, Merv and his three team members were due for a break, and Dave's bunch were to take over, digging snow holes and fixing further ropes. I had already asked Dave Nicholls what his exact plans were.

DAVE Our difficulty at the moment, of course, is that Merv has got about two-thirds of the way, or possibly three-quarters of the way up the Ridge, and has not found a satisfactory site for Camp Three. The important thing is that we get a site somewhere about half way, so that people who are carrying heavy loads can carry them half way up and then come back down again. And also, that we've got a safe haven there, perhaps not a very big one, in the middle of the Ridge. The important camp will be at the top of the Ridge, and we've got to make that about sixteen strong, so that we're in a strong position for going along the Ridge. So, tomorrow, I'm going to go up to talk to them there and get a de-brief on exactly what has gone on and what the options are for Camp Three, and then it'll be up to our team to have to site it . . .

Dougie Keelan had been in daily radio contact with Merv up on the spur, and was well aware of the problems.

DOUGIE The hazard of this route is not that it's the steepest, although it is steep, but it's the wind. And what's been happening – and they may be telling you this – is that while they've been forcing that route up on what is very often blue ice, they've been hanging on with their ice axes and the wind has been so strong it has whipped their feet from under them, and there they are, just hanging on with ice axes. It really gets very worrying and indeed quite frightening from time to time when that happens constantly. It is of course early days, it's not yet quite the end of March, and it's the transition of the seasons. Winter's fading, we hope, and Spring is coming, and let's hope that these winds do subside, but if anything is going to stop us, it'll be this wind. It certainly won't be lack of motivation or strength . . .

Standing there up at Camp Two, with Mount Everest towering behind them, Dave and Merv plotted how best to bring the beast to heel. As we filmed them, once again I was struck by the audacity of their endeavour. There is something grand but nonsensical about pitting oneself against such odds. Obviously I would never make a mountaineer – I lacked the basic instinct that drove these men from one expedition to the next, up one peak only to contemplate another even higher. And here they were taking on the mightiest of them all. Back at ABC, I wrote in my diary that night:

Big E frighteningly dramatic and huge from Camp Two. One feels right under it, but in fact it's a good half-hour walk across the glacier to the bergschrund. It looms menacingly, and looks to me so forbidding I would never wish to set foot on it. Dave Nicholls, by contrast, like a kid with a new bike, very excited and itching to get up on it and do the bit. His enthusiasm is infectious but not, for me at least, his aim. I'm too tired and exhausted physically and mentally to continue writing any more now.

Everest Blues

By Easter, at the beginning of April, the cumulative effect of discomfort, exhaustion and altitude was getting us all down. It was around the middle of the trip, six weeks out from England, with at least as many more to do, and all of those up here on the mountain. Our spirits were at a low ebb, our fingertips were cracking and splitting painfully and refusing to heal, and we were missing family and friends at home. Between ourselves on the crew, we very seldom exchanged words in anger and always made a point of apologizing for any flash of temper, itself all too understandable in the circumstances. But I detect a different tone in my diary around this time, with the prospect of a long stay up at Camp Two imminent.

Not a very satisfactory day. Nick in prima donna mood; Ian dreading everything; Al more concerned with getting up the Ridge than the filming immediately to hand; I'm as tetchy as hell with everyone; and one of our porters is ill and not working. Still no water for a wash, although to my annoyance Nick managed to get hold of some. Very fed up. Can't find the camera sheets, so our shot list could get very dodgy. I expect the next few days to be sheer hell.

31 March. Well, like most things you dread, it wasn't quite as bad. We came up slowly, Nick and I accompanying Ian. Left 10.30 in the morning and only arrived at 4-ish – it should take three hours, or even two. With the pauses it didn't seem too bad a slog, but when we arrived those here, especially Nev, were a real pain, ignoring our requests for tent space, refusing u. the tents already here which we could have put up, etc. No doubt they had had a very hard day on the mountain, but still. Luke helped empty a store tent into which Ian and I crammed our stuff and ourselves. It must be six foot by three foot at the most; very close quarters. We managed to find and purloin a gas cooker and heater – those in the Hunter Hut already in use and thus unavailable – and

cooked ourselves a high altitude menu: pressed chicken from a tin, rice in
pre-cooked pack with barbecue sauce; oxtail soup first. Every bit of water is
melted snow, and a long and laborious process it is.

The imperative need to consume vast quantities of liquid at altitude
– five to eight litres per day – has something of the 'heads you win,
tails I lose' about it. If you do not drink, you run a serious risk of
developing one or more forms of AMS – definitely to be avoided! But
if you do, not only is it a freezing cold and protracted business forcing
handful after handful of snow into a pot as it melts down to a
frustratingly miserable drop in the bottom; you also face the certainty
that all this liquid will demand to be drained off. It is quite common to
produce over a litre of urine overnight, to which end we all had pee
bottles. Learning the knack of keeping the polythene jar at a sufficient
slope to avoid an overflow in your sleeping bag is an early lesson. The
alternative – which is, I suppose, inevitable for women – is to extricate
yourself from your bag and venture out into the minus 20s or worse.

And accidents do happen: Charlie Hattersley managed to roll over
in his sleep, and burst his bottle; others, half-asleep, let their bottles
slip out of their hands. My worst experience was the most common
one: the overflow. It is very difficult to judge whether the jar will take
the load you are about to impose on it, and equally difficult to stop in
mid-flow. It was not for nothing that we turned our sleeping bags
inside-out each morning and draped them over the tents in the sun.
And when you are sharing a tiny tent, the problems seem to be
magnified. My diary again:

We expected conditions to be cramped here, and they are. It's also bloody cold.
An exceptionally cold wind has been blowing all day, in our faces on the way
up here, and there's still a bit now at 11.30 p.m. But some cloud has lessened
the wind. After cooking our meal, which wasn't too bad considering, Ian and I
went for the obligatory coffee, tea, or chocolate to Nick and Alan's tent. It's a
bit bigger, but then they've got all the gear. Another hour's wait for the snow
to melt, but quite a convivial evening of 'us v. them', and general whingeing
about our lot. Now back in tent with gas-light, three-quarters into the bag but
with jacket and gloves still on. Already a thick hoarfrost on inside of tent –
bodes well. My nose is pretty heavy, both blocked and running, this ever-
lasting but intermittent cold. Strange not to have spoken to a single expedition
member this evening, very unusually exclusive. Hope this is not an ill omen.
Time will tell.

In fact our relations with the lads were in general always good, or at least so it appeared to us. I believe our half-accidental, half-deliberate strategy of preserving a minimal distance, both physical and meta-phorical, in what were unavoidably close quarters, was a sound one. The basic understanding between us continued throughout – that they were there to climb the mountain and we were there to film them doing it – and we both got on with our respective tasks. So much for the lads; but the leader was a different matter. There were moments when my relationship with Dougie Keelan troubled me. I confided my nagging worries to my diary:

It's unfortunate but no surprise that I don't get on more positively with DK. He's obviously not at ease with me, and it's mutual. Can't work out whether he suspects, deep down, our aims are antagonistic, or whether it's just that he has a very full plate and we are another item to be digested. We seem to operate like two boxers before the first blow is exchanged – circling and parrying. But the analogy is wrong, because neither of us intends coming to blows, I'm sure. In the end, it's a difference of priorities that divides us: climb Everest versus make programme of Everest. Fuck it, I'll have another cigarette and a piece of Vicky's Christmas cake.

Dougie's fear was that we might so edit the series that the expedi-tion was made to look other than it was – an efficient military operation. This would obviously reflect badly on him and his abilities as a leader. He had on several occasions asked me about our intentions: how much commentary would there be? would the films be narrative? would they be analytical? I was unsure what he meant by the last, and said so. I gleaned between the lines of his answer that his worry was that we might compare this expedition unfavourably with other Everest attempts, or take a critical standpoint on the style or quality of his decision-making. I reassured him, not for the first time, that any criticism would be out in the open and come up as we filmed the series, not later in the cutting room. I was in no position to be critical from a climbing point of view in any case, and could only pass on opinions I had heard expressed amongst the lads. My aim had always been to avoid any disparaging editing later, and to use such conflict as arose, if any, as part of the continuing story – all grist to the mill. The risk in this area was that I might be thought to be going behind the back of anyone who confided in me. But I made no secret of my intentions and methods. Obviously, I failed to allay Dougie's fears, as later on, over several whiskies down at Base Camp, he turned to me one evening and said:

'Well, Mark, are you going to screw us or not?'

'No way,' I replied, genuinely surprised. 'And even if I wanted to, I couldn't. The way we're making these films – day by day, here on the mountain with you all – means we are as much part of the expedition as you are, even if our role is different. You've agreed as much yourself, Dougie.'

'Yes, I have, I know, but once you're back in the cutting room . . .'

'Dougie, you'll come to see the rough-cuts yourself. We've agreed that.'

I knew that nothing I said would convince Dougie completely. We had been over the ground back in England before we left, and several times since. And yet I had some sympathy – if I were in his shoes I imagine I would harbour some suspicions, given how television all too often portrays the Military. I had myself made a film about the Armed Forces in Belize – at the time, Britain's last foothold in the whole continent of the Americas – and had left out of the finished programme all material concerning the officers. The Ministry of Defence were not best pleased, but the film had always been intended to be light-hearted and a-political, and had deliberately been shot over Christmas when the mood was one of seasonal cheer rather than deep inquiry. I had made no secret of this film and, more to the point, I had always stressed that the Everest series was primarily about an expedition rather than the Military, and this was still my opinion. Unlike several previous television documentary series – *Fighter Pilot*, *Sailor*, *The Marines* – this one was always conceived and executed as a series about an attempt to climb Everest by thirty-six men who happened to be in the Armed Forces, not a series about servicemen who happened to be climbing Everest. It was indeed just as well this was so because, as I have already recorded, the military aspects of the expedition were barely perceptible, and we would have had a very thin set of programmes on our hands.

There were many occasions, however, when Dougie and I had serious and wide-ranging conversations, often over a scotch or two at Base Camp, or a pot of my espresso coffee to which he, amongst others, was very partial. Frequently differing in our viewpoint, as on the Falklands War, we still respected each other's opinions. Dougie, I have to confess, often floored me with a combined force of erudition and experience. I found it difficult to argue about the Falklands, except on a point of principle, with a man who had spent over a year in command of the garrison there. And again, discussing the British Raj in India, where Dougie was born, he would clinch a question by quoting Lord Wavell or Ziegler's biography of Mountbatten.

Before laying this topic to rest, I would like to say that I believe confidence increased between Dougie Keelan and myself as the expedition proceeded, and certain shared experiences towards the end put the seal, so far as I was concerned, on a firm basis of mutual trust.

Meanwhile, work continued on the mountain and the world went on its way, somewhere unimaginably remote from our day-to-day dilemmas. The BBC World Service, fading and hissing on my shortwave set, kept me tenuously in touch. I listened to live commentary on football matches on the Saturday evening (for me) sports programme, trying to imagine mid-afternoon at Anfield or White Hart Lane. When it came to the Cup Final at Wembley, we were all in the Hunter Hut at Base Camp. Conversation came to a hushed standstill as Wimbledon scored their single winner. Even in the snowy wastes of Everest, the British enthusiasm for the under-dog coming through on top was alive and kicking.

Luke Hughes and the Lhasa party had returned, with our two porters (who proved to be a very mixed blessing), all the oxygen and a first-hand account to flesh out the sketchy picture drawn on the World Service of the situation in Lhasa.

LUKE I think the riots are far more severe than anybody has actually let on. I spoke to one eye witness who watched a child of five's brain being splattered out all over the walls of the Jokan. More than eighty people are known to be dead and thousands of families do not know whether half their family have been arrested, shot or just removed. But the atmosphere actually in the bazaar is much better than I expected – it's quite friendly. All the Khampas, who are in the warrior class, if you like, of Tibetans are all very active but still quite friendly. There wasn't that awful oppressive tight atmosphere that I experienced just after the last riots which took place last year . . .

If it was difficult to imagine serious political protest on the streets of the Tibetan capital nearly five hundred miles away, it was yet more mind-wrenching to follow the course of the Kuwaiti hijack. One of the lads, who for security's sake must be nameless, was itching to be there on the runway at Algiers to sort it out. When not on a mountain, such activities were his stock in trade.

An incident reported on the radio which affected me far more deeply and personally was the execution in Florida's electric chair of one Willie Darden. Back in 1979 I had made a very different documentary series, called *Circuit Eleven Miami*, about crime and punishment in the Sunshine State. Filming in the State Penitentiary in Starke, Florida, I had met and talked to Willie Darden, and later interviewed him for the series. He was a quiet and thoughtful black man who had already spent years on Death Row, fighting appeal after appeal. It is not for me to say whether he was guilty or innocent of the murder for which he had been convicted, and I do not know: on Death Row, everyone you talk to claims innocence. But Willie made a deep impression on me as a man who, whatever he had or had not done before, had reasoned long and hard with his soul while living every day under the threat of electrocution. I could see his baleful but strangely gentle eyes in my own mind's eye as clearly as if it had been yesterday. And now, almost a decade after my conversation with him, they had put Willie in the chair and fried him, as the warders liked to phrase it. It was the one item of news in the whole course of the expedition that shattered the cocoon of timelessness Everest had built around me. I almost wept.

However isolated from reality I felt, it would be wrong to imply that our expedition was alone on the Rongbuk Glacier. Everest is a popular mountain, and from the North side alone there would be half a dozen attempts on the summit in 1988. The largest was a tri-national expedition, making their bid at the same time as we were, but by another route. Totalling almost three hundred Japanese, Chinese and Nepalis, this massive undertaking was a two-pronged attack from both North and South – Tibet and Nepal. The Tibetan contingent had their base camp across the plain of moraine, and a spectacular camp it was in comparison with ours. Their expedition had been funded by a Japanese commercial television station, and the aim, ambitious but ultimately successful, was to put representatives from all three stations on top on a Japanese national holiday and broadcast the whole event live. To this end, the camp flourished a forest of aerials, and transmitting dishes the size of a house. It put our portable film camera very much in the shade, but the whole enterprise was on a totally different scale. Their budget alone, reputed to be over $US6,000,000, was about twenty times larger than the hard-won sponsorship that funded BSEE 88.

Easter Sunday was just like any other day – except that we lost the Hunter Hut at Camp Two. The ill-fated designer happened to be at the camp when it happened.

KEITH HUNTER We started to put the thing up about three or four days ago, and then the weather changed and there was a lot of spindrift blowing onto the adhesive so we had to stop, and we put it in that hole over there and covered it over with a tarpaulin. When we came back, the day before yesterday, it was under about three feet of solid snow. So we spent about four hours digging it out and then another four hours building it. And we'd almost completed it as it got dark, and anyway we were dead on our feet, so we tied it down as best we could and went to bed. I woke up in the middle of the night – I suppose it was about midnight – and looked at it, and it seemed OK although the wind was getting pretty strong, and it was coming over that wind-break that we'd built, and I thought – well, it'll probably be OK. So imagine how I felt when I opened the tent this morning, and it just wasn't there. I've been right across the glacier looking for it. I got as far as the tarpaulin that was holding it down, but it's a very heavily crevassed area and not the sort of place to be on your own, so I came back . . .

Eventually, enough panels were either retrieved from down the glacier or sent up from the spares at Base Camp to patch up the hut. But it was never as strong as it might have been. It had had a chequered career from its earliest days, when Dave Orange had mis-taken a bottle of naphtha fuel for water in an identical container, and heated the highly inflammable liquid in a pan on the Epigas cooker. At the critical temperature, the naphtha exploded in a ball of flame, burning the roof badly and throwing Dave across the hut. He was singed and shaken, but managed to extinguish the fire, pale with shock. But Dave was soon back on the job, and I caught him as he was on the point of leaving Camp Two for his stint up on the mountain.

DAVE Myself and Dave Torrington and Kit's group are going up to Camp Three which is half way up the French Spur. There's two snow holes there, and we're actually going to finish the remainder of the fixed rope up to Camp Four which is on top of the West Shoulder. There's about a thousand foot of fixed rope remaining to be fixed, and once that's done we can actually start digging, I would think, about a twelve-man snow hole, or perhaps two six-man snow holes. From there, that's more or less our group's job finished. Two other groups will come up and start stocking Camp Four ready for the assault to get Camp Five set up along the other end of the West Ridge . . .

Manpower is the key to this style of mountain climbing, especially as the expedition had chosen to make do with its own members, and only had six climbing Sherpas. I asked Luke Hughes about this.

LUKE Well, that's always a problem. There's always a problem about a big mountain, and that's why some people climb Alpine-style and some people climb Himalayan-style. But this expedition has never made any bones about the fact that it was going to be a big Himalayan expedition – and a safe one. Whatever one's personal preference is, if you want to come along and climb on that basis, well, that's the basis that you have to come along on.

MARK Is it necessary to have a dozen or so places at Camp Three, and maybe even Camp Four?

LUKE I think it will be. Certainly at Camp Three, because there's no way that people can do the single load-carry all the way up – it's a hell of a long way. It's taking it all out of people just getting up to Camp Three. I think probably what will happen is that we will find that maybe we haven't got enough people to continue the siege technique all the way up the mountain, and then we will rely on the fittest climbers to be able to move, light and quick to finish off the mountain. But I still think you need a very sound base at Camp Four.

MARK So can you just tell me what the immediate plan is now?

LUKE Well, the immediate plan is to continue to push up behind Dave Nicholls and Dave Maxwell, who have found the old Japanese camp, plus all kinds of goodies up there – in particular, as far as we're concerned, nineteen bottles of oxygen which may or may not fit our regulators. But it's important, because that's effectively about fourteen man-loads up the Ridge, which obviously saves a hell of a lot of our own expenditure.

Camp Three as you know is fairly well established, and we've dug a big cave there and now it sleeps about ten. Dave Nicholls's group are responsible at the moment for pushing the route forward, and Kit's group, of whom I'm one, are responsible for supporting them. So our plan is to go up, occupy Camp Three, get supplied by Andy Edington's group who are coming up behind us, and then keep the supplies going up the hill so that Camp Four on the top of the Ridge can be as comfortable and as logistically sound as possible.

MARK Are you looking forward to getting up there?

LUKE Very much so, yes. As far as I'm concerned, this is it. It's terrific being here – I mean, you arrive at Camp Two, you know, the mountain's been so nebulous – well, perhaps that's the wrong word in the light of the present weather – and you suddenly come into Camp Two and you're right underneath it, and now there's the chance of getting onto it. And for all the myths and all the legends and all the history that one has heard about, it's marvellous to get stuck into the mountain itself. Absolutely terrific, yes, I'm very enthusiastic about it.

MARK And are you feeling pretty fit so far?

LUKE Yep, I'm feeling extremely good at the moment. I'm going very well and I'm pretty lucky, I think. Lots of hot chocolate . . .

It was a bar of chocolate, not the drinking variety, that did for me. On Easter Monday I bit into a Cadbury's Caribbean Delight, or some such delicacy, only to feel an ominous crunch that could by no stretch of the imagination be a piece of chocolate. Feeling round gingerly with my tongue, I discovered what I feared – a loose piece of porcelain and large gap in my front teeth. My precious crown had parted company with its foundation. High on Everest, this was not good news. I could not help remembering the medical handout at the beginning of the expedition: 'There will be no dentist. The doctors are prepared to act as emergency fang-pullers, but can do little more.' With visions of a choice between raging toothache and oral excavations performed by an amateur, I poked the yawning hole with my tongue. No twinges. I investigated further with mounting relief. I can now report, with some satisfaction, that the nerve appears to be quite dead. Mercifully, I had no trouble at all over the rest of the trip.

To pass the time between the short periods when we were actually able to film, we called on every possible game anyone could remember. One of the best, at least at filling in the hours, was 'Botticelli'. For those who don't know the game and may well need to fill in hours on Everest, the idea is that someone thinks of the name of a person, real or fictional, but likely to be known by at least some of the other players – for example Botticelli – and gives only their initial, B. The other players then establish B's identity by the tortuous and time-consuming process of thinking of their own Bs, say Bertolt Brecht, and asking: 'Did you write the *Caucasian Chalk Circle*?' If the questionee cannot answer, 'No, I'm not Bertolt Brecht,' the questioner gets a direct shot – are you alive? are you British? etc.

Al Evans chose a good one – it took over two hours before we finally gave in. First we had the initial, T, and then, as a concession, JT. And it wasn't John Thomas! We established the sex (male), nationality (British), the century (seventeenth) and trade or profession (agriculture) – that took no time, relatively speaking. Gradually, as we got nowhere, Alan gave us a clue – there's a pop music connection. To a seventeeth-century agriculturalist? We looked unenlightened.

'And he was an inventor in his own field.' Alan looked smugly satisfied at this particular clue, but it still didn't help. Well, I'll let you off the hook more quickly than Alan let us off. The man was Jethro Tull, inventor of the modern plough and resurrected as a pop group. Inventor in his own field? We groaned, but half the morning had slipped by.

April 12 was Henry Day's birthday, and for those at Base Camp, which included him and us, Dave Orange had baked a cake. Having no cooking colourings, he turned to ink to dye the icing a sickly shade of violet. But the overall effect, and more importantly the taste, was excellent. We duly sang Happy Birthday, and Henry side-stepped our inquiries as to his exact age. It was a cheery evening, and the Famous Grouse did a grand job of washing down the cake. The conversation plumbed new depths of triviality: we had been through all the serious topics weeks before. A survey was conducted as to what kind of underpants most people had, and how many of them. The answer, for those of you who might be interested, is that the average was three, and more people had slips than boxer shorts. Marks & Spencer's had obviously done a very good trade.

Earlier, there had been a strangely sombre moment when Andy Edington, one of the team leaders and supposedly at that juncture leading his team up the French Spur, walked unexpectedly into the Hunter Hut, took out a book and started reading. Conversation faltered into silence, but nobody asked what had happened. It seemed inappropriately intrusive at that moment. But it was an occasion I could not pass up, and the following day I asked Andy, on film, what had gone wrong.

ANDY I'm not at death's door, or anything like that – it's just that I've got this infection and they're worried it might get worse and they thought that I wouldn't throw it off very well. I suppose it's a bit like, if you're at home your doctor sends you to bed, not that you're going to die watching television, but you just recover quicker when you're in bed. So Andy Hughes, who was the doctor up there and is in my group, said – you go down. And I thought, if you're going to go down there's no point in dealing in half measures, so I came right down here, slid down the ropes to Camp Two and had a brew, walked down to Camp One, had another brew, and then just made it here in time for tea. I think coming down five thousand feet will help a lot. Last night I slept, no problem at all. I slept right through, which is unusual in the higher camps – you expect to wake up coughing or needing a pee in the middle of the night, but I just slept right through last night.

MARK Don't you feel that you were, in a sense, letting the side down?

ANDY Yes, I do. We're organized into these four-man groups, and time has taken its toll, each group has sort of lost things, and my group hasn't actually . . . we haven't missed a day through sickness or injury, and we were actually feeling our batting average was quite high. So officially, as I'm notionally the group leader, though it's a sort of collective thing, abandoning them up on the mountain to come down to the pleasures of Base Camp is a bit . . . I don't know how to describe it. When I heard they'd taken three inches of new snow last night, I felt a bit ashamed to be lying in luxury down here.

MARK I'm sure you noticed when you walked in yesterday, there was a kind of atmosphere in the hut. Did you feel it was sort of saying, ah-ha, so he's not made it?

ANDY Yes, that's true. One of the sort of qualities I think the team needs from individuals is not just technical climbing brilliance but sort of health and fitness, and I'm sure you'll have picked that up. But I suppose there's always a mental element to it as well. I mean, there are guys who perhaps get up there who've got sore throats and every-thing else, and show they haven't bottled out and they're still plug-ging away and hacking it. Whereas I didn't, I came down. In defence I'll just say that it wasn't actually my idea to come down, it was the doctor who said go down, and I can sort of self-analyse that and justify it to myself.

MARK So, mentally speaking, do you think you'll be OK? I mean your physical state's fine, you're a big strong lad, but mentally do you think you can hack it?

ANDY Oh yeah. I know what you mean, it's very easy to sort of say, well, I've gone so far and that's enough. But once you've been on a couple of these trips, you know afterwards you sort of look back when you're assembling your mental scrap-book or whatever, and if you haven't really pushed yourself as far as possible you feel guilty about it afterwards. And you know there's a couple of times that's happened to me. So – this is a once-in-a-lifetime trip and I'm definitely going to go back there for all it's worth, and see where I can get . . .

Where Andy got was as high as all but the few summiteers – he had laid his ghost and got on top of his problems, if not of Everest itself. Who was going to achieve *that* was still a very open question.

All Set for the Summit?

Sunday 10 April to Friday 15 April
Base Camp

Genius, it is said, is one per cent inspiration and ninety-nine per cent hard slog. Climbing Everest, I knew well enough, is hard slog all right, but at least as much effort, mental if not physical, goes into 'logistics', the minutiae of meticulous pre-planning. It is all too often boring and repetitive work, and a chance snow storm or an unexpected turn of events can throw all the best-laid plans. But it is an inescapable fact that, to get to the top, exact quantities, timings and locations must be decided for every oxygen bottle and face-mask, every gas stove and high altitude rations pack, every tent and sleeping bag, every rope-length and snow stake . . . the list could continue *ad infinitum*.

And then there is the vexed question of casting the stars – choosing the best-suited and most likely summiteers. This unenviable task fell, of course, to Dougie Keelan as leader, and he knew before he started that by definition he could only please a tiny proportion of the lads: those selected. This is not to say the rest go off in a huff, but there is inevitable disappointment if you feel you're going well and could match the performance of the men appointed; and, more rarely, outright criticism of the choice for what seem, to you at least, well-founded reasons.

On 10 April we eavesdropped with our camera on Dougie and Henry Day deep in consultation in the Base Camp Hunter Hut. With a shortlist of names in front of them, they weighed the pros and cons of A's fitness and B's experience; of X's recent load-carrying perform-ance and Y's state of mind and Z's state of health. Finally, as climbing a high Himalayan peak is almost invariably done in pairs for reasons of safety, there is the consideration of who will work best with whom up there on the hill. Physical strain is only one factor – almost more telling is the mental stress, the realization of the responsibility on your shoulders which weighs as heavy as the back-pack and oxygen bottles.

And all climbers know that, even on oxygen, the brain plays tricks on you at altitudes in the high twenty thousands. Decisions that would be straightforward a mile lower become agonizingly complex as you approach the summit and, even more dangerously, a course of action that demands careful consideration is undertaken thoughtlessly.

Henry Day had brought with him a computer to help out on logistics. As the man who is famous – some would say infamous – in the mountaineering world for his catchphrase 'It can all be worked out on the back of a fag packet', I asked him why he had swapped his cigarettes, not that Henry smokes, for silicon chips.

HENRY As you get higher, speaking personally, you get stupider, and it's very easy to forget things, very obvious things, and the arithmetic that's necessary to work out what loads need to go up the mountain is perfectly easy to do down here on the back of a fag packet, but higher up you're likely to get it wrong. Indeed, from last time I have actually kept the notes which I made at the time, and there's some glaring arithmetical errors. I mean, it's pathetic, apart from the handwriting deteriorating. So now the computer is there. It doesn't make mistakes in the arithmetic. The way I've set it up, it's a sort of perfect solution to aim for; you, or whoever is using it as a plan, can then say – Ah, what happens if we have a day of bad weather? What happens if somebody falls down on a job and doesn't deliver his load as planned? What happens if somebody is sick and needs extra oxygen? And all of this can be very quickly fed in and the significance of it worked out equally quickly . . .

Finally, perhaps the greatest test of all for the summiteer is the decision when to make discretion and survival the better part of valour, and turn back. Many mountaineers have died *after* reaching the summit, and all too often because they have continued when time was too brief or the weather too bad; in short, the temptation too great. Luke Hughes had been through this experience the previous autumn on nearby Shisha Bangma:

LUKE It depends really on the extent to which you want to survive, how much you want to achieve, and how, finally, you're prepared to make the decision. If I go to the mountains, I want to come back, I want to survive. If you achieve as well that's great, and if I was a professional mountaineer I would feel a greater onus, I think, to achieve. On

Shisha Bangma we were very close to the summit and we had the awful dilemma of knowing a storm had been forecast, and knowing that we had a very long way to go. We had covered most of the ground when we came out after a bivouac in a snow hole without sleeping bags and no food, and the conditions were down to about minus thirty-five. And we came out and there were sixty-mile-an-hour winds going streaming across the knife-edged ridge, and we still had another two hundred metres to go. But it would have meant that we'd have had a fifth night out in those conditions, and we had a very long way to go back. If we had gone on we might have made it – but we would have put the rest of the expedition in jeopardy. They would have then not known where we were, they would have had to come and look for us. In fact Nigel* did come out and look for us, because they hadn't heard from us on the radio for five days. We had a great old argument as to whether we were going to go on or not.

MARK And you were within two hundred metres of the summit?

LUKE Well, I think that was one of the most difficult decisions of my life. But I don't regret it at all . . .

Dougie and Henry, at the end of their deliberations, had decided to postpone the announcement of the composition of the first summit group until 13 April. I am not unduly superstitious, but I reckoned Dougie must be less so! We had a fair idea of the likely lads, but had been sworn to secrecy by Dougie and, whatever the temptation to reveal all, were determined to keep faith.

Meanwhile, the four-man teams were continuing their routine load-carrying to establish and equip the camps on the mountain. Just before they left Base Camp after their R&R† period, I asked Kit Spencer and his team – Luke, Tug Wilson and Charlie Hattersley – how they fancied their chances of selection as summiteers.

KIT I don't know, it's very difficult at the moment. Even down in Base Camp there are sort of rumours flying around, and until Dougie comes up with the actual definitive team lists for the assault we really don't know at the moment. I mean, the way we're going we'll be in a strong position. It could be that because we're going back up the

---

*Nigel Williams, also on this expedition.
†R&R = rest and refreshment or recuperation.

mountain and everyone else is coming back off it, effectively that we'll be fitter, better acclimatized, and you know, anything could happen. I mean, if we're in the right place at the right time, say at Camp Four by the end of this week, we could get some action in on the Ridge. And again, if they have problems in Henry's group, we'll have to plug the gaps and get Camp Five established. So it's very iffy and butty at the moment, and we'll just have to wait and see.

MARK How many people do you reckon are likely to get to the top at this stage? I know it's early days.

CHARLIE I think two groups of four is realistic.

MARK You don't, do you, Kit?

KIT I would tend to be slightly more cautious than that. You know, at the end of the day perhaps two. It very much depends on weather, and how the teams go. Weather will mean a lot – but at this stage, I reckon two.

MARK Only two out of thirty-six?

KIT It wouldn't surprise me . . .

One of Kit's team, Tug Wilson, had had trouble with a nasty throat infection, and would be unable to keep with his team as they went up the mountain; but, as he explained, at this stage of the expedition the teams were likely to split up in any case.

TUG When the guys start coming off the hill – there'll be people who are sick and people who are tired – they'll be restructured into the summit four and the support team. And I think there'll be a total disregard for this integrity of the teams, quite honestly. He'll just say, right, OK, you four are summiteers, you six are supporters, and it doesn't really matter if it's A team, B team, C team or whatever. You know, he's going to structure the best team possible for his initial summit bid, as he has to really, because it's the main aim of the expedition, to get somebody on top.

MARK Now what about Henry Day's role? He's just shot off at five this morning; how do you see his plan developing to set up Camp Five?

LUKE Somebody's got to set up Camp Five.

MARK You don't think he's jumped the gun?

LUKE I think the setting up of Camp Five is obviously the last really important bolt-hole for all the expedition camps. In a way, it's unfortunate that they haven't been able to push out some further camps already.

MARK Given that there is this master plan, which of course may change, if you're not part of the front rank, what then?

LUKE Well, nothing much. I've always said and I've always believed that one of the things about a very large expedition is that there are very rarely obvious outcomes, and I think right from the beginning we've all been absolutely clear in our minds that we're here as part of a team, with a team effort, and a team goal. If the team does actually succeed, that's one layer of icing on the cake. And the second one might be that you might actually have something to do with it as well. But I don't think I'm going to be unduly disappointed.

KIT I think it's important to have realistic aspirations about moun-taineering, certainly on this one which is, you know, the biggest, and it's quite technical at the top. Frankly, every foot of ascent I make now is something new for me because I've never been over twenty-four thousand feet before. It's really sort of a mental process of balancing everything out and saying, well, am I capable of doing it? Do I really want to do it? Are the opportunities there for me to do it? I mean, having said that – I'm trying to be fairly realistic about it at the moment – having said that, you know, I'm not done for yet, there's plenty of mileage left in me. I'm going reasonably strongly, I haven't had any problems with altitude yet, so we'll just see what happens at the end of the day. But the important thing is that even if I don't get to the top, it's the culmination of all our efforts if we do get two guys on top – if we get one guy on top and get him back down again, then we've cracked it. I'd be happy either way.

MARK What's the priority in the end then? Charlie?

CHARLIE Of course the priority, I'll tell you what the priority is, and that is however hard people push themselves, however hard they go, whether people get to the top or not, it's to get back in one piece. On this expedition we've been really lucky, there've been no casualties so far. I mean, statistically we should have three to four on this trip, so to me the priority is to get us all back in one piece.

KIT I think, you know, if you were really, totally, absolutely truthful, from the depth of your heart, you'd actually find that there probably aren't that many people who would in themselves feel confident in getting to the summit of this mountain. If you could get them to talk – and they won't talk, they'll know in themselves, but I don't know how they'd put it across – even if they feel they do actually aspire to the top of the mountain, they know they'll feel better in a supportive role, to push maybe those who they see as one of the stars to the top, the people who've got the natural ability to get to the top, because let's face it, you know, it's the biggest mountain in the world and you do need a certain amount of natural ability to get to the top of this thing, and it's not going to be easy, no matter what people say.

I believe there's probably a lot of psychological barriers that people have got to break through, again because there's the situation of this mountain – it's not technically that difficult, every single person here has probably climbed, technically, a more difficult route somewhere in the world than this one, than the West Ridge and up the Hornbein Couloir. But certainly I think there are barriers there to be broken through, you know, certain height barriers for everybody, and psychological barriers – everybody's got those. The people that are doing it have got to believe that they're capable of doing it as well, and they've got to believe in the deepest, most private part of the mind that they can actually do this mountain. They've got to believe in themselves. If they start sort of not believing in themselves they'll turn back at the first opportunity. They've got to believe they can do it, and it's up to other people, once the team's been selected, to support them and allow them to believe that they can do it. It has been done before, it's not impossible, and that's one thing you've just got to keep in the back of your mind as well. And it's down to the people that are in the front rank at the time, the conditions, the fitness and whether all the equipment works, the oxygen, etc – it's down to so many factors to get people on to the top of the mountain, and the weather is one of the most dominating of those factors overall . . .

It was an ominously accurate prediction; but the weather was manifestly outside everyone's control. What interested me, as a non-mountaineer who could not come to terms with the voluntarily imposed hardship and danger involved, was what drove these men to the mountains year after year. Luke had given me one of the most convincing answers:

LUKE Why am I here again? I don't know. Mountains are a passion – climbing is a very passionate sport. The reasons why it's passionate are very difficult, they vary for all kinds of people. It's not just because of the heights of extremes that you experience – exhaustion, happiness, elation, camaraderie, cold, heat . . . you could go on

30. 'In the history of load-carrying, the Granada crew is unique in being overtaken by the yaks.'

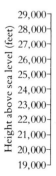
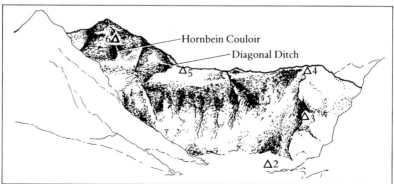

Hornbein Couloir

Diagonal Ditch

Approximate positions of the higher camps.

31 and 32. 'And then, closer to Advance Base Camp, came the blue teeth, 100-foot-high stalagmites of ice, melted into weird contortions by the sun.'

33. Advance Base Camp, also known as Camp One.

34. En route to Camp Two – 'this time, we made it ... over some very slippery scree which alarmingly kept sliding down into pools of ice many feet below.'

35. Al on the Lhola, with Changtse across the Rongbuk Glacier.

36. Nick about to 'knock the bastard off' – on film.

37. The posed publicity shot: 'Granada's crew at Camp Two just below Everest.'

38. Dougie on the radio intercom at Camp Two.

39. Interviewing Luke before he set off up the French Spur.

41. One for Nick's album – or is it for Arriflex's?

40. Dougie giving us a 'sitrep', with Changtse in the background.

42. There were occasional moments at Camp Two when I could enjoy the sun – not a pretty sight!

43. Roger Antolik with a forkful of tinned sardines.

44. My tent at Camp Two had to be dug out almost every day.

45. We were not the only ones with photographic gear: Roger's tripod and 1000mm lens case.

forever. I mean, it *is* extremes, it's the pushing of extremes, that has a lot to do with it, particularly on big mountains. You don't feel it quite the same way rock climbing, which is more athletic. But the opportunities to push those extremes don't come very often in civilian life; they do occasionally in military life, but sometimes in a slightly less constructive way than when on a mountaineering expedition . . .

But it was Pat Parsons who put his finger on the 'Catch-22' quality of my question.

PAT It's a good question, and it's one that you can't really answer unless you're a mountaineer, and if you *are* a mountaineer you don't need to ask it anyway, because everybody understands it. You know, life in the sort of humdrum way that it is in the UK, it's fine, but you've got to have some sort of challenge in life so you can fulfil yourself, and a mountaineer fulfils himself initially on small peaks, which seem big at the time. But then, as you sort of get more experienced and proficient, you raise your sights, and I suppose the ultimate sight for a mountaineer has got to be Everest. OK, it's not the hardest technical mountain to climb in the world, far from it, but it is the highest mountain in the world, and we know that for a fact now, and that alone will present, you know, an immense challenge. It's difficulties which we as a team have got to try and overcome. Now I always think that the harder the climb, the bigger the buzz you get out of it. So if we crack Everest, we're going to be buzzing for the rest of our lives – it'll be just brilliant . . .

Merv Middleton, certainly one of the most qualified to be a summiteer, was even more direct and characteristically frank.

MERV It's a labour of love, that's all I can say. I wear this stupid hat saying 'Because it's there', but that's not the real reason. It's competition, it's a bit of aggression, it's working hard and the pleasure of working hard, it's fun as well, and you come back to the elements, you prove to yourself, and to others I suppose, you can survive in the elements. I don't know, in the end it's an ego trip . . .

Gambling on a hunch that Merv might play a significant role in our story – and I was proved right! – I had talked to him at length at the beginning of April about his own expectations and experiences.

MARK After your starring début leading the climb up the mountain, I believe now you're starting on simply load-carrying – does that seem a bit of a pain?

MERV Well, frankly, it breaks my heart. We were chosen to do the first couple of thousand feet on the French Spur, which was a real pleasure. That was great climbing and it was good exposure. And then we had to drop back down. We had four or five days off, and illness struck. And now we're having to come forward again and load-carry. It's a real ball-breaker, but it's got to be done and you just get it over with. I think as time goes by, in the next week or so now, groups are on the Ridge, illness and physical problems will come out a lot more, and I suspect that our ten-day stint down low will very rapidly get reduced and we'll find ourselves back up there having to start to use men who are acclimatized as others drop out. It's a fact of life. It could be me who drops out.

MARK There's a kind of word going around that there's going to be a quick hard push, maybe even get up by the end of April. Do you think that's feasible?

MERV It's feasible in an ideal world, but the West Ridge is long – it's a mile and a half. In fact it's almost two mountains. You climb four and half thousand feet and then you've got a mile and a half which is not flat, like some people say it is. It's a thousand-foot climb, is that mile and a half, and the line of communications can be extremely long and drawn out. It will be very necky indeed to run out from the top of the French Spur and go for the summit.

MARK What about the weather? Isn't that going to be a critical factor really? Everything else seems to be going well.

MERV When we were here in 1984, the wind was minimal, virtually nil. From March right through to mid-April we had no snow, beautiful hot sunny days, and the main thing, no wind. You could hear the jet stream high up on the Ridge – the jet stream used to come down and clip the Ridge early on in March – you could hear it screaming miles away. It was pretty unnerving, but then it lifted up and it was beautiful. But now you have no idea of the days we're getting here – it batters the mind more than anything. You can climb in it, but you're a lot slower because it's a lot more methodical, you're a lot more prone to cold injuries, and wear and tear on equipment is higher as well. The old fixed rope, rubbing backwards and forwards across the snow and ice, however hard you try to protect it, the wear is there, and there's a lot of traffic going up and down these ropes. And that's the risk in a big expedition like this.

MARK You mentioned that you'd been here before, and I know that yesterday was the anniversary of your mate's death up here. Can you just tell us about that, and what happened?

MERV We came here in 1984 on a multi-Services expedition to the North Face of Everest, more or less a vertical line from the summit straight to the bottom. It's been done once before by the Japanese, and we were hoping to make a second attempt with a British ascent. Exactly the same time of year four years ago, in fact, yesterday the 3rd of April, we were on a ledge at about twenty thousand feet. We had a camp at the base of the North Face and the snow conditions were as you see them today – very little snow; the wind was very, very strong; the mountain had been swept clear – and you couldn't really have anticipated any sort of avalanche danger. And then a huge ice serac, which has never been recorded, fell from the North Col, from Changtse. It fell about three and a half thousand feet and travelled two and a half miles in a matter of seconds. The only thing that saved us – it was a climbing team of five up there at the time – and the only thing that saved our lives was the actual shock wave of the impact of the ice. It created parallel avalanches off Everest, minor ones, but the shock waves were enough to destroy the tents and flatten the ice. Actually the shock waves enabled us to be thrown quite clear – we travelled about forty yards down the glacier – but unfortunately one guy was killed, Tony Swierzy. He was in a tent which had been fairly well buried, and instead of the tent being blown clear, it was just crushed under the ice. The total summary of injuries was that a guy, Andy Baxter, had a broken shoulder blade and ribs, Brummie Stokes had broken vertebrae in the neck, and there was frostbite all round. It was a very bitter day – it happened first thing in the morning – and it took about three to four hours for the rescue team to get up. Even so, we were in good spirits – we were a very strong team.

MARK What actually happened to *you*? Were you all right?

MERV I was the fortunate one. It was my turn to brew the tea that day. I was just sort of sticking my head out of the tent as this thing happened. There was a big crump in the sky and my ears nearly popped at the noise. They erupted with blood from the shock waves. I looked up and saw this thing coming, and grabbed the other guy's legs who was in the tent with me, a guy called Graham Cook, and by the time I dragged him out of the door it was upon us and we were airborne. We were travelling down the hill in light underwear for about forty metres. It was quite traumatic, running about afterwards at 7 in the morning in the pitch dark, trying to find items of clothes to put on.

The whole thing was a tragedy when it happened, and then there was just amazing good luck afterwards. We found one of the guys buried, unconscious, and by sheer fluke found a duvet and a sleeping mask and an oxygen ball, and I put him on the oxygen. He went from bright blue round to cherry red, and started to breathe again. I raked about in the snow and came across a radio, and the radio was just falling apart, the antenna hanging off it – you'd never have thought it would work. I just turned it on, and as I turned it on someone came across the air with an impromptu radio check saying – is anyone out there? I was just able to sound the alarm immediately, otherwise we would probably all have died in the passage of time, because we were pretty well incapable of helping ourselves. It was a superb team effort, to carry out that rescue.

MARK Doesn't that sort of thing put you off? I mean, here you are again.

MERV Perhaps I'm a fortunate person – I've been in an avalanche three times before . . . It doesn't really. The mountain is inherently safe, the dangers of the North Face at this time of year are predictable. The North Face route is a much more logical line, it's a straight line, a plumb line from top to bottom. Nine thousand feet does away with all the objective dangers and what not. The West Ridge in many ways is inherently harder, it just makes you much more aware . . .

Physically and psychologically, I was in another world from Merv's, and I was still suffering from my 'Everest blues'. Frequently, I had to drive myself to concentrate on the job in hand. I've never had this problem on any other project, and indeed, now I am back in 'civilization', my interest and involvement has returned to its normal level. But my diary is littered with exhortations to myself, even on 13 April, the day Dougie was to announce the first summit team.

We are definitely going up to Camp One tomorrow and Camp Two the next day. Not looking forward to it, as it's probably for the duration, until Everest is climbed. My thoughts are far fuller of getting back, my holiday in France, Vicky, the kids, the house plans – anything but the series. But I'm still trying to put in as much effort as I can, if that's not contradictory. Boredom makes the

time pass so slowly, and allows one so much thinking time – a bad thing.
Home can become an obsession, like a steak or a pint, and I can't afford to let
it. But I can't avoid thoughts of 'this time in a month or so' either.

That was written in the afternoon, before Dougie's announcement.
Later that night, after we had filmed the much-anticipated naming of
names, I had obviously cheered up.

Excellent evening, starting with Dougie Keelan's briefing and announcement
of the summiteers. Johnny's reaction a picture! At last I feel the thing is taking
off and has become exciting. I hope I'm right. A breakthrough with Dougie,
too – having a good long chat. All in all, even scotch allowed for, a significant
evening.

Moods are prone to sudden shifts on Everest, and mine were to
continue vacillating between excitement and enervation. But it *had*
been a good evening, for the series and for our egos. Everyone had
gathered in the Hunter Hut at the appointed time of seven o'clock, just
after supper, and Dougie had addressed the assembled company.

DOUGIE I realize that some of what I may say may sound contentious
and certainly some of the selections, but I can assure you they've been
done in consultation with those whose judgement I value on mountaineering, professional and military, and in terms of experience . . .

Again, as everybody has sensed, the time has come for a major
re-grouping of the expedition out of our original eight four-man
teams, because probably two-thirds or at least half of all the teams
have gone by the board now, with folks dropping out with injuries or
chest infections or whatever . . .

Well, enough of that by way of general preamble. Once Henry has
got Camp Five established – and we hope that will be within the next
five or six days – and once we're happy that the weather is holding, we
are ready to go for the first broad summit attempt. I know you're all
waiting for names, but I'll give those out in just a moment – first, the
groupings.

I would see each of the two groups as consisting of four summit
members supported by a further six – ten in all. At Camp Three and
Four we will have twelve bed-spaces and at Camp Five, ten. So the ten
people will move from Camp Five on towards Camp Six, the assault
camp, where there will be two of the lightweight tents set up, and I
hope it will be somewhere half way up the Hornbein Couloir where

there is, if you look at it, that little tributary of ice up on the left – somewhere in that area, no lower than twenty-seven-and-a-half thousand feet.

The whole group will move up there, get that camp established plus its oxygen stocks for one go, and six will come back to Camp Five for the night, and wait in case of an emergency while the four do their big thing.

In a broad sense, that's how I see the strategy for both of the two main summit bids that we're going to make taking place. OK?

Now, what you've all been waiting for – names. Now the second summit group is – there are still two names that I'm not going to put in, two out of the four, I'm deliberately ducking the issue at the moment because my mind isn't quite made up. We need, we feel, to hang on a little bit longer to see how people are going. But the first group, the four that will go, will be – Nicholls, Maxwell, Moore and McLeod. These will be supported by six who will come from the following – Orange, Torrington, Miller, Last, Lowe, Parsons, Andy Hughes, Edington. OK?

The second group, the summit four, will be – and as I've said, I'm only going to give two names at the moment – will be Middleton and Garratt, and two more to follow; and they will be supported, with two out of these names to be picked nearer the time to join the summit two – Williams, Bell, Morning, Howie, Pelly, Atkins, Vlasto, Taylor, Hardy, Spencer, Luke Hughes, Hattersley and Henry Day – we'll have to see how he's faring after what's going on right now. Now, if amongst those names that I've given in the supporting role there are drop-outs, for one reason or another, then I can see no reason why the Sherpas can't jump in there. And the final point of this particular theme is that, of those names going to the summit that I have mentioned, there can of course be a lot of change – there can be injury, there can be infections, there can be a collapse of acclimatization – and when that happens, of course one of the supporters steps in, and I can't predict who that's going to be. It's very likely to be a natural selection, I think you'll agree, and there would be, I suspect, not a lot of dispute about who would jump in – it would be whoever was going best of the supporting group at the time.

Now, timings. It's not possible to be precise in this game, as we all know, but we're talking in an ideal world about twelve days hence – in other words, just inside this month – and I wouldn't deny that it would be extremely nice were we to achieve the first bid in April. Now I think you don't have to be a great mountain genius to work out that the odds are stacked much higher for success for the second group than the first group, on the grounds that there will be the knowledge that the first group will have gained of the route and the conditions of the fixed ropes. Secondly, it's slight later in the season and every week, as we know, counts at the moment in this pre-monsoon season, and the winds get a little warmer, we hope a little less and so forth. Thirdly, of course, you will have had a little bit more rest, not that that necessarily should make all the difference because the first group will have been pretty well and truly rested.

Right, I don't think I really have a great deal more to say, I hope you accept these selections – there's bound to be disappointment, there always is in a big expedition where you can, by virtue of the logistics at the time, you can only put a limited number up. If we get these eight up it'll be terrific, and the fact that you're not one of the eight, I'm sure you'll agree, you'll all be quite sanguine and men of the world enough to know how to take it. It's the old Olympics ethic, isn't it? It's the taking part that really counts, and nearly everybody in this expedition has taken part with a great vengeance and has contributed enormously to what I'm sure we all agree will be an ultimate enormous success . . .

The majority of those names were no real surprise; but Johnny Garratt, accompanying Merv Middleton on the second wave, could not possibly have been certain of his selection. Immediately after the briefing, I spoke to him.

MARK Surprised?

JOHNNY Happy, yeah, so happy, just over the moon.

MARK Did you think it would be you?

JOHNNY No, I mean everybody had a chance, you know. I think as Dougie said, it just came down on the day to being in the right place at the right time, being fit enough, so everyone started with the same chance. I'm just really so happy I'm going to get a crack at it.

MARK And you, Merv, not quite so surprised?

MERV I refuse to be serious.

MARK Go on then, be not so serious.

MERV Well, I'm chuffed to hell, I can't deny it. I really can't disagree, it's great.

I then went on to talk to Dave Nicholls, perhaps of all of them the most likely not only to get a place, but to be selected as leader of the first summit team along with his climbing partner, Dave Maxwell, known as Max.

MARK Congratulations, what can I say?

DAVE Thanks very much. I'm personally absolutely delighted and very honoured. I feel that we represent all the efforts of the team, and since we're the first ones to crack it we've got an extremely important job to do, and I'm very confident, unless we get a blizzard, we'll get up there, absolutely certain of it.

MARK As was said, you've got the hardest job because you're trail-blazing.

DAVE Yeah, we are – it's a psychological barrier to bring everybody across the Diagonal Ditch and then up the gully. There is the crux, of course, of the climb in the top of the gully and we don't know how much rope is there, what's fixed there, and we've got to break through that first. But having said that, you know, both Max and I have been up to the top of the West Ridge, we've seen how much it lies back, and we're confident that there won't be any technical difficulty to stop us . . .

The next day we were to set off up the glacier again to cover the summit bid when it took place, which would be before the end of the month if Dougie Keelan had his way. Before we left, we interviewed Pat Parsons who was still having great difficulty with his eyesight, and Dave Orange who was having almost as much trouble with his breathing at high altitudes. I certainly had an idea of how he felt. Even the walk up to Advance Base Camp was strain enough, as my diary for the day records:

A killer day! Started well enough – two short bits with Pat Parsons and Dave Orange to add to the Base Camp sync bank, and then eventually set off about 11. It took one-and-a-half hours plus a rest, to get to the East Rongbuk River, and then the climb up the steep hill did for me. Nick branched off lower (Ian is staying at Base Camp with his chest and cough) and I struggled on, Tug overtaking me about 4 o'clock at the top of a hill. Finally arrived at 6, barely able to put one foot in front of the other. The endless ridges up and down before you arrive are incredibly dispiriting. A bad journey. And to be followed by a bad night, the first for some time, like they used to be, awake at 4 and no sign of more sleep. Writing this at 6 a.m. Far colder up here, frost inside the tent and freezing cold hands, even in gloves, from holding this note book. Feeling wretched. What a pity, thought all that was over.

To add to my depression, a potential conflict of interest arose between Dougie Keelan and myself over our need to get Alan, with Roger Antolik to help him, up onto the West Ridge to film. Dougie needed all the available sleeping places in the Camp Three and Camp Four snow holes, as well as all the oxygen with which they were stocked, for the summit team and their supporters as they came through. It had been decreed that oxygen would be used at Camp Four and above – in other words, from about 24,000 feet to the summit. I could understand that the laboriously sited oxygen was at a premium, and equally that bed-spaces went first to the climbers and only second to us. But we needed shots along the Shoulder, and I had hoped to be in a position to film the summiteers on their way through. It was one of the few direct them-and-us conflicts of the whole expedition. Finally, after much discussion of the dreaded 'logistics', it was agreed that Al and Roger could follow Dave Nicholls and his team up the mountain, a day behind them, take the film we needed of the mountain and views across into Nepal from the elevated position of Camp Four, and then welcome the victorious – we hoped! – summiteers as they came back along the West Ridge to Camp Four.

If At First You Don't Succeed . . .

Saturday 16 April to Saturday 30 April
ABC and Camp Two

The summit date had been set for 25 April, or as close to that Monday as was possible. Climbing up a camp a day from Base Camp, where the summit team was to gain as much strength as possible, takes six days, ending up in the yet-to-be-established Camp Six in the Hornbein Couloir. From there, a little under 2,000 feet takes you to the top and, all being well, it's a day's work to get there, and back down to Camp Six.

Henry Day was up at the far end of the West Ridge with Ted Atkins, the boatered and bow-tied joker of the expedition. I hadn't actually seen the tie or the headgear since we arrived on the mountain, and assumed he had left them in Kathmandu to sport on his return – it was hardly a suitable sartorial style for the howling gales of the West Ridge or the rigours of life in a snow hole. Their task was to dig out a third snow hole, or erect sufficient tents, to put in Camp Five as close as possible to the bottom of the second leg of the climb – up the Diagonal Ditch and the Hornbein Couloir, through the Yellow Rockband, and on to the summit. Dougie, like Merv Middleton, had always talked of two mountains, one on top of the other, with the West Ridge as 'an easy walk' between them. Easy or otherwise, it meant that having done that section you were only half way. And only now were Henry and Co. putting in Camp Five, with Camp Six yet to be established, and less than ten days to summit day. I spoke to Nigel Williams, himself now selected, with Steve Bell, as the final pair of the second summit four, along with Merv Middleton and Johnny Garratt. Nigel had had health problems up at Camp Four. How did he reckon the others would fare?

NIGEL There's a lot of guys I'd rather see go there before me almost, because I know that they're more capable and I just know roughly where I stand in the pecking order, and that's fine. Also, I think, there's a lot of people who think, oh yes, you know, I'd love to go, but they just do not have any idea of the commitment, leaving Camp Six and going on up that ridge, on your own or with your partner. And the worry about getting back down, which has frequently been the problem in the past for other expeditions. Very few of the lads have been above twenty-one thousand feet, in fact; a number have been on expeditions, but not many of them have been to peaks much above twenty-one.

MARK And then there's still another eight to go.

NIGEL Yeah, exactly, eight thousand more feet, and I mean, I think one or two of them haven't even been in a snow hole. A snow hole is actually more comfortable than a tent, and yes, it's all a big game. I mean, none of them have touched oxygen and really had to live at twenty-four thousand feet, which is where life starts to get quite unpleasant. You're out of breath just putting your boots on before you've even crawled out of your tent and sorted out your oxygen and de-frosted it, got it into your rucksack, strapped it all up so that it's comfortable, because an eighteen pound long cylinder, it doesn't sit in a rucksack very comfortably, and that's about all you can carry anyway, you know. So up there, there's a lot more problems than there are just sort of picking up a box of food and zipping from Camp Two to Camp Three in an hour and a bit.

MARK One of the things that occurs to me is, that very few people have ever made it to the top of Everest by the end of April, and it must be tempting to Dougie, and to this expedition in general, to try and crack that particular barrier. Do you think that's a factor?

NIGEL I would hope not too much, just for the sake of breaking a record or something. I think there's a possibility we'll have Dave and Max and Al and Terry on the top before the end of April, and it would be absolutely marvellous. It's what? the 15th, no, the 16th today. The weather is due to go bad, although the weather forecast hasn't been that reliable. And if it does go bad, it might make it impossible because the back-up still isn't there, I think, at Camp Four and Five. And I think you're going to need it, I think it's going to take a bit longer than people realize. So there's a chance, but I'm not really sure. Great if we can do it, but I just think that you need more people up there making more of a logistic build-up . . .

Dave Nicholls, the leader of the summit team, was also expressing serious doubts about the feasibility of the schedule, given the unpredictability of the weather. My diary recalls the yo-yo of our hopes and expectations at Advance Base Camp.

17 April. Dave Nicholls arrived with sobering expectations of the timetable – it seems everyone agrees more carrying is needed to set up Camps Four and Five than Dougie had anticipated. It's cloudy, cold, and now has just started snowing.

18 April. Two inches of snow or more overnight. Cloudy this morning and general decision to delay all moves by 24 hours. But then the sun came through and it has been one of the best days to date. Can it still be the 25th April, a week today, as Dougie hoped on the 13th? I doubt it, but still hope for it.

19 April. Yesterday's 1800 radio call very positive. Merv's group coming up today; Dave Nicholls's group off from here at 9 a.m.; and Al Miller's support group up from Base Camp tomorrow. Get the camps equipped, and then go for it within a week. But . . . this evening snow falling again here at Advance Base Camp, despite weather forecast for five good days. And we're back on the see-saw.

20 April. People are now talking about April 28th for the summit, just over a week, but it's got to be guess work and very dependent on the weather. Even so, it's cutting it fine for Dougie Keelan's self-confessed aim of an April ascent. I'm right behind him, but for different reasons. Further rumours are putting Henry as the final eighth summiteer now Nigel is out. I wouldn't be surprised – he's been acclimatizing at Camp Five for days and must have Dougie Keelan's ear more than most.

21 April. Summit bids now anticipated 29th April to 2nd May, with a second a week later – not good news. Everything weather-dependent as always. Nick happy up at Camp Two: Ian and I will go up probably on the 24th, i.e. Sunday, as Dave Nicholls and his three will set out from there on the 25th or 26th, all being well.

22 April. Beautiful weather, after two days rather cloudy. Long 1800 radio call – Dougie announcing 29th April summit bid, if the weather and load-carriers go to plan. Dave Nicholls and three to go up to Camp Two on Sunday 24th, Ian and I with them. So that's when it will start, with the second bid a week later. Good to know, to have a date. And, by chance, it's the transmission of my 1968 programme. Fingers crossed on all counts.

23 April. 1800 radio call: bad news. Snow thick and dangerous between Camps Three and Four. Merv and Johnny couldn't get to Camp Four. At least twenty-four hours delay. Dave Nicholls and us now going up to Camp Two on Monday 25th earliest. General disappointment and let down, none less than I, for my own reasons. Feel very sorry for Dave Nicholls and the rest of his group.

24 April. Back to square one. Fine, sunny day, and so all to continue with original plans. Dave Nicholls etc. to Camp Two today: me and Ian too. Now sharing tiny tent with Ian, not ideal for either of us but there's not much accommodation up here at Two. Dougie in very gung-ho mood, seeming set on 29th April. Let's hope the weather holds.

25 April. Sunday* dawns fine and sunny, wind getting up by 11. Filmed breakfast and preparations for leaving, then Dougie bidding the four farewell and God speed. Genuinely moving, I hope – it was in the event. The prospect of their next five days or so truly horrendous, at least to me, and surely in some ways to them.

DAVE NICHOLLS We feel that we have every confidence. Yep, the weather's the crux, it is the crux, but it's looking a little more settled, but we can't be sure. It's a terribly exciting moment, two years' worth of planning and here we are at the final launch. It's really quite a moment.

DOUGIE We'll be talking twice a day on the radio and we have every confidence in the four of you. There are at least thirty-two other climbers who are putting their hopes in you. We couldn't have a stronger team. I'm sure of that, and we'll all turn up trumps.

DAVE Cheers, Keith mate. Thanks for the breakfast. What is it now? In five days' time we'll see you back down here.

KEITH HUNTER Five days' time, if you play your cards right, you'll get another good breakfast.

DOUGIE Cheers then.

KEITH All the best . . .

To a chorus of 'Good luck, good luck' from those of us left at Camp Two, Dave, Max, Terry and Al set off across the glacier to the foot of the mountain proper. I turned to Dougie:

---

*I had lost count of what day it was. 25 April was a Monday.

MARK I don't know about you, Dougie, but I found that quite emotional.

DOUGIE Well, I did too, really, because it's the culmination, as somebody said, of nearly two years' planning, the culmination of a great deal of effort over the last eight weeks to get as far as we've got, and here we are at the launch, and we've launched them off up the hill in as safe a mode as we can. I can't think of a better or more suitably qualified or tougher and stronger and more robust group to do it. And they go, as I said, with all our thoughts and all our prayers.

MARK Yes, it's a touching moment. It must present to you, although they haven't got there yet, the beginning of the climax of the whole saga.

DOUGIE That's right, and in this next week we're going to be biting our finger-nails a bit, keeping our fingers crossed for the weather, hoping that they go well. I'm sure they will, and I think really that waiting period which we've got to fill in is going to be pretty tough. But it's over to them now . . .

Jottings in my diary reveal the momentous events of our day, now there was virtually nothing to film at Camp Two.

Cooking tonight for the second time in Nick's tent: his turn tonight, mine last night. Dougie retired to his tent after lunch and hasn't been seen since. Heavy snow storm started 6ish. Merv, Johnny and Richard Pelly all arrived at Camp Two in a white-out at 7.45, having been from Camp Four all the way to Camp Five, at the far end of the Ridge, and back down in one day. But amazingly cheerful and none the worse for wear. Snow stopped but then resumed 10.30 and is falling thick and hard now at midnight. It must be bad news for tomorrow's work on the mountain and summit bid on the 29th April – almost certain delay.

26 April. Lot of wind and spindrift in the night, but warm enough in tent and two sleeping bags. Awake and reading 3 to 6 a.m. – just not tired – and up at 10. Radio call left progress along the Ridge pending, to see what conditions were like. Then at 1 o'clock, confirmation all were en route. We could see Al Miller's support group leaving Camp Four about midday. Did shots of route, ridge, etc. plus a longish sitrep with Dougie.

DOUGIE Now the plan, weather permitting, is that the summit team will go up to Camp Four, and as we look up at the Ridge now, I can see all four of them approaching Camp Four, which is a good time for them to get in and rest. Tomorrow they'll move along the Ridge to Camp

Five – where Al Miller's group will have got in tonight, and will have set up the camp and dug out the snowhole which Henry Day and Ted Atkins prepared about five days ago – that is tomorrow, Wednesday, one loses count of days, the 27th.

Then Thursday the 28th, they move up new ground to Camp Six through what we call the Diagonal Ditch, with a height gain we hope of about two thousand feet. It's actually much more leaning back than it appears when you look at it from here. As I look at it now, over your shoulder, it looks enormously steep. In fact it does lay back, and we don't anticipate any great technical climbing difficulty.

So, Thursday night, there we will have, all things being equal, Al Miller's group supporting Dave Nicholls's four at Camp Six at about twenty-seven-and-a-half thousand feet, in what we call the Hornbein Couloir. We hope they'll get in there in good time on Thursday afternoon, so that two of them will stay and dig out the shelters and prepare the platforms for the two tents, and the other two will climb on up, we hope about five or six hundred feet, to fix rope over what we believe will probably be the crux, in other words the most difficult part of the whole climb, towards the top of the Hornbein Couloir. And if they can do that the night before or the afternoon before when it'll be relatively warmer, because the sun doesn't get on to it until about midday, it'll be much, much easier on their hands. And they'll be able to start out for the main summit bid on Friday, that's Friday the 29th, with the knowledge that the rope is there to see them over the difficult bit, and then they'll go whizzing up to the top . . .

Dougie allowed himself a smile.

DOUGIE They've got a radio and we will be on listening watch down here, and I don't think we'll actually see them wave from the top, but at least we'll get the word when they're there, and we hope we can pass it out live . . .

My diary again:

27 April 8 p.m. Now it's started snowing again, but only briefly. As I write, in forty-eight hours Everest might be conquered. I must admit to real excitement at the prospect.

28 April. Dave Nicholls and his three off from Camp Five about 9 o'clock, not by 8 as they intended. But then they seemed to make very slow progress,

reaching the large snowfield below the Hornbein Couloir only at 1500. Bodes
ill for getting Camp Six established as high as necessary, or it will be a killingly
long day for them. We can't do much – thin cloud on hill makes long lens shots
look even softer and milkier than they normally would. Hoping against hope
that Andy Hughes, with our Video-8, is managing to get something up there,
and maybe even Al Evans at Camp Four on the end of the twenty-to-one.

I find I've only five and a half packets of cigarettes left – going to be a bit tight
until the mail-run arrives. There should be several letters for me, with luck,
which will make the protracted stay up here for the second and maybe even third
attempts slightly more acceptable. There's a lot of cloud approaching from the
south over the Lhola – probably yet more snow sooner or later.

11.30 p.m. Strong winds and thick snow drove us into the Hunter Hut. A
day of shifting expectations. The 1800 radio call found the summit four well
short of the Hornbein Couloir, having had a hard time fixing ropes earlier, and
Dougie very inclined to call them back down. To be decided at 2000. Then,
Dave Nicholls made a powerful plea for a further advance recce, with try for the
top if possible. Dougie agreed. The chances are thin but all hangs on tomorrow.
Weather tonight terrible – snow, wind, violence. Hope they're above it at
Camp Six, even if it is lower than intended.

29 April. Horrendous, gusty storm all night. Dead quiet, then as though the
tent were about to take off down the Rongbuk valley. Difficult to sleep through.
But the day dawned and proved a real downer, a dire disappointment. Dave
Nicholls decided to turn back on the 12 o'clock schedule, but would first go on to
site Camp Six proper, rather than the temporary one they'd put in overnight.

Waiting impotently at Camp Two at the foot of the mountain, I
asked Dougie what the implications of that decision were.

DOUGIE What he said was, that he didn't stand a chance of getting to the
top today, and that was abundantly obvious last night because, for
reasons that aren't quite clear to us yet, the four summiteers and their
six supporters didn't get nearly as far into the Hornbein Couloir, to the
projected place for the top camp, as we'd hoped. I think it was probably
a combination of the oxygen bottles, which seemed to be under-
charged and therefore ran out much sooner than we'd planned, and
perhaps loads, which were rather large and heavy in the circumstances.
Perhaps a combination of a whole host of reasons – it's very difficult to
tell.

But it's happened and we've got to live with it now, so there's no point in looking back and deciding what went wrong. We must pick up what we can from what's happened, and make sure that the second summit bid is a total success.

Now the difficult decision last night was what to do with Dave Nicholls's group. They were not nearly so far as they should have been, as I said, but they were none-the-less well up on the mountain, and on the one hand we could have pulled them off and thereby saved the oxygen for the next lot, because we haven't got a limitless stock. Or else we could have said – well, you're up there, and a lot of people have helped get you as far as you have, so go as far as you can tomorrow, safely, do a recce up the Couloir for Merv Middleton's group, which as you know follows next.

So I decided anyway, after a lot of heart-searching, to give them the chance to do a recce and get as high as they could today. But, as you see, they're making quite slow progress. They've hit a difficult spot fairly low down in the Couloir, and at twelve o'clock we had that radio schedule, as you know, and made the decision that they would go on to the projected proper Camp Six site, the top camp, and then go and try and recce the crux of the climb, which is a sixty-metre stretch towards the top of the Couloir. If they can get up that high and look at it, and see if there are any old ropes from other expeditions there, and then let Merv know what *is* there, and how difficult it is, and what the snow's like and so on, then at least they would have achieved something. It gives them a sort of morale boost as well, that they would have achieved a personal high altitude best.

At the moment, I'm pondering away on the logistics for the second bid, and I think we've probably got to boost up the support party, so that we can reduce the individual loads a bit to make sure they get there. Others have done this route, indeed have done what we hoped it would be possible to do this time, but, to be fair, we are slightly early in the season – it's still April – and there were some ferocious winds last night, and it does undermine.

MARK I imagine you must be deeply disappointed, as leader.

DOUGIE Well, I am, deeply disappointed, obviously, as this was our first carefully planned summit bid, which is now going to fail. But you know, you pick up the pieces and make the best of it. You pick up what's good and what's been achieved from this, and throw that back into the second bid, which is what we're going to do. So, yes, I'm disappointed, I won't deny that, and I'm sure they are too. It's a chance of a lifetime to be selected for the first summit bid of a major Everest expedition, but it just didn't happen for any of us . . .

Dougie smiled bravely. My diary concludes the story of that bitter day.

Charlie Hattersley arrived, full of grumbles from Camp One about the planning and operation of the first bid. It would have been possible for them to continue up, but the support team were knackered and the summit team would have used oxygen designated for the second bid. Not surprisingly, the day was really blighted. We had all built such hope and expectations on it. To see them crawling so slowly up the Hornbein Couloir, each step affirming more positively that they could never make the summit, was heartbreaking. On top of everything, the weather was perfect for summit bids – fine, not too much wind, and clear. Now, the second bid will be postponed until, at the earliest, the 7th May, a two day slip, and all the momentum and excitement has dissipated.

So that was it. The first attempt had failed, and a complex combination of factors was to blame for the failure. The weather, to be sure . . . but was there not an element of human error? Nick and I decided we must confront Dougie with the question that all the lads were asking – why go for an April ascent when we were, increasingly obviously, insufficiently prepared? Wasn't it imposing a load on the summiteers that was more than they could cope with?

DOUGIE Well, as things turned out, that is so. But the plan when it was conceived was based on the evidence of previous expeditions that have been in this area and was, in fact, very well founded. We've got more oxygen up there now than any previous expeditions have had; we're working on much wider margins than many previous expeditions have done, and when I say many previous expeditions, we're actually only talking about three or four. I consulted our Sirdar, Chowang, who's of course been up there before, and his view was that it would take about six to seven hours to get from Camp Five to where we hoped Camp Six would be.

Well, conditions vary from year to year. It may be that in the Diagonal Ditch, which is the bit that took them the time, and where we know this year there is far less snow, the going was much harder. Certainly it took them much longer than we'd envisaged and planned. If you're implying that the plan was a flawed plan, I would dispute that, because others have done that route in the sort of time-frame we were looking at, in numbers that we were looking at, and at the end of the day they didn't get there.

MARK You don't feel in retrospect, or with hindsight, that perhaps you needed more backup, more support, more oxygen, and that you were really flying a bit of a kite, going a bit light on it?

DOUGIE No, I don't think we were going light on it. It's easy to be wise after the event, and I have no doubt now, now that we know what the conditions are like up there, which we didn't before, that it would be wisest to get Camp Six, the top launch camp for the summit, firmly placed. But the traditional way of doing these things is usually to launch a summit bid with a number of supporters who place the top camp and then return, leaving those who are going on to the next stage of the summit to go on from that camp. It's a time-honoured way of doing it, and we were certainly not doing any differently this time. I mean, it's a disappointment when a plan doesn't work out, but Everest is never easy, by any route at any time.

MARK If you could write off the first attempt as a sort of dress-rehearsal, what are the lessons that have been learnt, can be learnt and will be put into effect for the second attempt?

DOUGIE Well, it's become clear that they were exhausted after the heavy carry from Camp Five, which didn't get as far as we'd hoped to locate the top camp, and therefore we must have a concerted and separate effort to get the top camp fixed firmly before we put the summit climbers into that camp for them to go to the top the next day. That's the conclusion I draw from this.

MARK Finally, and this may be a bit of a nasty one, if anyone is going to lay the blame, would you lay it on the mountain, the climbers, yourself – or none of those?

DOUGIE I don't think you can. I think it's entirely wrong to apportion blame. There are far more failed attempts on high Himalayan peaks than successful ones, and certainly that's true of Everest. Everest hasn't been climbed, except for this winter, for about three years now. If you want a scapegoat, I will very willingly be it. But with hindsight, now that we know the conditions and what they are there – the fact that there isn't much snow; the fact that the Diagonal Ditch is much more tricky than we'd been led to believe – perhaps we should have been a bit more cautious and placed Camp Six as a separate phase of the operation rather than bracketing it with the summit bid. I'm prepared to go as far as that, but then, as I said, it's easy to be wise after the event. We've got a very strong second summit bid in the pipeline which is being wound up at the moment. It remains a disappointment that we didn't succeed the first time, and I hope we will the second . . .

On the following day, Saturday 30 April, the summit team arrived back at Camp Two – it's a far quicker business descending Everest than ascending. The first was Terry Moore, a reserved and reticent RAF man who, for those reasons, had not featured greatly in our filming. But his recent ordeal and its unsuccessful outcome were too much, even for Terry's sang-froid. As he approached across the glacier, Dougie went out to meet him with us in hot pursuit.

I thought I detected an expression on Terry's face that, in the midst of his emotion, said: 'Oh God, the film crew, at this of all times.' If only he knew, we felt almost as down as he did – not that it would have been much comfort to him. As Terry fought to control the tears of frustration and disappointment that welled up in his eyes, Dougie offered what commiseration he could. Tactfully, this took the form of congratulation on their achievement in the circumstances. And Dougie was right, the summit team had done everything in their power to reach their destination, and were themselves in no way to be charged with any personal or collective failure. If fault there were, it was with the planning in the beginning, and the weather in the end. Dougie himself may have felt he had let down his chosen summiteers, but there was no hint of acrimony in Terry's distraught responses. It was a moving moment for all of us, witnessing the two mens' emotions stripped bare on the freezing glacier. For them, it could not have been more painful had it been their bodies, not their feelings, that stood naked.

Soon, Dave Nicholls arrived with Dave Maxwell and Al McLeod. As Dave saw Dougie approaching to welcome them back, he raised his arms in a gesture of despair.

DAVE Well, we failed, didn't we? . . .

It said it all. Again, Dougie did his best to offer comfort and encouragement.

DOUGIE Well, it wasn't through want of trying – not through want of trying at all. And I'm glad to see you again, and don't be discouraged.

Nobody in this world could have done more than all of you did. You have the feelings and thoughts of the whole of the expedition behind you, I can reflect that view coming all the way up the line. And congratulations on getting as high as you did – a magnificent achievement in human terms. You didn't get there, but I don't think anybody else could have done in the circumstances. And everybody's back in, and that's the most important thing for you all. But that apart, I think your mountaineering has been enjoyable and interesting . . .

Dave gave a wry smile.

DAVE Well, nothing comes easy in mountaineering, and Everest least of all.

DOUGIE All I can say to you, if it isn't blindingly obvious, is that on your achievement in the last two or three days, the expedition will succeed with subsequent bids . . .

No words, though, can anaesthetize the sting of failure, even when the fault is none of your own. As soon as Dave had recovered his breath and had a cup of tea, I spoke to him.

MARK Hindsight is obviously a great informer after the event, but do you feel now, Dave, that you had sufficient in manpower and equipment and just sort of physical climbing ability – was that one of the problems?

DAVE No, it was one of the frustrations – physical climbing ability. There were other factors, reasons that we didn't get to the top, and they were outside our control. In terms of climbing ability and physical ability to get there, we all had it, and that's what's so frustrating. And that's why I felt so inwardly depressed and bitter after we had to come back down again. And when I spoke to Dougie on the radio and he said, well that's it, it was like a knife going in, just sliding straight into me, because you know, we were there, we were fit, we were able to go and the weather was good. But the fact that determined that we couldn't go there was, as I say, outside our control, and those I think I have described already – you know, that the plan was too ambitious for the conditions and we put too much on the summit team. It was too much responsibility in terms of leading the route and trying to establish the camp and all the other bits and pieces . . .

Dave's partner, Dave Maxwell, had discomfort to add to his burden of disappointment – he had contracted frostbite on his two big toes, and by the next morning they were a deep blue-black, as though they'd been trodden on by an elephant.

MAX Well, that's just part of the game. I'd actually had a bit of a problem earlier in the trip when we were fixing from Camp Three to Four, when the jetstream was still on the Ridge. I've obviously been trying to look after them as well as I could, but once we got in the Couloir, you know, it was bitterly cold and it was very difficult trying to keep them warm at all. Once we started down, I suppose trying to come down without any oxygen didn't help at all, because the effect of oxygen is to keep you warm. So that didn't help. And then I felt I was warming gradually as we got towards Camp Five on the way back, but, looking at them at night, you know, with a fading headtorch, I couldn't really see any positive signs of frostbite, so I just wrote it off as a bit of frostnip, hoping that the feeling would come back.

MARK But it didn't?

MAX No, they actually started to blister on the way down from Camp Five, and I only discovered when I took my boots off last night, which was quite late, how bad they were . . .

Al Miller could do little to treat them, and Max was on his way down to rest at Base Camp in any event. But by the time we were next down there, they were largely recovered and Max was desporting himself on his Base Camp gym, an improvised affair of large, empty gas cylinders, tent poles and plastic storage drums. Whenever the next mountain beckoned – for it could not be this one, on this expedition – Max would be fit and ready for it.

Having got over the disappointment at the first bid's failure, I, like everyone else, was turning my mind to future attempts. My main concern was to get footage high on the mountain, and, in particular, on the summit itself. I had persuaded Dave Maxwell to take with him our lightest Video-8 camera, which weighs only four pounds or so, and use it *en route*, and above all, on the top. I knew full well it was asking a lot: every ounce counts at that altitude, and the summiteer's mind is as pared down as his pack. One thing matters, and that is getting there. In such circumstances, even thinking of filming, let alone the added effort of doing it, is wasted concentration.

But this was of little comfort to me, trying to produce a TV series about climbing Mount Everest that might well have no footage of its culminating glory. I had used this and every other argument I could muster on Max before he left, piling on the moral pressure as thick as I could manage. But in vain! When I asked Max, he confessed that on the final day he had left the camera at the improvised Camp Six. His excuse, not that he really needed one, was that he knew in his heart that morning the bid was doomed – they had too far to go in too short a time, and the conditions were against them.

But I was more anxious about the next attempt; this one, after all, had not got to the top, and so the question of summit footage did not arise. What if, at the last moment, whoever I managed to persuade to carry and operate our camera felt as Max had felt, and left it behind? My sense of impotence was overpowering. All I could do was beg, beseech, plead – and hope.

. . . Try, Try and Try Again

Sunday 1 May to Wednesday 18 May
Camp Two/Base Camp

The next bid was already under discussion, with the advantage of the first as a recce to learn from. My diary for May Day:

Dougie and Henry Day have decided to have a rolling second bid starting next Sunday, May 8th. A whole week of waiting, and then some! First group to leave here on Wednesday. It's going to be a long and boring vigil, probably over the next two weeks. Hell's bells! And there's nothing we can do but stay here and stick it out. I can't face the walk down, and up again, for the sake of a day or so's R&R. However, I do feel our coverage of bid one and its failure is good, and will certainly make an episode. There's a lot of chat, with all the post mortems. Just need a success to round it off.

2 May. Summit party now to be only two – Merv and Steve Bell – on the 8th, and then another four the next day or the day after, and possibly a third a few days later. But I reckon we'll leave after the return of the first and second groups, and go down to Base Camp. We've all had quite enough up here.

The enforced inactivity until the climbers got back on the mountain was made worse, ironically, by excellent weather. The sun shone and the snow stayed away – ideal conditions for 'knocking the bastard off' as Dougie frequently put it. And there wasn't a single man on the mountain! Inevitably, my thoughts jumped ahead to the end of the month when, whatever the outcome, we would know what it was and be on our way back.

A plan hatched some time back was coming to fruition: our wives and girlfriends were to fly out to Kathmandu to spend a week or so with us, while we put our feet up and indulged in whatever luxuries Kathmandu could offer. Several of the lads' wives were coming out as well, and the prospect for all of us was understandably enticing.

The plan for the 'recovery' from the Rongbuk Glacier was

necessarily well advanced: the yaks have to be ordered in good time, as do the CMA trucks which were to take us back over the route they had brought us along at the beginning of March. Adding to the need for fixed dates was a decision by members of the Higher Management Committee to come not just to Kathmandu to welcome the expedition back, but to the Friendship Bridge on the border between Tibet and Nepal. I could not imagine all that 'top brass' in the squalor and chaos of Tatopani, but at least it meant we all now knew the day to set our sights on – 23 May. By great good fortune Vicky, together with Nick's wife, Annie, and Al's wife, Andrea – poor Ian's Lynn was too pregnant to make the flight – had been booked on a plane for that very day. The news came by letters, arriving on 3 May.

Spent the whole morning reading and re-reading my letters. Great! Also, on top of news from home, confirmation from Dougie that we shall be in the first group crossing to Nepal on 22nd May, and that the girls will arrive on 23rd May at Kathmandu Airport. All excellent news and very cheering prospect. It makes the intervening time somehow more bearable – at the moment! Although no doubt there will be plenty of frustrating days. But the end is in sight, a light at the end of the tunnel.

In the absence of any filming, we sat discussing endlessly the ins and outs of the journey back and our reunion with 'the girls'. The major open question was whether we could reach Kathmandu on the Monday evening, 23 May. The lads were all to camp at Tatopani after the official meeting on the Friendship Bridge, and carry on to Kathmandu the following morning. And before we even got to the bridge, we had the long drive from Xegar to the frontier, the double hurdle of customs with all our film gear, and the final obstacle of a massive landslip between Tatopani and Kathmandu. Five miles of road had disappeared.

It wasn't looking good, even allowing for the summer time three-and-a-quarter hour time difference in our favour between Chinese and Nepalese time. We plotted out the day, estimated the hold-up at the customs, calculated the duration of the walk – even the run – through the road block, and the more we did our sums, the more hopeless it looked. It now seems a little absurd to have been so obsessive – what difference would one more day make after more than a hundred? But at the time, out there on the glacier in Tibet, it seemed of paramount importance to get to Kathmandu as fast as we possibly could. And yet we knew there was nothing we could do to speed things up. In the end we either would, or more likely would not, make it through on the Monday.

The snow returned for a couple of days, holding up progress as before. But on 5 May the weather picked up and the tri-nation expedition got to the top. Our second summit team watched their first summit team from Camp Two.

MERV Their top camp is about eight thousand five hundred metres, it's about five hundred metres or less from the summit. See the three tents, three orange dome tents. The wind is screaming and one of the tents is inverting all the time in the wind.

DOUGIE Look, they're there. Slap bang on the skyline, you know, where the North Ridge joins the North East Ridge, just dissect the line from the summit to the North East Ridge. Can you see them?

MERV Well, Dougie, in a few days' time . . .

DOUGIE Yep, four days and we'll be in the same excitement as they are, no doubt. I'm absolutely delighted, I must say, for them, and indeed for us, because, as I say, it does mean that the snow conditions and the wind and so on are tolerable.

MERV But when you think they've been planning for two to three months now, they stated the date, a week ago they stated the time, and to the minute the guy stands on top, that's a good performance! And in those conditions it's not easy. When you look up there and see that spindrift coming across, it must be doing sixty miles an hour. They're clawing their way right along the top now.

DOUGIE You'll be the next ones on top.

MERV No problems.

DOUGIE Well, it's quite a thrill, actually, isn't it, to see that? It's a real boost.

MERV I reckon you'd probably be able to see them, if somebody was on the top now, you'd be able to see them clearly.

DOUGIE Well, I put my telescope on just now and I couldn't. I suppose there's just too much spindrift in the way . . .

They had disappeared over the brow or into the blown snow, some yards short of their goal. This raised a new worry for me – what if our lads were similarly to disappear, eluding the reach of our telephoto lens? Not only might we have no Video-8 at the summit, we might not even get long-distance film of it either!

But now, at last, our own second attempt was getting underway. My diary for 5 May:

After a somewhat wakeful night, very cold again and clear, the sun came back, and with it the resolve to get moving. So, a busy morning filming everyone packing up and getting off. Sixteen altogether going up to Camp Three or Camp Four today. The Six Sherpas to Camp Four plus Henry and John Vlasto from Camp Three, and the rest to Camp Three. The next four summiteers arrived at Camp Two to go up tomorrow. Everybody, including us, far more cheerful and positive, and, as last time, a real sense of anticipation and occasional emotion as they left. I'm delighted. I think some of the stuff this morning should be good, and purely psychologically it's great to be making the series again rather than sitting around in the cold getting depressed.

6 May. Despite more snow overnight, everyone moved on up. Sherpas to Camp Five with loads, and back to Camp Two perhaps tonight. Merv and Steve to Camp Four; Nigel, Johnny, Luke and Richard, Camp Two to Camp Three. Filmed four summiteers before leaving. Fairish – Richard Pelly was good. Send-off as usual. Weather, bright and sunny in the morning, deteriorating as usual again in the afternoon.

To fill in the time until they were all high enough to make it worth filming them, I decided to walk over to the Lhola with Al Evans and the camera. From the top of the pass, really a col between the West Shoulder of Everest and neighbouring Khumbutse, one can see down into the Khumbu Glacier and Nepal. It proved to be the expected exhausting haul, especially carrying the tripod. But it was worth it for the sheer grandeur of the views both ways. The dreaded Khumbu icefall lay below us, a giant-sized stream of white icing left to dry out and crack. Beyond it was the southern tri-nation Base Camp, like a town compared to our tiny hamlet.

Everest looked quite different from here. I had grown so accustomed to the twin-stepped silhouette from Camp Two that it was disconcerting to see the summit almost obliterated by the end of the West Shoulder, which itself looked far steeper end-on than it did in profile. The abstract formations in the glacier were fascinating – Daliesque slashes in glistening white fabric, cubist sculptures in granite and basalt, and Henry Moore holes in towering pinnacles of blue-green ice.

Our little Camp Two, down on the glacier, looked like a child's toy. Indeed, the spectacular scale of the panorama reduced man to midget and less. Once again, I felt the mountains ridiculing our efforts, as careless of our fate as we would be treading accidentally on an ant. Reason told me to stop anthropomorphizing, but in a land-scape of these dimensions and grandeur, reason comes a poor second to gut reactions. I left the Lhola chastened and subdued, but quickly found my conscious mind fully occupied with the scalding heat as I crossed the reflective bowl of snow. Although cold is a more common complaint on Everest, it is easy to feel like a chip in boiling oil. The sun cuts fiercely through the thin atmosphere, and the glaring whiteness of the snow bounces back its burning rays. There are recorded instances of sun-burn on the inside roofs of climbers' mouths as they pant, lips apart, across a glacier. And we all suffered cracked and blistered noses and lips, despite the constant application of total sun-block glacier cream.

8 May. And a real downer. Despite all the hopes and expectations of today, by 4 o'clock, as last time, it was obvious it was no go for this attempt. So the two advance summiteers, Merv and Steve, their support group and the four back-up summiteers all turned round and are on their way down. Disaster. And there will be a third go in about a week. So Alan and I will pack up and head off tomorrow, with the dreadful possibility of coming up again, and being delayed for leaving. Haven't felt so depressed, for all these reasons, in the whole trip. Very bad for the film, as the third go is a long shot given the conditions, and it was snow conditions that stopped them today. The only hope is that days of good weather will improve things around the Hornbein Couloir. Some hope! And it all looked so good only this morning. Christ, what a bastard! The sum-up is, via Dougie Keelan: 'The mountain's not in climbing nick by this route.' Well, that covers a multitude of disappointments. Ironically, it's been beautiful weather down here, if a bit breezy. The old currant bun's still shining at 6.30 as I write, a rare occasion. It doesn't brighten my feelings, though, or anyone else's. I feel desperately sorry for Merv and Steve and the other four, and Dougie. The only guy who might benefit from all this is Dave Nicholls, who's up here in case. Poor sods, especially Dougie, who now sees the possibility of failure staring him in the face.

9 May. Would have been summit day! But in the event a tremendously gusty wind from half way through the night. And they had planned to get off at

4 a.m. Merv had even bet me a half pint of beer they'd be on top by 1 o'clock, lunchtime. Despite the wind blowing spindrift against the tent like a sand-blasting machine, the sun brightened the morning and we did a bit with Dougie and Henry in our pink tent about the selection of the final four – Dave Nicholls and Al McCleod – a second shot for both of them – and Henry Day and Luke. So Henry has got his chance at last!

Then, packing again and off to Camp One, an exhausting but not unpleasant walk. Overtaken by Johnny Garratt, who stopped for a cigarette and riled against Henry's inclusion and thus his exclusion, and the organization in general. Why had Camp Six not been installed first? Why was bid two a carbon copy of bid one, writ larger? It seemed to me he had a point. I remember Dougie telling me just after the first bid that the one thing they would do was put in Camp Six before the summit team arrived there.

As everyone arrived at Camp One, called up from Base Camp and down from the hill, to total twenty-odd by the end of the evening and threaten, unsuccessfully thank God, the sanctity of my tent, it became clear there was massive disagreement with Dougie's choice and plan for bid three. But Dougie stuck to his guns as regards personnel, if not tactics, and retired to bed, leaving Merv, Dave Nicholls, Simon Lowe et al in the twelve-by-twelve, arguing furiously. Even Luke got a basting as the fourth man, but Henry took the brunt of it. I went to bed by 12, leaving them to it.

10 May. Dougie called a briefing at 10.30 and put his case, quite well. There ensued long discussion and argument as to dates, back-up equipment, back-up team, timings and logistics, and who would be in which support group, carrying oxygen, or putting in Camp Six and rope fixing. I packed again, and for the first time tried the 'middle route' down. Far better, if rather a lot of boulder-hopping. Met Laurie Skuodas and Lincoln Rowe on the way up, also very critical of Dougie in general over the summit attempts' planning. So there's virtually no one at Base Camp except Max and his frozen toes. Base Camp now a warmer and much more pleasant place, both Advance Base and here now almost devoid of snow. ABC has a puddle in the middle which is, I guess, the lake of its other name. The frozen snow at Base Camp has largely dried up and shrunk. Spring or maybe even summer has arrived.

Weighed myself on a hanging balance – a hundred and fifty-six pounds in clothes and boots. So without them, I'm now well under eleven stone. Ian is even less, and was over thirteen, as was I.

Dougie Keelan down here too, and washed and changed is a different man despite all the criticism rolling around. His decisions made, he can now only

*wait and hope for good weather, and he was in an expansive mood. We talked
about the series, the difference it would make if the expedition failed, and
Charlie Hattersley's attack on me and television in general this morning –
'Superficial, parasitical, uncreative'.*

*Rod Caird, on the phone, had stressed the impact of Japanese TV's live
pics from the summit. But what can we do if the lads won't take the Video-8
up there? Also a nine minute and very enjoyable chat with Vicky. She seems
in good fettle and looking forward to the trip out here. I still can't wait for the
23rd, now less than a fortnight, and away from Camp Two life does seem
more tolerable. Woke up wide awake at 5 a.m. and decided to write this,
which would have been impossible higher up. Although chilly, it's certainly
not freezing in the tent, which is a marked change. Tomorrow, well, it's today
now, we'll have to sort out who goes up again for the final bid. Perhaps all of
us, although I'd be delighted to avoid it and the long slog there and back. We'll
see.*

Life at Base Camp was now almost enjoyable. Wind permitting, I
even got in the occasional sunbathe. I was luckier, or just more careful
of the sun's intensity, than Steve Bell. Doing the same at ABC, stark
naked, he burned his buttocks badly, and put himself out of the
running for any more mountaineering on this expedition. But it was
no great loss – he had had his chance alongside Merv, until the attempt
was aborted.

We finally caught up with Lincoln Rowe, the expedition artist, who
had succeeded in getting his visa some time before, but had always
managed to be in a camp we weren't in. We wandered off across the
Rongbuk Glacier with him, as he picked a spot to site his easel, and as
soon as he put pencil to paper, interrupted his inspiration with our
questions.

MARK Do you ever use photographs, and if not, why not? It seems
slightly perverse to be out here with a brown crayon in these days of
advanced photographic techniques?

LINCOLN Well, maybe, but I don't use photographs. Partly as a matter
of principle, and partly because they really don't give you much
information. I think people really want a personal look at something,
and the difference between the two, really, is the time element. What
I'm doing, just now, is watching the mountain and absorbing the
changes in the light and the atmosphere over a great period of time,
and the painting itself is an accumulation of that experience. And

likewise, when I'm back in the studio in England, I work from drawings such as these, using Conté, and when I draw, it's the recall, I can reproduce virtually any kind of light or atmosphere that I want to. I can impose a change on the subject which a photographer can't do. I can move things around and so on. And I think, at the end of a day's work, I've got a much more powerful image, a much more composed kind of image, and a much more personal view.

MARK Do you ever do figures, or are you really a landscape artist only?

LINCOLN I've done all sorts of things in the past. I'm quite happy using any medium for any subject matter. But occasionally I use figures, in landscapes, just to give scale. I mean, for example, something like this – it's just so vast, so huge, that you can't have any idea of how big it is unless you've got something to scale it by. So a few tiny figures, perhaps coming out of a tent or climbing along a ridge. It's just something that gives it that little extra bit of zap.

MARK What about the costs? Do you have to actually pay for your expenses as part of the expedition?

LINCOLN I do, like all the other team members. I contribute my share towards the costs – five hundred pounds. But it was decided that my contribution, by way of sponsorship, would be in the commitment to the work, and the expedition getting the use of the exhibition I hope to have at the end of the day. But on top of that, I've bought all my own equipment, art equipment and so on. And of course, it isn't a commission, in the sense that it's non-remunerative. So my only return is from the work that I actually produce on the expedition. Which is again why this last month and a half stuck in Kathmandu has been a bit of a blow. But it's a cracking day today, and I'm going to make the most of the next two weeks up here . . .

The evenings of those few days of relaxation before the third and final bid were often enlivened by the Famous Grouse. Trivial Pursuit was resurrected, and on this occasion I'm glad to say Granada did a little better, but was still just beaten. It's amazing how frequently we knew the answers to the climbers' questions! The game gave way to another discussion of the series, but I think it was an indication of Dougie's growing confidence that the usual doubts were never raised, and we talked instead about the music that might be most effective, Dougie insisting that emotion and mood were everything, that we should avoid being too factual and narrative and that we should, above all, go for the 'feel' of the experience. I was almost forced to play devil's advocate, and argue that this was a *documentary* series, that it had to tell a story, that while one impressionistic half-hour might tickle an audience's fancy, a series of them would meet with a mass switchover to another channel. But I was delighted with both the tone and thrust of Dougie's and the others' thoughts. The end result would, I felt sure, need to be a combination of techniques and approaches, to work at its best. But, as I write, this has yet to be resolved in the Manchester editing rooms.

Before Dougie left Base Camp to supervise the final bid from Camp Two, whither we would have to follow him shortly, I capitalized on the previous evening's *bonhomie*, and asked him for a retrospective interview intended to lead into the last-ditch attempt on the summit. Sitting in the middle of the valley with Everest towering over his left shoulder, Dougie dealt with my questions thoughtfully and honestly.

MARK I don't know whether you expected it, but there was quite a bit of criticism of your choice of the final summit four, and in particular of one member. Do you have anything to say about that?

DOUGIE No, and I stand by my selection of all four of them. I only heard comment about one, and I'm reassured that people did comment, one or two of them anyway, did see fit to come to me and have a word and say, look, I'm not too happy about that. But time will tell. It's not appropriate to go into people's backgrounds and so on at a time like this, but I stand by my judgments on that, and we'll see what happens.

MARK Do you think the plan as it now stands, and its modifications from previous attempts, covers every eventuality?

DOUGIE No, of course it doesn't. How can it? There are so many imponderables in the high Himalaya, particularly on the top of Everest, that you can't possibly cover them all. All you can do is set yourself up as best you can, giving yourself a fair and safe chance, and hope it will all go well. One of the imponderables, of course, is the weather. We can't possibly cope with the snow conditions or the fact that the night before there might have been a six-inch dump of snow up there which would make it very unsafe, as indeed happened on the second bid. I believe that we've got a balanced team, we've got a very strong support team, we've placed the oxygen and the food, and the camps are now well stocked, which has been the effort of the last three

46. During the summit bids: while Dougie maintains radio contact, Nick and Al take a break from filming the minute figures up on the mountain.

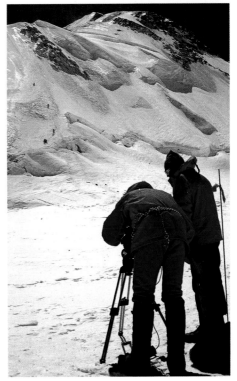

47. From the foot of the French Spur, the ascent appears artificially laid back after the initial climb.

48. Nick and Al pulling the camera rucksack
up the French Spur ...

49. ... to film the lads crossing the 'bergschrund'.

50. Al on top of the West Ridge above Camp Four, with Nuptse in the background.

51. Oxygen was used at Camp Four and above – Al with sleeping mask in the snow hole.

52. It was very difficult to operate the camera with gloves on – but you couldn't leave them off for too long.

53. Al warming up again in the snow hole, with Merv Middleton to raise his spirits.

54. All dressed up and *somewhere* to go: Terry Moore.

55. Looking back along the West Ridge past Camp Five from the Diagonal Ditch.

56. Looking up the Diagonal Ditch.

57. Dave Nicholls in the Hornbein Couloir.

58. Leaving Camp Two for the last time:
Nick kept going on the glacier ...

59. ... while I stopped for a cigarette.

60. Another day, another cigarette – at the East Rongbuk river between ABC and Base Camp. The solid ice of March was melting in May.

61. At Pang La, the final photo-call – and a much warmer one than on the way in.

62. Filming the last shot. Our Base Camp may be half demolished, but Everest impassively awaits the next expedition. '... representing, as it does, so many memories, so many mixed emotions and physical extremes, it is a view I shall never forget.'

or four days, and we've kitted and coped for all that we reasonably and realistically can. But there's always, to coin a phrase, the fuck-up factor, and you just can't cater for that. I hope we'll be successful and I'm confident we will.

MARK I don't in any sense want to be depressing, but if the worst happens, how much will it matter to you personally if this expedition fails?

DOUGIE By failing, you mean not getting to the top?

MARK Yes.

DOUGIE Well, it would be a blow, of course. I should be very disappointed, because we've got thirty-six excellent climbers, and behind them not just the Defence Establishment but all sorts of people, in all sorts of walks of life. And there are all the sponsors – they will be disappointed, but they will be disappointed for our sake, I suspect. I can to some extent temper my disappointment if that happens – in other words, if we don't get up on this bid – by consoling myself with the thought that we will have done our best. I don't believe that any other expedition could have done better. We've worked extremely hard – if we added up the number of pounds of weight that people have lost slogging up and down those slopes, that indeed would be an indicator. But the fact of life is that Mount Everest is never easy, particularly by this West Ridge route, which is one of the hardest routes on Everest. The fact of life is that in certain conditions it's unclimbable safely and sensibly, and I believe to date all our operational mountain decisions have been sensible. So I can console myself with that, and I console myself also with the thought that we'll have counted everybody out and everybody in.

MARK You've taken me exactly to my last question. It seems to me that perhaps a civilian expedition might have taken greater risks – might even have risked human life. Where do you draw the line between the taking of risk and the achieving of success on the top of the mountain?

DOUGIE That's a very hard question to answer, actually almost an impossible one. You intrinsically take a risk by setting foot on the lower slopes of Mount Everest, let alone on those higher, bleak, dangerous slopes towards the top. It's a sort of calculated judgement all the way along. In other words, it's the balance of probability of survival – it's as simple as that. When the group on the second bid got to that snowfield and stopped, they made the operational judgement, which I supported entirely, that the snow slope was unsafe and that there was a greater chance of it avalanching and killing them than there was in their getting across safely. It's a dividing line, and very difficult to generalize . . .

On 15 May three days before the intended date for the final assault, we were on our way up again – Nick and I to Camp Two; Al and Ian to Camp One – to get maximum coverage of this make-or-break bid. Whether it was the effect of the now-familiar climb up the valley, or the feeling that the die was cast and I had no cards to play, my diary records a sense of irresponsibility shocking as I read it now, a month or two later.

15 May. Will film the 1800 radio call in case Merv reports Hornbein Couloir impassable and Dougie calls it all off. I'm appalled at my total insouciance. I know I'll regret it later, but I'm powerless to affect the outcome, and I've had it up to the ears with Big E. Any definite decision would be welcome. And it would, with luck, avoid my walking up to Camp Two, although that's not really a factor. Wait and see, it could be all over and a failure in an hour's time.

But it wasn't, quite. Merv will make one more sortie early tomorrow and report to Dougie at 9. Meanwhile, the summit group will stay at Camp Four for an extra day until the way is clear – if it is. We should all know by 9 o'clock or 1300 latest, and the signs aren't that good. Strange atmosphere amongst the lads at Camp One, all playing Botticelli, joking, watching videos and the film Mona Lisa, and seeming, every one, not to care or give a shit about the situation, with the one exception of Pat Parsons.

But by the next day, I had partially recovered my enthusiasm.

16 May. Well, all change with the 0900 radio call, which we covered half-heartedly in the cold, Nick having had a rather sleepless night. Merv and group progressing to put in Camp Six. Eventually they all but got there, a hundred and fifty metres short, and returned to Camp Five, where the summit four arrived from Camp Four. So tomorrow they go up to Camp Six, put up the tents etc, and make their bid on Wednesday 18th. Finally, Nick and I set off to Camp Two again, having heard on the 1300 radio call that Merv etc. were getting on well, and virtually to the Hornbein Couloir. It was devastating – the sun was hot, our loads seemed heavier and heavier, and the path across the boulders, mud-on-ice, rocks etc, quite terrible. Arrived 5-ish to find Camp Two much depleted – only four tents – and we both to sleep in our pink Granada tent. It's bloody cold this evening, but that's good for up the hill, so never mind. Gaslight and cooker both flat out to provide some heat, and the prospect of returning on Wednesday – only forty-eight hours! – after the summit success (or failure) some encouragement. Thank God, and fingers crossed. What a change of mood and expectation since last night. We could still be in there with a success.

I did not know it at the time, but Terry Moore, up at Camp Five with Merv Middleton, was to pass the time waiting for the sum-miteers' return by interviewing Merv on one of our Video-8 cameras. Terry asked how the support group had got on.

MERV We pushed out, me and Terry Moore, and got away just before seven as dawn broke over the North Col – a beautiful sight, one of the best sights in the world. But so, so cold, the coldest I've ever been in my life. My feet are frostbitten, not badly though, and my fingers are still tingling as I sit and wait up here at Camp Five. We pushed out into that Couloir, but the snow was so deep – calf- to knee-deep – and I wasn't carrying a load except for a full bottle of oxygen, while the guys coming up the steps I was making behind me were carrying two or three bottles – thirty or forty pounds. It was just push, push, push, push. It just hit everyone at the same time, we'd fixed new rope up to about eight thousand one hundred and fifty metres, and we just ran out of steam. We looked at each other, all realizing it was going to be the biggest effort of our lives just getting back to Camp Five that night . . .

So I came up on the radio and said the height we were at, eight thousand one hundred and fifty, was as far as we could go. That was it. It was very much an ultimatum, an ultimatum the summit team back here at Five accepted. They had to accept it, but they accepted it gracefully.

The support team, all of us, were absolutely on our last legs – we just lay comatose when we got here, for twenty-four hours, on oxygen.

I think the assault team realized what we in the support team had done when they set off the next day, up the trench through the snow, on and on and up and up, I think they realized the work that had gone into it, and respected it . . .

My diary picks up the story.

17 May. Brilliant and hot start to the day but usual clag [cloud cover] built up around lunchtime and by 3 or 4 snowing, not too heavily, the sun still filtering through. All progressing OK up the hill. Main drama at 2.30-ish, missed on camera, when Henry suddenly announced he was turning round and giving in. Now, he's supposed to get back to Camp Five, but cloud covers the hill and we can't see. No doubt people down the hill feel he's got his comeuppance, and wasted a place on the summit four. Still, he sounded wretched – I hope he gets back OK.

Merv Middleton, still waiting at Camp Five for the return of Dave Nicholls and the now depleted summit team, was the first man to set eyes on Henry Day.

MERV Henry Day arrived back here absolutely chinstrapped. I think he was about five minutes' walking off the point of total collapse. We'd seen him coming for about half an hour, stumbling and falling. Eventually he arrived and just collapsed outside the tent for about twenty minutes, waving us away whenever we tried to help him. We got him to take a brew – a hot orange – and then he managed to speak. I said, 'What went wrong?' – initially we had heard it was oxygen, but I instinctively knew it wasn't because there was a cache of five bottles available to him – so anyway, I said, 'You're absolutely shagged, mate.' He turned and looked at me, and said, 'Those boys are in a different league from me' – insinuating that he was absolutely blown. And looking at his condition today – all this was yesterday – he's still . . . I mean, he's still the walking dead . . .

18 May. Third and final summit day. Awake early and listening to radio calls. Weather bad, sleety snow and high winds. Merv reported 40-mile-an-hour gusts at Camp Five, and summit pair got off about 8 a.m., leaving Luke to return to Camp Five and down, as he couldn't go on by himself. The tone of the radio calls fairly low-key, lacking total enthusiasm from Dave and Al. And Dougie in awkward position of not being able to ask them to take unnecessary risks.

Merv knew there was more to Luke's abandoning the bid than met the eye. Luke had been close to the summit on Shisha Bangma, and made the decision to turn back. Now he had been within striking distance of the summit of Everest, and had left others to go for it. It didn't make sense.

MERV Three is never a compatible number – the pressure is always on the third guy. There was Dave Nicholls and his partner, big Al McLeod; then there was Luke, with his partner, Henry Day, gone. So the emphasis is on the third guy to prove himself. And Henry had left with one of the two cookers, with visions of bivvying out or some such. So he'd taken a cooker, and no one had thought to take it off him. Very, very easy to do at eight thousand metres – oxygen starvation, you don't think rationally . . .

Then they had to erect two tents. The summit tents are tiny, big enough for two at the most. So that doubled the workload that night before, digging out a space for two tents. They must have been looking at Luke, wondering, 'Why is this guy here still? He's a problem . . .'

So you'd got three guys, two tents, and one cooker. It doesn't work. So they had to split their options, two guys use the cooker and leave early, leaving the third guy to follow on later . . .

They made the only decision they could. The only decision, to my mind, that would have been even correcter – I know that's bad grammar – would have been for the leader, Dave Nicholls, to have said to Luke Hughes, yesterday, 'I'm sorry, mate, but you're out of it. Help dig us in, and then you'll have to go.' And that's the cold, hard logic. But they took the gentleman's way out, and the three of them stayed. What happened was inevitable . . .

Then Luke arrived here, having had five or six hours to resign himself to his fate, that he wasn't going to be a successful ascendant. I think half his chirpiness was because at least he was doing something. He arrived here in good spirits, a smile on his face, and it was bloody good to see. He'd had a hard two days, he'd got a bit lost, alone on the ropes in very dangerous conditions, and I think he was bloody glad to see two faces here, expecting him. He had a couple of brews, and a scoff later, and was a changed man . . .

If Luke was putting a brave face on his feelings, at least his physical problems were over. All he had to do now was to escort his exhausted erstwhile partner, Henry, down to the safety of Camp Two – which he eventually did. But for Dave Nicholls and Al McLeod, Everest was still there to be conquered, and they knew all too well that it was them – or no one.

So did Dougie. He had joined Nick and me in our pink tent, both because it was marginally more spacious than his and, more importantly, so that we could film him as he followed Dave's and Al's progress on the radio intercom. We could see nothing up on the mountain, thanks to the worsening weather. I can do no better than let the story tell itself.

DOUGIE The choice is yours, Dave. I mean, if you're going well, you're well up on time, it seems to me, and as long as you think you're in with a reasonable chance for the top, with a safe return, my advice would be to continue. But please feel under no pressure from here at all. You're the man on the spot, and whatever you do we'll support you. Over.

DAVE Thanks very much. We'll have a bite to eat and a drink here, and I'll have a chat with Al and I'll come back to you. Roger and out . . .

Time passed, and the radio crackled back into life.

DAVE It's pretty uncomfortable up here, with all the snow on the rocks, and it's building up. But I think we'll probably give it another hour and then take stock and have another look. Over.

DOUGIE OK, Dave, fine. Just let me try and establish where you are. You were at the top of the Couloir – have you gone through the zig-zags yet? Over.

DAVE No. No, we have to do the zig-zags yet. Over.

DOUGIE Right. So we've got you with the crux just in front of you? Over.

DAVE Chowang was saying, you know, keep out to the right and then go back left again where the snow is. I was intending to have a look at that, rather than sort of go waltzing up. This looks like quite a steep pitch. Over.

DOUGIE OK, Dave, fine. Well, we're behind you as ever and we'll talk in about an hour. Over.

DAVE Yes. I find it strange about Merv's comments, you know, it's clear on his side of the mountain, and yet it's snowing on this side and has been since we set out almost. Over . . .

Merv was still keeping a waiting watch in support at Camp Five, which was located just under the summit pyramid, and occasionally in the lee of the howling wind.

DOUGIE Well, it's not clear now. He came on just now and said it's far from clear, and it's blowing quite hard down with them. Also perhaps the North Face was protected in the beginning, but obviously where you are that's not quite so. Over.

DAVE Yes, that's the case. Over.

DOUGIE OK, Dave, fine. We'll remain here and see how you get on. Over.

DAVE OK, Dougie. Roger and out . . .

Base Camp then came on the radio, having not received the last transmission, and asked Dougie for a progress report. Dougie gave it.

DOUGIE Dave Nicholls called half an hour ago, three-quarters of an hour ago, and said they'd stopped for a break. They were going quite well, they were at the top of the Hornbein Couloir, but with the snow they were a little hesitant. Anyway, they're going on for another hour, which should be for another half-hour or so from now, and then I'll get a call again. The weather here at Camp Two is just awful, it's sort of raining and sleeting, and at Camp Five it's been snowing amazingly hard. So all in all, things aren't looking too good. Over.

KEITH HUNTER (at Base) I got most of that, Dougie. There's little I can say. Over . . .

There was another long pause, during which Dougie, Nick and I exchanged not a single word. And then Dave Nicholls came back.

DAVE Dougie, I'm afraid the news up here is bad. It's bloody awful weather up here, really snowing and blowing a hooly. We've had about five inches. I'm in the middle of the crux at the moment, and things just don't look good. Over.

DOUGIE Well, it has to be your decision, Dave. If you can get back down now . . .

Dave, in his anxiety, forgot or ignored radio-call discipline, and cut in mid-sentence.

DAVE I'm desperately disappointed, but all my mountaineering wisdom is telling me, and in fact before I started on the crux, it's telling me to go down. But I said, bugger it, we'll go on and have a look. I saw a bit of sun coming through but, you know, the snow's just piling up more and more now, and I can't see how it's worth taking the risk. You know, if we go by that forecast that we had before, it'll get even worse. So in terms of mountain sense, I can't see any way out of this. Over.

DOUGIE No, I think that's true. I do see your disappointment after everybody's efforts, but sanity must decree that you get down in one piece. OK, David, we'll call it off. You do your best to get back in one piece. Over.

DAVE I would dearly love to go on, if I could see any way of going on, but I just think we're risking too much if we do. And to think yesterday we'd have been up. Over.

DOUGIE Yes, but you know . . . you can't win 'em all. Over.

DAVE Well, we'll go as carefully as we can. It's going to be bloody tricky getting back down, I assure you that much. When I get back to Six. I'll let you know. My intention will be to get back to Five eventually. Over.

PAT PARSONS (ignoring the rules again in the heat of the moment) Dave never mind the bloody mountain, mate – you just get down in one piece and take it easy. Out.

MERV (at Camp Five) Hello, David Nicholls. Just look after yourself, mate. We've got a welcome here when you get down.

DOUGIE Roger, OK, out to you. Hello Base, over.

BASE Hello, Base here. Over.

DOUGIE Keith, you will have heard that. That's it, I'm afraid. Everybody has done their best, but sanity must prevail and to continue in these conditions at this time of day would be really being stupid, would be putting the lead two's necks right on the block. Quite rightly, the decision has been made, without any demurring, to come back down. It's a pity and it *is* a disappointment, but we can live with that because everyone has done their best. Had we had yesterday's weather today, I have no doubt we would be putting two people on top in the next two or three hours. Over.

KEITH Couldn't agree more, Dougie. Over . . .

The abject disappointment in Keith's tone of voice spoke volumes. But it could not compete with the tone of voice of Dave Nicholls, twice leader of a summit bid, and twice unsuccessful. When he reached Camp Five later that day, his beard thick with frozen snow, he spoke to Terry behind the Video-8 camera.

DAVE I was close to tears. I was, really. It was a terrible decision. This was our last chance – we'd spent what? – three months' worth of effort out here and two years' worth of planning, we'd raised a quarter of a million quid for this thing, all to get on the top. And our final, final effort was to get two, just two, up there. And then to have to say 'We're going to have to go back' – a dreadful decision to make . . .

Five thousand feet below where Dave spoke those words, and almost 8,000 feet below the crux at the top of the Hornbein Couloir, where he had earlier taken the decision to turn back, Dougie, Nick and I sat in our tent. The radio was now silent; it had carried its message from near the summit down through all the camps. Dougie put down the intercom and there was a long pause before he turned to me and spoke.

DOUGIE Why, why did we have to have weather like this today? We couldn't keep them up there, we couldn't delay it another day, we'd delayed it one day already to get the stocking right up at Six. *Why* did we have to have this weather, today of all days? It's done for us, at least as far as the summit is concerned.

MARK Yes. All that effort that everyone put in, all your planning; such a tragedy.

DOUGIE Well, it's not a tragedy yet, it won't be a tragedy in human terms, I hope. We've been sensible, and our planning has been without fault, our judgement I think has been without fault. But at the end of the day, when you're on the world's highest mountain, if the elements are against you there is not a lot you can do actually, and if you look at the two that are up there, you know, Dave Nicholls and Al McLeod, I mean they are both in their separate ways extremely competent mountaineers in a technical sense and in experience, and both have climbed the North Face of the Eiger so both are fit, both have mountaineering as their main supreme hobby and both have been going extremely well throughout the expedition. I don't believe you'll find anybody else who's prepared to take more risks, more justified risks than those two.

Where do we go from here? Well, I don't think we need to put a brave face on it, because our performance speaks for itself. We've done our best, and it's been a pretty good best, I think. At the eleventh hour here, we've been defeated by this atrocious weather which you can hear beating on this tent now . . .

It was almost one o'clock, five in the morning back in Britain. And now it was over – eighty-nine days of slog and smiles, sun and snow, all for this outcome. I had a large lump in my throat and had only just managed to put a few questions to Dougie. He had answered ably enough. No doubt he had met greater challenges and greater danger in his time as a Royal Marine, but surely he cannot have experienced greater disappointment. Dougie's face was a study of a man cheated by fate, and my heart went out to him as we sat huddled in the pink tent with the sleet still thrashing on the nylon. Nick obviously felt the same as I – when Dougie stopped speaking, he put the camera down, reached out to lay a hand on Dougie's shoulder, and said: 'Well, it may not have ended the way we all dreamed. But there's no doubt it's been the greatest experience of my life.'

I echoed his every word, but could not, at that instant, speak. Dougie looked at each of us in turn, and a rare and precious moment of unspoken sympathy united the three of us. Graciously, Dougie said: 'Thank you, Nick. It's been a real pleasure for me, having you all as part of our team. I know your disappointment is as great as any of the expedition members'.'

I'm sure he was right; and not, I can honestly say, because the series would lack a triumphant finale – that realization came only later. It was quite simply that all the preparation and individual effort of fifty-two men, each in his own sphere, had come to naught.

But had it? Was the summit the only goal? Almost immediately, I, who had carped and complained incessantly about the hardships, felt deep down that it had all been worthwhile. I may not have enjoyed it, but I knew I would not have missed it for the world. That instinctive reaction to the initial telephone call, back before Christmas, had been correct. I had seen sights few human beings have been privileged to see; I had done what I would not have thought myself capable of doing; and I had learnt about myself and my fellow men. Experience is a wonderful teacher – and as Nick so aptly put it, there is no doubt that this expedition, with all its trials and tribulations, had been the experience of a lifetime.

Back to the World

Thursday 19 May to Monday 23 May
Camp Two/Kathmandu

And now we were on our way home. Gathering our gear together, we packed our rucksacks and trudged down across the glacier for the last time. As planned, by the time we arrived at Advance Base Camp, Alan and Ian had left for Base Camp to film the reactions there and start the process of packing our twenty-nine boxes of equipment. My diary is curtly matter of fact.

19 May. Everyone pretty sanguine about the failed attempt. The 'bad weather' line not universally accepted by any means, but none the less, the result is a fait accompli. Could call the last episode Whether Weather. Staying at Camp One today and will go on down to Base Camp tomorrow.

That Friday, Nick and I finished the packing of the film gear at Camp One ready for the yaks to carry down, and set off for Base Camp. Nick was going like a train, and I soon suggested he carry on ahead. I was in reflective mood and preferred the prospect of wandering down in my own time, alone. As I walked, I looked for small pieces of the different rocks that littered the glacier, to take back as mementoes. But, as my eyes sought out the orange, the black, the green-and-grey fragments, my mind tried to make some sense of my conflicting emotions. I was delighted, there can be no doubt, to be walking down to Base Camp for the very last time, in the certain knowledge that I would never again do the arduous climb in the opposite direction. Yet already there was a creeping nostalgia for 'Big E', as Dougie was wont to call the massive mountain, now, step by step, receding into the distance behind me. I was desperately looking forward to Kathmandu, Vicky, a real shower and a good meal. But would I miss the close camaraderie of the last three months?

On the last day at Base Camp there was a good example of the tightrope relationship between us, the film crew, and them, the lads.

159

There was a party atmosphere, and tongues were untied by the remaining bottles of Famous Grouse. But behind the banter there was, I like to believe, a genuine liking and respect between us, developed over the three months together on the mountain. We filmed intermittently, and Nick and Ian happened to be rolling when someone called for speeches. The cry was taken up, and I felt that the time had come to say 'thank you'. Considering the scotch we had all consumed, I was at least to be commended for my brevity – and I *did* mean what I said, however it came across on that glacier in Tibet. The transcript typist attempted to convey the mood along with the spoken word:

Someone shouting in background about making speech.
bleep
Lots of shouting and frivolity.
Someone shouts, 'We love you, Mark. We're all fond of Granada'.

MARK Thanks a lot, everyone. Thanks very much for putting up with it, and I only hope you feel that the thing we end up with justifies all the problems there have been. Yes, I'm sure you'll say: 'impossible!' But seriously, thanks.

Someone shouts, 'It's almost been a great pleasure to have you with us, mate.'
All laughing.
'Delighted.'
'Cheers, Granada, it's been a lot of fun. Yes, three cheers for Granada.'
All clapping.

MARK Well, let's hope it's all worthwhile, come November or January or whatever.

Someone says, 'Not January, we'll be in Norway! November!'

MARK Well, whenever . . . Thank you!
bleep . . .

Dougie's speech was longer and more thoughtful, befitting his role as leader. He too had taken his fair share of Famous Grouse, but his words came from his heart rather than his slightly inebriated head.

DOUGIE On an entirely personal note, if I may, please can I say that of course it is an enormous disappointment and regret and sadness that we didn't get up, but I do believe we tried as hard as we could and we were seen off on three occasions by conditions which in the main were outside our control. One can't help feeling that there was somebody up there who had it in mind that we were not going to be allowed to get up this time. But we started with thirty-six climbers and we've got thirty-six back, so that in itself is a significant achievement. Finally, I'd personally say to you please, folk, it's been an enormous privilege for me to have been appointed as your leader, to have had the response, the friendship and the willing acceptance of the sort of decision-making which from time to time it's been necessary to put out. It's an experience I shall never forget. I hope that the friendships that I've been able to make will be sustained – I feel sure they will. And I hope the friendships that you've made will be sustained. I cannot think of an expedition of this size where there has been such little bickering, such little contention, and such general co-operation and friendship. And I thank you all from my heart for all of that. Many thanks.

(All clap Dougie, shouting 'Well done'.) . . .

He summed up the expedition admirably, if not quite reflecting my own feelings towards it all, now at last emerging from the amorphous continuum of daily events. I don't expect to have made that many lasting friendships myself among the servicemen – as Luke had remarked, servicemen and media-men are two different breeds. And in his 'Thoughts on Granada' piece, Luke had identified another influence our presence exerted on the lads. . . .

LUKE There was a tendency for everyone to appear utterly, boringly, sensible. Rash actions and hotheaded decisions have little place on a mountain, but there are times when boldness is required. Risks are involved and people must be found to take them. I'm left with the lingering thought that we might have pushed the boat out further (especially on the summit bids) if there had not been the beady eye of Granada's lens recording every detail for the Great British Public, wise after the event, to judge whether the right decision had been made. Dougie, I suspect, was under far greater pressure in this respect than any of us appreciated at the time. There is a certain bitter-sweet satisfaction in knowing when to turn back on this kind of venture which is in direct proportion to how fond you are of your family. On this expedition we played very safe, more fearful than usual of what might be said if one of us failed to return.

Another result was that everyone was impressively loyal to each other when the camera was around. Four months of living together in aggressive conditions is bound to throw up tensions. Sometimes these are aired explosively, and would have made marvellous television. But there was no way the team would start griping about each other with the knowledge that the arguments would be immortalized on celluloid. That said, if any of the climbers were using the little video cameras at the higher camps in the privacy of the snow holes, indiscretion abounded. This might be considered to indicate that the loyalty was inspired less by the presence of the camera than by the presence of Granada.

I am quite sure that when the programmes are released, we will all be grateful for the recording of some sensational footage, and some memorable adventures. We may regret the absence of many of the lighter moments that should have been more part of the action. I suspect the crew were surprised at the slow pace at which everything tends to happen on a big mountain; frequently they missed opportunities to film simply because of the time it took to get the whole system set up. I'm sure our sponsors will also be grateful for the publicity the film will give them. The Services may even find recruiting figures are up for a period. But most mountaineers go on these trips to climb mountains, not to be part of massive PR exercise. When I go back to finish the job, I do not expect to be distracted from the task in hand . . .

Of one thing I am quite certain: I will not be with Luke when he goes back to finish the job. My time on Everest was over on Sunday 22 May 1988, and I was far from sorry. And yet, now I knew we had reached the end, the whole experience took on a new quality. This perception was even stronger as we waved goodbye to the rear party, whose task it was to clear Base Camp and leave the Rongbuk Glacier as we had found it three months earlier, and headed north. My diary:

22 May. Off! And at 10 a.m. Finally drove back down the track, even bumpier than I remembered. Leaving mountain behind couldn't resist looking back with mixed feelings. Three months of my life given to Everest, and what in return? Professionally, time will answer that. But personally? As Nick said, an experience, and of some weight. But affection, more intimate feelings? Difficult, but not the unalloyed relief I expected, despite what I said to the others. Knowing it was over, and we were on our way to Kathmandu, made it much easier to see the whole thing through less jaundiced eyes.

At the atrocious hotel in Xegar, in May much warmer and more acceptable than in February, I did not sleep much. Excitement, and a sudden attack of the runs, kept me up most of the night. Nick was awake too, and we chatted through the hours of darkness until it was time to leave again, thankfully at the early hour of 7 a.m. Back in our Toyota, we re-traced our journey of all but a hundred days earlier. A film run in reverse, the route brought back memories at every land-mark. On the Pang La, Nick's stone scratched with his name stood there still, while mine had disappeared; at Xegar, the patchwork quilt of fields, in February frozen and dry, were beginning to show short sprouts of green. Further on, the distant peaks of the Himalayan range stood out all the more starkly for having lost the carpet of snow that lay across the landscape in front of them. And as we embarked on the perilous descent from Nylam to the border, any fears of falling over the precipice were distracted by the exquisite pleasure of seeing our first flowers for months. The valley grew greener and greener as we dropped down, the slopes on each side feathered with luxuriant forests, and the road itself invaded by flowering bushes bearing clus-ters of yellow, puce and crimson. And the air became warmer and warmer, and damper and damper. By the time we reached Xangmu, we were all sweating in the steamy heat, a forgotten and not entirely welcome sensation.

At the Chinese customs we hit our first hurdle in our race for Kathmandu. The film and film equipment were no problem, but could they see the video tapes please? Apprehensively, we dug out some of the tiny cassettes from the cooler boxes stacked on the lorries. Faces fell: they had only a VHS player. We asked Mr Deng to explain once again that all our tapes contained only material shot on the mountain. What was their query or concern? Finally, we got to the bottom of it: rumours had reached them – how, I have no idea – that we had had pornographic movies up there on the mountain. *Clan of the Cave Bear,* I wondered, or that film *Spring Fever* about pubescent tennis stars in Florida? The customs officials were shown the pre-recorded tapes, and soon seemed reassured by their printed labels and Sony trademark. Nothing under the counter about those!

Relieved and anxiously eyeing our watches, we set off down to the Friendship Bridge, to find the top brass from the Higher Management Committee looking most un-officer-like in shorts and leisure shirts, and not on the bridge but a short walk into what was technically

Tibet. My planned sequence of a bearded and dishevelled Dougie shaking hands with the spick and span, multi-starred Generals and Air Marshals in the no-man's-land of the bridge fell flat on its face.

And so too did the camera. To shake hands with Sir John Sutton, Nick shifted the Arriflex from right hand to left, and it slipped from his perspiring palm to the concrete floor, the lens taking the initial impact. Cursing and apologizing, Nick checked it out. Disaster! The image was totally out of focus. We had filmed for three months in the most rigorous of conditions, and done no more than scratch a filter. Now, on what might well have been the last sequence we were to film, the camera collapsed on us. And all the spares were sealed in their boxes and buried on the trucks. It was obviously an omen: we were not intended to film this meeting, which by now had happened anyway, as Dougie was only minutes behind us. I was not greatly bothered – it had not panned out as I had envisaged in the first place, and it was hardly essential material.

So we crossed into Nepal and took a beer or two while the visa formalities were gone through, tapping our fingers neurotically the while. We had managed to hire transport from Tatopani to the road block, and it was still only three o'clock in Nepal, thanks to the three-hour-plus time gap. Finally, we were on our way, scattering chickens and dogs to right and left, as our rented Land Rover revved its way out to the open road. We looked at each other, we looked for the umpteenth time at our watches – we might still make it.

And then, in a village called Barabeesi, just short of the landslip, the Land Rover stalled. It resisted all attempts to revive it, so while three of us set about hiring local porters for our rucksacks, Alan set off at a run for the far end of the road block. We had been told that taxis were available for the two-hour-or-more journey to Kathmandu, but that there were no departures after five o'clock. It was half past four, and there were ten kilometres to cover. Alan was already a disappearing dot in the distance as Nick, Ian and I set off at a cracking canter, exhorting the poor porters to keep pace with us. Sweating like pigs in temperatures well into the eighties with humidity to match, we reached the end of the road block in well under an hour, even taking an enforced pause while a section of hillside en route was dynamited out of existence.

Alan had pulled it off – two little Toyota taxis awaited us, bribed with Granada funds to get to Kathmandu come what may. The porters were paid off, handsomely, and we were on the last leg. As darkness fell, and with it our first rain since leaving England, we arrived at the Summit Hotel and settled our account with the taxi drivers – six hundred rupees each, including waiting time, or about fifteen pounds. For a trip of over two hours!

While Ian announced our arrival at the desk, as the poor man had no one to greet, we walked into the hotel bar, lit only by candles as the whole of Kathmandu was having one of its customary power cuts. We saw the girls, sitting with their drinks at the far end of the room. It was a moment to savour – they had not seen us and were not expecting us this early, if at all. With three months' growth of beard, our lips cracked and blistered, our faces burnt red-raw, and our filthy and sweaty clothes hanging limp on our slimmed-down bodies, we must have looked an uninviting trio.

'Hi!'

As one, Annie, Andrea and Vicky looked up. A long, long second of incredulity passed. And the next, we were in each others' arms, embracing and then stepping back to take in the reality of the reunion. Celebrating with a bottle of duty-free wine, another first for us, we told them the story of the day. It had been a long haul, as on Chinese time it was now eleven o'clock, and we had got up at six. But it was by no means over. Two things were essential – a long shower and a good steak.

I have to say that neither quite came up to expectations, but I'm not sure that our inflated expectations could have been fulfilled. It was delicious to feel clean again from top to toe, but a shower is just a shower and I could not milk as much pure pleasure from it as I had imagined. And steaks in Kathmandu – well, let's say it's not the best place in the world for beef. I also have to say it did not matter a jot. We were back, we had suffered no major setbacks, and we had done what we had set out to do. Everything felt just wonderful.

We filmed nothing in Kathmandu. This was not due to the damaged camera – we now had access to our other cameras – but because I felt increasingly convinced that the story ended, so far as the expedition was concerned, on the mountain. On the day we left Base Camp, Everest was magnificently clear. We had filmed the lads departing in the back of the lorries, up and past camera, leaving the camp, yet to be shut down, in the foreground, and twelve miles behind it up the Rongbuk Glacier, dominating the frame as it had in so many previous shots we had taken – Everest. In this particular contest between man and mountain, the mountain had won, and it seemed fitting to end on the imposing sight of this, the highest peak in the world, impassively victorious. Time will tell as to whether the final programme does indeed finish in this fashion. Other endings may suggest themselves. But in my mind at least, the enduring image of those three months spent at its foot is, and must be, Everest as seen from the Rongbuk Valley. Those who can compare, say this view is the most impressive of all. I cannot say; but representing as it does so many memories, so many mixed emotions and physical extremes, it is a view I shall never forget.

Appendix A

A Note on the Camera Equipment

As it may be of interest or value to some readers of this book with a professional interest in mountaineering camera-work, I am adding this appendix, which concludes with a list of the equipment we used.

I want to begin, however, by expressing my heartfelt and most sincere gratitude to the three 'oily rags', Nick Plowright, Alan Evans and Ian Hills, who did the work while I supposedly did the thinking. In the event, we each participated in the endless discussion of how best to do the job we had collectively taken on. Nick in particular far exceeded his duties as a cameraman, and was a tower of strength to me as producer-director, often suggesting a sequence, prompting me in an interview, or just filming without being asked when it was necessary. It is customary, even obligatory, for producers to thank their crew; but in this case, I can only say I mean it from the bottom of my heart, and hope that the series, when it hits the small screen, will do justice to their dedication. They deserve a resounding success.

And now, a few thoughts based on our experience. Our major problem was that we were a small crew of only four, and I had no technical abilities beyond occasionally deputizing as sound recordist. There is an apparent contradiction between my frequent moans about boredom and inactivity, and my conviction that more personnel would have helped. The fact is, when things happen, they happen up and down the mountain, and we could only, at best, be in two places at once. Another two crew members, providing a third sync channel, would have been an undoubted bonus.

In the same vein, it would have been a great help to have far more porters at our disposal: we had two in Tibet, of whom one was sacked for inefficiency after a short time. By Nepalese standards they were excessively expensive – about £1,300. Not that the porters would see that money; they came perforce through the auspices of the CMA, who would pocket the lion's share. The expedition members frequently helped out, but this was an unsatisfactory solution, as it put us in the position of asking favours, which is awkward, however graciously they may be granted. It also meant we did a lot of carrying ourselves, which is, to say the least, detrimental to the business of filming proficiently.

On a previous Everest film, made by the BBC and in Nepal where porters and Sherpas were readily available and cost relatively little, they called upon the services of a small army of load carriers who worked exclusively for the film crew. If such an arrangement had been feasible, we would have welcomed it with open arms and unladen shoulders.

The other undeniable coup pulled by the BBC was the inclusion in their team of Mick Burke, the well-known mountaineer and cameraman, who so tragically was never to return from that assignment. It is commonly accepted that he reached the summit with his ACL camera, and that they are both still there beneath the snow. The loss of such a man speaks for itself. But Mick was able to do what we could not: namely to get professionally shot footage all the way up to the summit itself. I have mentioned earlier the expedition members' excellent contributions using the Video-8 format, and also their reluctance at very high altitudes to act as unpaid cameramen. We had, of course, Alan Evans as a climbing cameraman, but it is rock-climbing rather than mountaineering that is Al's forte, and he had never operated at the altitudes we were at. As luck would have it, he suffered more than any of us from symptoms of AMS, and in the event made only one sortie to Camp Four at the top of the French Spur. This itself was no mean achievement, but it left five thousand feet of mountain beyond our reach.

In planning the shoot, we tried to strike a balance between having sufficient equipment to cover the three main camps without constant shifting of gear from one to another, and the obvious need to keep weight to a minimum. Perhaps the most difficult item to estimate was film stock. In the end, we took two hundred rolls of Eastman 7291, and fifty of the 400 ASA 7292. This gave us a rough shooting ratio of sixteen to one, which proved in the event to be more than adequate. We exposed 160 rolls of film (or 64,000 feet, or twenty-eight hours) and with the help of the lads, we recorded almost twenty hours of video tape.

We had decided as a policy to use the Arriflexes whenever possible, for reasons of quality and consistency. But it proved an irresistible temptation to pick up a Video-8 camera when a potential, rather than essential, sequence presented itself – e.g. the daily radio checks between camps. The strike ratio on the Video-8 material is likely to be very low, but the cost of tape is negligible and it is better to be safe than sorry. Even then, though, we missed much.

The 'box Brownie' Video-8 camera, the M8, was more reliable and simpler for amateurs to use than the V90 with its multiple buttons; but the V90s have a zoom lens and provision for a better microphone than the on-board condenser. Both did sterling work in very adverse conditions.

Nick professed himself very happy with the Arris, one of which had been 'winterized'; and with the Zeiss ten-to-one lenses (one winterized); less so with a now rather ancient Angenieux twenty-to-one lens (unwinterized), which proved impossible to zoom smoothly in the temperature, and had no motor drive (our fault).

Ian used three recorders: the Nagra IS, Nagra SN and Sony Pro-Walkman (sync adapted). We shot least footage on the Sony, but that was as anticipated. Their principal purpose was to allow single-man operation, by attaching to the Arri, but this put an all but impossible demand on that operator, and we found it far more satisfactory to work in a minimum of two per team on the many occasions when we were not all four together.

To carry our equipment, we had prepared two very successful improvisations beyond the standard silver boxes and carbon-fibre cases. The first was 8 Crichton cooler boxes, of fifty and eighty litre capacities. In these lived the film stock, protected to a degree from the excessive temperature variations; and the Video-8 equipment which came in flimsy cases of their own. The Arri and Nagra to be used 'on the run' each had a specially adapted Berghaus rucksack with semi-rigid sides and a suitcase-like format. These were padded out with pre-cut solid foam to accommodate a camera with ten-to-one lens and pistol grip, and a spare magazine in the outside pocket; and the Nagra IS or SN, with gun-mike and windshield, spare tapes and spare film stock. If necessary, a tripod could be strapped on top of either rucksack, but that made it unpleasantly heavy. On the trek, however, our porters managed this without complaint – and were paid at the Nepalese rate of around £1 per man per day. It may be exploitation, but it's the system.

As for batteries, we had eight on-board rechargeable Arri batteries, with solar panels to charge them; ten lithium cells, which were excellent but expensive; and an almost infinite number of Duracells. The solar panels were a mixed blessing, heavy but essential. There was a very temperamental generator, which ended up at Advance Base Camp, and no other charging capacity.

The one serious omission from our equipment was a set of two-way radios of our own. Due to a misunderstanding, we were under the impression that the expedition equipment would include enough spare radios for our use, but this turned out not to be so, and although we frequently made use of the expedition radios, it would have been infinitely better to have had our own. You live and learn.

List of Equipment

To be forwarded to Base Camp

No.	Description	Country of Origin
1	16mm Arriflex SR II camera	West Germany
2	400' magazine	
3	Zeiss 10–100mm T2 zoom lens	
4	16mm Arriflex SR II camera	
5	20–1mm Angenieux lens	France
6	6 lithium batteries	UK
7	1 set of head and legs	West Germany
8	filters/accessories	UK
9	Kodak 16mm stock	France
10	Nagra IS recorder	Switzerland
11	Micron transmitter	UK
12	Micron receiver	
13	Arri-Walkman recorder	Germany/Japan
14	box of tapes and batteries	West Germany
15	cables and accessories	UK

Appendix A

For the Trek

No.	Description	Country of Origin
1	16mm Ariflex SR II camera	West Germany
2–4	400' magazine	
	400' magazine	
	400' magazine	
5	4 on-board batteries	
6	variable speed control	
7	16mm Arriflex SR II camera	
8–10	400' magazine	
	400' magazine	
	400' magazine	
11	4 on-board batteries	
12	variable speed control	
13	5.9mm Angenieux lens	France
14	5.9mm Angenieux lens	
15	300/600mm Canon lens	Japan
16	9.5mm Distagon lens	West Germany
17	9.5mm Distagon lens	
18	Satchler panorama head and legs	
19	Satchler panorama head and legs	
20	Zeiss 10–100mm T2 zoom lens	
21	Zeiss 10–100mm T2 zoom lens	
22	2 solar chargers	UK
23	4 lithium batteries	
24	Kodak 16mm stock	France
25	filters/chargers/accessories	UK
26	Nagra SN recorder	Switzerland
27	SQN 3C mixer	UK
28	Nagra SN recorder	Switzerland
29	SQN 3C mixer	UK
30–32	Sennheiser 416 microphone	West Germany
	Sennheiser 416 microphone	
	Sennheiser 416 microphone	
33	Micron transmitter	UK
34	Micron receiver	
35	Micron transmitter	
36	Micron receiver	

No.	Description	Country of Origin
37	Arri–Walkman recorder	Germany/Japan
38	4 ECM 50 microphones	Japan
39	cables/batteries/accessories	UK
40	¼" sound tapes	West Germany

N.B. Some of the trek equipment was repacked in Kathmandu and sent direct to Base Camp. This still left more than enough to be carried on one back or another.

Appendix B

Dramatis Personae

Team List – British Services Everest Expedition 1988
(as supplied by the BSEE 88 Project Office)

Lt Col G D B Keelan RM	Dougie	Leader
★ Lt Col M W H Day RE	Henry	Deputy Leader/Oxygen
Col R H Hardie OBE	Dick	Chief Medical Officer
Sqn Ldr K E Hunter RAF	Keith	Base Camp Manager
★ Cdr R C Pelly RN	Richard	
★ Maj D V Nicholls RM	Dave	
Maj C B Spencer 7 GR	Kit	
Surg Lt Cdr A R O Miller RN	Alastair	Medical Officer
Capt C W Hattersley RNR	Charlie	
Capt P H Parsons RM	Pat	Equipment
Capt A J S Edington RE	Andy	
Capt M H Bazire RAOC	Martin	Rations
Capt S P R Lowe R Sigs	Simon	
★ Capt G N Williams R Hamps	Nigel	
★ Capt J P J Garratt Gren Gds	Johnny	
Capt D G Strutt Queens	Duncan	
Capt J G B Gittings Coldm Gds	Giles	Project Team
Surg Lt A S Hughes RN	Andy	Medical Officer
Lt S F Gray DERR	Simon	
Lt J Vlasto R Sigs	John	
★ Lt S Bell RMR (TBC)	Steve	
Flt Lt L J Skuodas RAF	Laurie	
Chief Tech P N Taylor	Nev	Asst, Oxygen
★ SSgt E M Middleton	Merv	
SSgt D M Orange	Dave	
CSgt A D Wilson	Tug	

★ Sgt D Maxwell	Max	
Sgt S J Last	Steve	
Sgt W Batson	Bill	
Sgt J L Morning	Jim	
★ Sgt T G Moore	Terry	Asst, Equipment
Sgt D A Howie	Dave	
★ Cpl L A Hughes	Luke	
Cpl T Atkins	Ted	
★ SAC A McLeod	Al	
Gnr D Torrington	Dave	
LCpl A D Wilson	Andy	Project Team, UK
Maj J N Fitzgerald	John	Project Officer, UK
Mr L Rowe	Lincoln	Artist
Capt F R Antolik	Roger	Project Team/ Granada Liaison Officer

★ Member of a Summit Team

Granada TV team

Mark Anderson
Nick Plowright
Alan Evans
Ian Hills

Sherpa climbers

Chowang (Sirdar)
Angnema
Gombu
Gopal
Bhadri
Lakpa

Sherpa cooks

Kharmi
Tenzing
Manbahadur
Tashi